A TIME TO REFLECT

JOANNA WARRINGTON

A TIME TO REFLECT

Previously published as 'Gambling Broke Us'

DISCLAIMER AND BACKGROUND TO THE BOOK

The places in the book are real and based on notes I made during a trip to New England in the summer of 2018.

The names, characters and incidents portrayed in this book are the work of the author's imagination or used in a fictitious way. Any resemblance to actual persons, living or dead is entirely coincidental.

CHAPTER 1: PANDORA – 2018

I live in a shabby little town. Somebody has to live here. Approaching the town, a welcome sign reads *Welcome to the Heart of the South,* suggesting it's full of romantic, gooey-eyed people. It also implies it's a pretty town, but in reality it's anything but that. No couple would want to come here for a romantic weekend, as the buildings are offensive, in a Prince Charles kind of way. But we do like our signs. There's one that says, 'Don't be a tosser, take your litter home,' and a poster with a fairy holding a rubbish bag with the message, 'There are no poop fairies here.' But people don't care. Coke cans and crisp packets litter the park and doggy poo bags hang from trees like exotic fruit.

Half the shops are boarded up, teenagers stand idly outside the KFC and drunks languish across park benches, staring into beer bottles. The best thing about living here though—and I suppose I had better be positive—or I'll piss a lot of people off, is that it's easy to get out of, being near the motorway and the airport and having a fast train link to London. People live here, not because they want to be here, but because they can get out of here. However, I'm not a celebrity screaming get me out of here, I'm just a sensible middle-aged woman. A famous comedian joked that the town is about as exciting as walking from one end of the curtain to the other. Recently the town's biggest event was Waitrose opening a new store, but with that out of the way, and the novelty of visiting the store for a free cup of tea starting to wear thin, I feel the need to escape. Living my life in some dull *Groundhog* remake, I need to break the cycle otherwise I'll go mad, especially when my school friend's annual Christmas letter arrives from Rhyl with an update on the health and wellbeing of her three cats. So, my niece, Ellie and I book a trip and we leave in a couple of days for Boston. That's Boston in America, not the Boston in Lincolnshire which returned the highest Brexit vote in Britain and is where the humble carrot is grown.

The landline ringing startles me as it's a once in a blue moon occasion. If it's not a junk caller it must be my brother, Jules, the bad apple of the family.

My brother's gravelly voice at the end of the line greets me. As I've been blanking him because he's given me so much stress over the years, we haven't spoken in months. Deep breaths, Pandora, I tell myself.

'Mandy's having a baby.'

'No way.' My heart sinks to the floor as I try to match his cheerful tone, but this is the last thing he needs right now. Ellie, his daughter from his marriage to Vicky is twenty-two. Does he really want to be a father again?

'I'm going to be a daddy again.'

If anybody needs a daddy it's Jules who desperately lacks the support of a father because ours has died. I can't believe what I'm hearing. My brother is most definitely neither daddy nor hubby material, being the kind of person that starts a project then leaves it by the wayside when the going gets tough. With his few redeeming qualities, it makes me sad to see a smart woman like Mandy think that a guy like my brother is her only option as a boyfriend or her child's father.

'I thought she dumped you?'

'She did.'

'Why?'

'The usual reasons.'

After contemplating whether to encourage him to take a moment to assess his circumstances, I decide against it.

'When are you going to learn?'

'I know you don't want to talk to me, and things are difficult after what happened with Mum, but I need a favour.'

'I know your kind of favours.'

'It's not about money—don't hang up. You've got all this time with Ellie in Boston. Can you break the news to her?'

'Oh, for fuck's sake, Jules. You're a grown man. Tell her yourself, she's your daughter. It would be better coming from you.'

As ever, my brother wants me to do his dirty deed, being too weak and pathetic to tell Ellie himself. I've spent a lifetime breaking news to Mum and Dad, watching their disappointed faces, making excuses for him, and picking up the pieces when his life turns to disaster, which it always does. He's a car crash.

'It's about time you started acting like a father to Ellie, rather than pretending to be one. She's twenty-two. Time's running out if you want to make a good impression.'

Ignoring my sarcasm, he persists with his request.

'I wish you wouldn't keep doing this to me. I'm not some super-human being,' I tell him.

Although I miss our parents, it's at times like this that I'm grateful they aren't around. They would be horrified at some of the things that have happened lately. He wasn't a good son, and I'm sure their health suffered because of him, although I wouldn't be cruel enough to say that to Jules.

'Maybe not, you've had your fair share of relationship disasters.'

'Only one disaster and that wasn't my fault,' I remind him.

'But you're a great auntie, almost like a replacement mum.'

'Don't say that, don't even think it. I'm a separate person. My relationship with Ellie is special, it's a niece and auntie relationship. Vicky was her mum. Still is her mum. Her love for her hasn't gone away just because she died. She won't ever forget her, so if you're thinking that will happen, I'm telling you it won't.'

Jesus, my brother has some fucked up ideas about life.

'She can't be replaced or brushed under the carpet.'

'Enjoy Boston,' he says in a flat, despondent tone as the conversation ends. Since Vicky's death Jules has never taken Ellie on holiday, apart from a grim camping trip to Wales, when she was ten, but it was aborted after two nights due to heavy rain. For Jules borrowing a car and a tent from a mate, and a gas stove to heat tinned beans was a generous act.

CHAPTER 2: PANDORA - 2018

Purging our parents' home of all their possessions was the most daunting thing I've ever had to do. I stopped Jules going to the house, after what he did. I took his key away from him and told him I was in control and I was sorting it all. Mum and Dad appointed me as executor. They knew Jules couldn't be trusted.

Mum died six years ago, and Dad went years before that. It has taken me six years to sift through everything and there are piles of boxes in my basement. Our parents never moved to a new house from their beautiful fourteenth century cottage. It was in the country, with geese and chicken in the garden, and a vegetable patch and pond for dad's koi carp. Their belongings amounted to years of accumulated stuff. What am I supposed to do with Mum's Girl Guide badges and sash, her Cunard ticket across the Atlantic, Dad's first driving licence and my grandparent's gas masks? It's difficult to erase their lives at the tip. And sad too. Every item is part of our childhood and heritage, but it has to be done. Ellie doesn't want anything. Her generation prefers cheap furniture made of pressed sawdust and glue to fine antiques. They post their dream lives on Pinterest, by way of decor photographs.

I can't keep putting it off. I live minimally and continually purge my own stuff. Something new comes into the house and something old goes out. That's the way I like things to be. I have to do it myself. I can't let Jules help. I don't trust him, after what he did when Mum died. It was so disgusting that I never will again.

Speaking to Jules has made me think about our childhood and so while I'm waiting for Ellie to arrive, I prise open the oak chest that contains my parents' papers. There's so much to sort but I don't manage to get beyond Dad's diaries. Reading them is a trip down Memory Lane during the early nineteen eighties. I flick through the pages, my eyes settling on the passages about Jules.

'The Jules saga goes from bad to worse. We can't talk about anything else. Last night was the fourteenth consecutive night he was in late. At midnight I locked the door in what I was sure would be a futile attempt to teach him a lesson. When we finally heard him at the door, he barely tried to open it and went away. We didn't sleep for worrying where he'd gone. In the morning I found him asleep in the stables. He was wearing his best coat and was partly covered by the horse's blanket. After only two weeks in his new job, he's going to be late, but he doesn't care.

We went out for lunch with friends and discussed Jules. They suggested that we subsidise him so that he can live comfortably in a flat in town. No way is that an option. He's got to learn what things cost the hard way. If I subsidise him he'll never learn. After years of trying to make him see our way he is ultra-determined to do it his ...'

I read about my dad's work in Luton, and the progress of his tomato plants. His life as a civil servant amid cuts and chaos leaves me yawning. I'm about to put the diary back in the chest, when a page farther back catches my eye. It's dated 1974 when Jules was nine and I was eleven. It's as if I'm meant to read this particular extract because the diary falls open at the page.

'I can't stand liars and my son is turning into one. Maybe I've gone too far this time, but he makes me angry and I can't help it, I snap. He, brings out the worst in me as a father, but he leaves me with no choice. The boy needs a firm hand and discipline. Maggie is too soft, so I waited until she was out shopping with Pandora to teach him a firm hand as I can't teach him a firm hand when they're around. She lets him get away with murder. I challenged him and he lied to me. Yet again. This time it was hidden under his mattress. When is he going to learn?'

Pondering the words, I try to fathom out what he's talking about. It means nothing to me so I should ring Jules and read it to him over the phone, but something stops me. Whatever happened all those years ago will be used by Jules to justify his actions when Mum died. I hate it when people hark on about their dreadful childhoods and how it has impacted on their life. Jules had a good childhood—we both did. We had chores and sometimes it was hard, but nothing to complain about. But something doesn't add up. What was Dad talking about? I'm curious to know more and my mind conjures up all sorts of images.

CHAPTER 3: PANDORA – 2018

I love Ellie as if she's my own daughter. After Vicky died, she came to live with me and saw Jules most weekends. What option was there? I couldn't leave her with him. He was in no fit state to raise a little girl. My offer of taking her to stay with me for a few days while he took stock of what had happened, somehow ended up as a permanent arrangement.

I've had five miscarriages. I can't carry a baby. Getting pregnant was never a problem––but carrying them to full term was. When Ellie came along, she put a smile on my face and turned my sad mood around. Without her, my life would have been incomplete. She was a treasure, as if somebody above had given her to me, because I couldn't have my own. She gave me reason to celebrate, and in times of need I hope I've been a reassuring guide. When she stages her silent battles with her dad I'm the confidant when she needs a listening ear.

The doorbell rings. I've been waiting in for Ellie's Love Island personalised water bottle she ordered to arrive, in time for our trip tomorrow.

I smile at the postman. 'My niece will be happy.' I squeeze the packet and sign for the parcel.

'Let me guess,' the delivery man says. 'Love Island bottle?'

I laugh. 'How the hell did you know?'

'I've delivered over three hundred of the damn things this past week. If you hadn't answered the door, I could have done you a favour and binned it.'

Ellie arrives by train from Bath where she's worked since graduating last Summer. She's working as a housekeeper while she waits for a place at teacher training college. She slings her case onto the back seat and joins me in the front, she smells of freesia, spice and youth. Her long blonde hair looks like clear honey and is flicked into neat commas. There are scratched flecks of darkness under her eyes, but mine are drawn to her trim figure and the sleek yellow dress she's wearing.

She jiggles in her seat as we manoeuvre through rush hour traffic, dodging the pot holes the council haven't bothered to repair. 'America, woo, can't wait, can't wait,' she sings. Despite a year of working she's still a teenager at heart and her delight always buoys me along to book more holidays for us.

After dinner we repack the case and set our phone alarms for four.

'It should be very hot, probably as hot as it is here. Boston is on the same latitude as Rome, and Rome is boiling at this time of year.'

Britain has been basking in an unprecedented heatwave for several weeks. If it remains like this while we're away, I'll feel cheated and my beloved hydrangeas will wilt.

'Please don't start going on about the weather being just like 1976. I'm sick of your generation droning on about the summer of 1976,' Ellie grumbles.

'Well, it is like 1976. I remember your father and I playing in the paddling pool that whole summer. We didn't bother wearing shoes it was so hot. A horse trod on his toe that summer. Your dad was always having accidents and getting into scrapes. He was clumsy. His body was covered in bruises.'

'I can't imagine Dad as a kid. He hardly talks about his childhood.'

'I think I'll take a raincoat and fleece just in case.'

'Auntie you won't need them. What the fuck.' She gives a morose shake of her head only seen in young people.

'Language. And actually, I might need a hat and raincoat. It's best to be prepared. Do you know that Boston has the dubious distinction of having the tenth most unpredictable weather in America. Things can change quickly.'

'Sorry I swore, but literally you will not need them,' she says in her best matronly tone, ignoring my information, gathered from the depths of the internet. 'And you've packed all wrong. Put all the heavy stuff at one end otherwise it's all lopsided and please can we take your new hairdryer?' She stretches the word please, like chewing gum, emphasising the importance of the addition of my state-of-the-art Dyson hairdryer.

I'm updating my Facebook status. Ellie tells me off for being on Facebook. I'm too old apparently, and aunties shouldn't be friends with nieces. But today she tells me that actually Facebook is for old people—and it's now okay for me to be on it. She checks my posts all the same, despite it being for oldies, to find out my adventures into the online dating world—another area of life that I am too old for. 'Off to the land of the free,' my post reads. 'Planned holiday well. Trump will be here while we are there, you're welcome to him, ha ha.'

It's President Donald Trump's first visit to Britain while we are away. Protests are expected in every town that Trump visits. A twenty-foot balloon depicting Trump as an angry baby clutching a smartphone is expected to be flown above Central London. The mayor has given permission for it to be seen. Some people are saying it's no way to treat a U.S president, but to me it sounds like a right laugh. I'm slightly sad to be missing the excitement, there's going to be a big demonstration in London next Saturday, against his visit and I feel as if I'm missing out on the fun. Trump's reaction to the flying baby is sure to create a Twitter frenzy. I wonder if he will throw a paddy and feel unwelcome in Britain. Theresa May, our Prime Minister, thinks she can tame Trump, but he always thinks he's right.

CHAPTER 4: JULES – 2018

Surprised his sister answered the phone, Jules was glad she had. She'd been ignoring his messages for months. After their mum died, he thought they'd fallen out for good because he'd made a terrible mess of things and only had himself to blame. As far as he was concerned it took a strong person to say sorry, and, he'd said it many times over, but Pandora didn't appreciate how hard that was for him. All she could say was, 'It's just a word, sorry makes no difference. Sorry won't bring Mum back. It's just one word against a thousand hurts.'

Standing huddled in the doorway of the NatWest bank, using their Wi-Fi Jules sheltered from a torrential downpour, a fork of lightning knifing through the gun metal sky. The country had basked in a glorious heatwave for several weeks, but it looked as if the weather was finally on the turn. He hoped not because he would be homeless in three weeks' time.

Although he accepted that he'd been a crap father to Ellie, there were periods when he really tried to focus on her and put her first. But it never lasted long. The problem was he always slipped back into his old ways. 'A leopard doesn't change its spots' was a refrain that most women he had met hurled at him. If only they could think of a new analogy, as that one was tired and boring. Jules knew he was a prize idiot, a wanker, a tosser, a loser and all the other negative words they chucked at him, but they didn't understand him. Beneath that, if it wasn't for the one problem he had, he could show himself to be a decent guy, the perfect partner, and the perfect dad. The baby could be a new lease of life for him, a reason to change, if only Mandy would let him prove himself. At this moment he made an enormous promise to himself. *I'm going to make a go of it this time around. I messed up with Ellie and now it's too late but I'm going to be the dad this child will be proud of.* He wished he knew how many times happiness had come his way, only to be rejected because he was so consumed with all the bad things and was unable to recognise anything good.

According to Jules, Pandora had always been a stuck-up cow which was why he teased her relentlessly when they were kids, even telling her they weren't related and that she was in fact the milkman's kid. The fact was it didn't feel as if they were brother and sister. They looked alike but that was as far as the similarity went. One day Jules hatched a plan, telling their mum he wanted to learn how to write a signature. Giving her a folded piece of paper, he asked her to write her signature on it and stuck the paper on Pandora's door. On the other side of the paper he had written a note that said 'Dear Pandora, I have been keeping this a secret, but I have to tell you that you're the milkman's daughter, signed ...' Pandora cried her eyes out, and Jules got a right bollocking.

It had been plain to see in the way they'd treated her that she was the parents' favourite, but Jules told himself he was being pathetic carrying his angst for years and should forget the small things, let them slide over his head. But over time he began to focus on the small things, magnifying them in his memory bank. For instance, there had been hardly any photos of him around the house, but Pandora's had taken pride of place on the mantelpiece and it always looked as if her food was better presented on the plate than his. Years later, when his current problems were kicking in, he noticed that his mum's credit card PIN number was Pandora's date of birth, which pissed him off. Had it been any other number, he didn't think he would have withdrawn his mum's pension.

Pandora was the blue-eyed girl with the cute blonde curls, who couldn't do anything wrong. Whatever she did, she came out smelling of roses while Jules became the black sheep of the family. She won all the school awards and certificates, and he got all the detentions. He'd never thought of himself as the jealous type but that all changed the day he cut up her gym, music and swimming certificates. His dad made him write to the awarding authorities, explaining what he'd done and asking if replacements could be provided, and mostly they were. In one case though, the man responsible turned up in person, with replacement certificates and chocolate bars for him. Apparently, his office had found Jules' letter hilarious.

As teenagers, Pandora and Jules were poles apart. Her bedroom was organised and her bed made in the morning. She had a neat row of teddies along the pillow and a pin board on her wall displaying her revision plan. By comparison, Jules' room was the black hole of Calcutta. Food was another matter. Miss Perfect, Prim and Proper Pandora had a small appetite, but Jules ate enough to feed a small village and their mum would say, 'I can't wait till the boy leaves home because the food bill's going to go right down.'

There was one more call Jules needed to make before he returned to his flat—if he could call it a flat. It was actually a bedsit, but flat or apartment sounded better. In reality it was more like a hovel, but for the moment he was just grateful to have a roof over his head—after all beggars couldn't be choosers.

Mandy answered. And on the first ring. Wow, two people answering his calls in one day. That had to be a record.

'Jules, stop fucking ringing me.'

'Don't hang up.'

'What do you want?'

'I just want to be part of the baby's life.'

'It hasn't been born yet.'

'But soon it will be, and I want to be there when you give birth.'

'No fucking way.'

'I'm going to change. This is a fresh start. Just give me one last chance Mand. Please. I'm begging you.'

'You can beg all you like. We don't need you.'

'But this time I'm turning over a new leaf. The baby's my incentive.'

'I've lost count of the number of times you've said that.'

'But I will. I have good reason to.'

'I can't hear you Jules. Bacon Airline is just flying overhead.'

'Ha-ha. Let me take you out for a meal, so we can talk.'

'I'm not falling for that one. You've promised meals out before. They don't happen.'

'Okay. It will happen. Curry. Saturday, seven. Meet me in The Monkey Temple.'

She hesitated and Jules thought she was going to end the call.

'All right, I'll be there.'

Her quick response unnerved him. Was she playing games? He didn't know. He'd have to think of something to be able to pay the bill at the Monkey Temple, he could have kicked himself, of all the bloody places to choose—but he had to pull out the stops on this one and a limp Maccie's burger was not going to cut it.

The line went dead. He desperately wanted to be a part of

his child's life. He'd fucked up with Ellie, but this was his chance to be a good father.

Jules braced himself against the rain as it came down like a handful of nails, waiting for it to ease before heading back to his bedsit, reached down a short alley next to Greggs Bakery and a kebab shop. The tantalising smells drifting through his window were pure torment through weeks when he had no money.

The seriously riled sky mirrored his emotions. Opening the door to the Victorian building where he lived the hallway reeked of weed and damp with takeaway leaflets littering the floor. The timer on the light gave him precisely twenty seconds to climb the stairs to the second floor before it plunged him into darkness and left him groping for the keyhole to his bedsit. Colliding with strange characters on the landing in the pitch black wasn't a pleasant experience. He safely reached his door, the plastic doormat curled at the edges, creating a tripping hazard for women who entered his bedsit, but he was used to it. Once inside, the fluorescent lightbulb, a quirky-looking twist of frosted glass, resembling an ice cream cone spiral flickered to life, leaving the room in gloomy faded light that was inadequate for reading. His life was compacted into this one room. It was where he ate, slept, shagged and contemplated his life.

Flicking the kettle on in the kitchenette, he realised he was completely out of tea bags and the milk was on the turn. He would have to wait until Monday when he could nick a few teabags from work. Not considering himself to be a scrounger by nature he hated doing this but what option did he have? He couldn't keep returning to the food bank. There were more deserving cases and they didn't always have the brands of food he liked.

Unfolding his sofa bed, he put on the sheets and duvet that he kept in the corner of the room and hadn't been washed in weeks. He normally took his washing over to his friend Simon's house, but Simon had a new girlfriend and he'd become the unwanted guest that came just to do his washing and cadge a meal if it was going. He felt like a gooseberry, but it didn't matter if his sheets weren't washed regularly. His duvet smelt of him, which he found comforting and better than the pungent washing powder. When the bed was out, there was just enough room to slide sideways around the bed, backed against the wall.

He lay awake as the worries that his daytime activities held at bay came sneaking back under the cover of darkness, unpicking the threads of his miserable existence. Replaying the conversation with Mandy over in his head, had he really promised to change? Deep down, he knew it was an empty promise in a landfill of them. She of all people knew that. Out of all the women he'd dated since Vicky, she understood him. All he needed was a few more weeks and he'd come good—it was the promises talking. 'Please be patient Mandy. I know I can do it. Please believe me. For the baby's sake,' he whispered into the empty room, trying to convince himself that this time he would make it right.

He got up to check the fifty quid was still in his Keep Calm And Carry On mug at the back of the kitchen cupboard. The money was stopping him from sleeping, wondering whether he could turn fifty quid into a hundred. He'd done it before, loads of times. The money made him nervous. He knew exactly how long it had been in the mug. Ever since his last pay cheque, having put it aside to take himself and a friend, Rusty to the local football match at the weekend. He owed Rusty big time. Despite being unemployed, Rusty was always bailing him out and had put him up when he was last homeless. He couldn't let him down again and gamble away the money. Panic set in and he pressed his cheeks and made fists with his hands. None of these pacifying actions ever soothed the panic he felt, they were simply reflex responses to his troubled mind. He closed the kitchen door hoping it would help him forget that the money was there, knowing that would never happen. Money always made him jittery.

The front door slamming and the cackle of laughter crushed any hope of sleep that remained. It was noisier on Friday and Saturday nights, being in the drift zone between pubs. It was too early to get up and he tossed and turned as thin, curtained daylight pushed into the room.

When the wall clock nudged eight, he took his towel and soap and headed along the corridor to the shared bathroom, finding the floor covered in clumps of hair and nail clippings and trails of spat toothpaste mapping the sink. Nobody bothered to clean it. Whose responsibility was it anyway? He'd never found that out in the year he'd lived there—everybody's he supposed, but he'd never bothered.

He peered into the cracked mirror, confident he could finally win a shed load of money to sort out all of his problems —tonight was his lucky night. Mandy agreeing to come out with him was an omen—it would bring him luck. Thinking about Ellie he wondered if Pandora had told her about the baby yet. It would be easier coming from Pandora. She'd think of something, a way to soften the news. In any case, it was getting harder and harder to meet with Ellie as she expected too much of him, fancy dinners and trips to the theatre, laughing when he insisted on going to the pizza restaurant for her birthday.

'Pizza, that's so yesterday Dad. It's my birthday, I want to go to a fish restaurant and eat prawns and salmon.'

'I can't eat fish.'

'You eat fish.'

'No, I don't,' he'd lied.

'Alright, what about Mexican?'

'Not sure about that. Too hot.'

'Or Greek?'

In the end, he'd ignored her pleas and goaded her into the

pizza parlour, feeling dreadful that he'd let her down—again—but he had vouchers for that particular restaurant. The vouchers meant the meal had only cost him two pound fifty.

He turned the taps on. Steam clouded the dank air as water filled the dirt tinged bath with its mould speckled sealant around the edges. He thought about the beautiful, four-bedroom house he'd owned with Vicky—Ellie's mother— all those years ago, with its mod-cons. Despite the warmth of the bath water he shivered when he thought of Vicky's ghastly death. All it had taken was one split second to change every-thing, and now here he was limping from one day to the next, hoping for things to change. No matter how hard he tried to erase the ugly details of his wife's death from his memory it seemed impossible. In his mind's eye, he could still see the blood splattered across the wall, her stiletto wedged between the spindles of the staircase and Ellie's piercing cry from her cot.

His life was like a game of snakes and ladders and he was the snake. The past was another lifetime and it was hard to believe what had happened. But soon his current existence and all of the lies he'd told to cover up what was going on would also be a thing of the past.

CHAPTER 5: PANDORA – 2018

Excitement kicks in as I check the bags one last time before opening the windows to let the breeze filter into my stuffy bedroom. It's late before I close my eyes and try to sleep but it's too hot and sleep won't come. It's times like this I'm grateful I don't have a man in bed with me. Spooning in this hot weather would be hell.

Heat prickles my neck and warms my face, another hot flush. The last boyfriend called the beads of sweat angel drops, cute I thought, until he dumped me a week later. It feels as if I've been sprayed with Ralgex. I wish the hot flushes would go away and return in the depths of winter but there's no logic to nature. Along with the aches and pains, creeping weight gain and poor memory it's just one of the perils of being over fifty, a life marker that sneaked up on me so surreptitiously that I barely noticed it, until the big occasion, celebrated in a cloud of alcohol and sweat.

I've adjusted to the idea of the fifties and I'm embracing the decade—fifty is the new thirty. I could relax, slink into old age willingly without a fight and resign myself to the fact that I will never meet a long-term partner. Instead I put my feet up on the patio and writhe in fury as I watch my bamboo work its way around the garden, clipping every fresh shoot as it emerges. In the absence of a resident pet panda I'm unlikely to win. So, I must give up these small battles. I'm not going to be thrifty in my fifties either. With money to be spent from my inheritance I'm going to travel. It's the flighty fifties not the frumpy fifties and, dare I say it filthy fifties too, when opportunity permits. I shall ignore warnings about the fifties and beyond being a sexual desert. Damn it, the desert below, like the bamboo will be beaten. An oasis will flow in those nether regions, with the aid of supplements and tubes of medicated jelly.

The agony of watching friends have babies is thankfully in the distant past. Some of my friends have confessed they regret having children. That always makes me smile. It's acceptable to confess to barren women like me, to offload about how dreadful it's all been, but not to another parent. Images used to smash into my consciousness of breastfeeding and pushing prams. Somewhere along the way, I accepted that I wasn't going to be a mother. I'm content with my role as auntie, it was the closest I got to motherhood, fun but without the usual motherly responsibilities.

In a desperate bid to cool down I grab the sheet from the bed, bundle it into a plastic bag and chuck it into the freezer for half an hour. I've been looking forward to the trip for months but now that I'm hours away from arriving at the airport I feel unsure of myself and the decision to go with Ellie. I realise that in the absence of a partner I'm clinging to her like a marine mollusc. I love her to bits and her company is great, but the sad fact is I have nobody else to go on holiday with and I'm too scared to go alone. After this trip I need to address my fears, stop being a pathetic wreck and take the plunge on a solo trip. I can do it. I have to do it, because Ellie won't want to come on holiday with her old aunt for much longer.

I sit on top of the freezer eating an ice pop while waiting for the sheet and a thought hits me like a truck. I haven't arranged the travel insurance. I switch the computer on, and its glow fills the room. This is typical of me to forget the most important item on the packing list. I've stocked up on travel miniatures from Boots and sanitary towels, just in case my luck is down and a rogue follicle is stimulated, after all this time without a period. At my age insurance is important—I'm far more likely to fall down a ravine pissed than to welcome home the red river. I'm at the computer for some time, reading the small print, confused as to what the policy covers. When it comes to clicking the basket, I'm bombed out because I've taken too long and have to start a fresh search. Twenty minutes later and with two hours left until my alarm goes off there's a whirling egg timer in the middle of the screen after I enter my credit card details. Fractious in the heat and with tiredness sweeping over me I give up and go to bed. Ellie can sort it on her phone as we head for Heathrow.

CHAPTER 6: JULES – 1975

'Jules, Pandora, your tea's ready,' Maggie called.

Can we eat it in here?' Jules replied. 'We're watching Scooby Doo.'

Maggie appeared at the door, rolled her eyes but as always, she let them eat their tea in front of the TV. Stray chips got wedged down the sofa and there were crumbs on the carpet, but it was home. Maggie wasn't hard on them. She didn't have a presence about her that instilled discipline. She was a softly spoken, a tiny, brittle whippet of a woman.

'Okay, but just watch your dad doesn't catch you.'

Nobody heard George's key in the door.

'What's going on? Why aren't they eating at the table?' George plonked his case on the coffee table and loosened his tie. He glared at Jules. It was never Pandora's fault. He worked away all week in Reading and came home on Fridays. The family could have moved to be with him when George got offered the job in Reading, but they decided not to because they loved the cottage and it was, 'a rare find.' They'd muddle through and George would take lodgings through the week. Jules didn't like living in the countryside. It was too quiet, there was nothing to do and it was too far from his friends who all lived in town. He'd tried to persuade the rest of his family they should move to Reading. Everybody got used to the arrangement and in time Jules preferred it being just the three of them, Dad in Reading working all week. It was a calmer household. Their mum was a wonderful cook and she let Jules help her make his favourite meal, Cottage Pie. He'd stand on a stool at the kitchen sink peeling potatoes and chopping the ends off the sprouts. He collected the eggs from the chicken hut. And best of all, his mum would reward him with a shiny two pence piece for helping to prepare dinner. His dad would never have allowed this. 'Boys don't belong in the kitchen. He's a little Nancy if he likes cooking.'

Maggie defended them as she always did.

'They're okay eating tea in the lounge, children's TV isn't on for long and they can go up in a bit to do their homework.'

'Let me see your hands.' George asked Jules.

Jules put down his plate on the carpet.

'Don't put it on the carpet. Christ, it's like dealing with pigs in a trough in this house. And you've got ketchup all over your hands. You're an animal. Get into the kitchen and eat it in there. I will not have my kids treat this place like a barn.'

As George bent down to pick up the plate, he noticed a pink smudge on the arm of the settee. 'And ketchup on the sofa. For God's sake Jules, you can't be trusted with anything. This sofa cost me a fortune. It's going to need specialist treatment to get that out. It's coming out of your pocket money.'

Jules gulped. Please no, he screamed inside. It was like staring into blackness and being unable to pull himself out. He'd wanted a new bike for so long but saving up was proving next to near impossible because his dad took pocket money away from him for minor misdemeanours. How many new hiding places could he come up with he wondered, with a sinking sense of helplessness. An image of Captain Pugwash and the Black Pig sprung to his mind. He felt like Tom the Cabin Boy on the sinking ship who throws his last rope, with no saving hands to grasp it.

'George, that stain has been there a while. You probably haven't noticed it. I did try to get it out, but you know what ketchup's like,' Maggie mumbled in Jules' defence. Jules felt a tear prick at the back of his eye. Bless her, he loved her to bits. He wished that one day his father wouldn't come home. It was a fantasy but as soon as it popped into his head, he felt guilty for wishing it.

'Don't protect the lad, he knows what he's done. You're too soft on him. I'll deal with him later. How have they been this week? You both behaved yourselves... Jules?'

'Jules has done lots of jobs for me, he's earned himself some pocket money and Pandora's had too much homework to help with chores.'

George looked at Jules as if waiting for confirmation of this from him. It unnerved Jules. His dad had the piercing black eyes of a raven guarding a churchyard. It was dreadful to think it, but his dad reminded him, in looks and manner of the serial killer, John Christie. He had the same egg-shaped bald head, bulbous nose and wore a similar pair of round framed glasses. His clothes were dated. He hadn't emerged into the seventies yet and could have stepped out of a black and white movie as Humphrey Bogart.

'Has he now,' George smirked. One eye was ever so slightly wonky making him look creepy. 'He can tell me what he's been doing while you're at Girl Guides with Pandora.'

His mum helped at the Girl Guides and Jules had come to dread Friday evenings alone with his dad.

Jules kept his eyes fixed on the TV and swallowed hard. He was surprised that Dad hadn't switched it off. A feeling of panic grew in him, a temporary paralysing fear. He didn't want to be alone with him.

Pandora was in the kitchen eating her dinner, sensing their dad wasn't in a good mood and meant business.

'You did that on purpose,' spat George.

'No, I didn't. It was an accident.' Jules cowered away from him even though he knew that his dad would never slap him when Pandora and Maggie were in the house.

After tea, Jules and Pandora watched the *Magic Roundabout*. It was Jules' favourite programme. He imagined running away from home to work on a funfair. It was an exciting job, with bright lights and music and laughing children boarding rides or winning teddy bears. And best of all, the money flowed freely through slot machines. He loved the idea of pumping coins into an amusement arcade. It was a game he longed to play but he was never allowed to when they holidayed in Great Yarmouth. At least his money would be safe in a machine, away from his dad and he'd have some fun in the process. Sometimes he dreamt of money, his active sleeping brain came up with all sorts of crazy ways to keep money safe. He even made up a story called *Mr Money and His Adventures*. A favourite film was *Willy Wonka And The Chocolate Factory*. He dreamt he had the winning ticket.

It was an ordinary and routine Friday evening. Their parents didn't go anywhere socially together. Most of the time, Maggie had her hair in curlers, like Hilda Ogden in Coronation Street and she'd put a headscarf over them when she nipped to the village or to her friend's house over the field.

As soon as Maggie and Pandora left the house Jules went upstairs hoping his dad wouldn't notice. George was engrossed in the Daily Mail.

Jules was halfway up the stairs when he heard the paper rustle and his dad get to his feet.

'You've got no appreciation of money. You need to be taught a lesson,' he called from the lounge, as Jules reached his room. Pulling the latch across for extra protection, he hoped that and his weight leaning against the door would keep the fury away from him.

He heard the deliberate thuds on the stairs, his father was taking his time, to prolong the agony Jules was going through and by the time he reached the door, warm urine was trickling down Jules' trouser legs and he was shaking in fear.

'Unlock the door,' he thundered and kicked at the timber.

'I don't want you to come in. Leave me alone.' His heart was pounding in his chest.

'You'll open it now otherwise the punishment will be much worse.'

Jules unlocked the door and went to sit on his bed. His dad was framed by the door, the landing behind him in darkness. Jules was terrified. His dad was slight in build, but he was strong and menacing. The pulse in his forehead beat a rhythm and cold eyes pierced him like spurs. Spittle formed at the corners of his mouth and at that moment Jules wanted to crawl into bed and protect his savings stitched into the mattress of his bed. He'd worked for his money and that was more important than protecting himself. After the last time his dad had discovered the money under the mattress, he'd got wise and come up with his plan. His mum had given him the money. He'd completed his chores. The ketchup was an accident. Surely there was allowance for accidents. Nobody was perfect.

'Where is it? Where have you hidden it this time? I work bloody hard all week so that you can live in a lovely house. Other kids would kill for what we have.' Jules glanced towards the window, perhaps looking for escape or just to have a focal point to disappear himself into, he didn't know himself, but the view over the lake and open countryside beyond was an inky blot.

'Do you think I enjoy staying in a shabby hotel in Reading, with cockroaches scuttling around me, being away from your mother? You ungrateful little shit.'

This was the first time Jules had heard about cockroaches and the hotel described as shabby. He had the impression the hotel was nice, and he'd mentioned the landlady's full English breakfast each morning, with two rashers of bacon and an extra sausage if he wanted it. It never sounded as if he was in any kind of hardship working away.

Being called a little shit made him want to smack his dad across the face, but he was weak and sad, and he wanted to run as far away as his legs would carry him and never come back. It didn't feel right that a parent should say these things. He doubted any of his friends' parents would say such cruel things. A tiny part of him questioned himself. Maybe he deserved it.

'I've already spent it.'

'What on? Show me.'

George saw him flinch, as if his words had been hurled with violence and when Jules couldn't produce anything his dad stepped forward and grabbed his hair.

'Liar. You're asking for it this time. You either hand the money over or I take the belt to you.'

He unbuckled his leather belt. Jules didn't want his dad to know that he'd wet himself and suffer the ridicule and extra lashes.

Jules pulled the sheet from his bed and when his dad saw that he'd sewn the money into the mattress, George lost his temper and like a crazed monster whipped the belt from his trousers. He grabbed Jules' shoulder, yanked his wet trousers down and beat him.

Silence followed when it was over. Jules tried to stay calm and not give his dad the satisfaction of his cries.

'And don't you dare tell your mother otherwise they'll be more to come.'

When his dad left the room, he grabbed the fluffy rabbit his grandma had bought him years ago and clutched it tight to his chest. He couldn't buy what he wanted with his money because it was never in his possession for long enough, but rabbit, with his chewed ears and faded fur was a faithful friend to him through everything he suffered.

'And get yourself ready for a photo shoot. Clean yourself up and come down to the studio,' his dad called from the stairs. As if by instinct, he tucked rabbit under the blanket. He dreaded the day his dad took his anger out on poor rabbit. He didn't know how he'd cope without the toy, especially at night when he cried himself to sleep after the beatings.

Jules presented himself at the studio door. George was a keen photographer. He had an expensive camera, a Hasselblad, tripod and numerous lenses and a darkroom to develop prints. A member of the local club, he entered competitions for his black and white portraits and frequently won. He'd gained a reputation, and this led to his being asked to give talks to other clubs. Jules wished he preferred landscape or animal photography to taking pictures of people. It meant that he and Pandora were roped in. He was always thinking up new settings and poses. Last Saturday they had to get up at four in the morning to capture the heavy mist for pictures in the local graveyard. And in the summer, he liked to take pictures of them down by the old fishing huts and boats on Hastings beach, while Maggie sat on a deckchair painting a picture of the beach and the people. It was tedious and made Jules loathe photography which was a shame because it could have been an interesting hobby. But the trips to Hastings were happy ones. When their parents weren't thinking of painting and photography, they went just for a day out and took the cable car onto the cliffs. These were days when Jules felt an intense love for his dad. On the train, his dad pretended that the silver buttons on the seats were the engine switches and that by pressing them Jules could control the engine. The view outside was, according to his dad a moving picture and somebody was on board to wind the picture along.

'I need a few good pictures for the next competition. Take your clothes off. Leave your underpants on.'

Jules hated having his picture taken in the studio. He was usually there for hours while his dad ordered him to stand in different poses.

George barked his orders while he positioned his camera on the tripod and set the lighting at Jules' feet.

'Stand next to the screen with your back to me and your foot on the chaise longue.'

While Jules was getting into the right position it occurred to him what his dad was doing. A sense of disbelief hit him like a rock. He was trying to get the lighting right to show off the marks on his back—as if they were an artistic creation. But no amount of art could change the truth. His dad had unleashed his temper on him, and this was evidence of an act of violence, pure and simple and Jules loathed him for it. This wasn't art. It was barbarism. The pictures would earn him cash because his pictures were popular and sold in several galleries in the area. But if by chance they didn't sell Jules knew that he'd be blamed for not posing in a natural enough way because his dad would be embarrassed that the pictures hadn't sold.

Afterwards, Jules was expected to take an interest by joining him to watch the photographic film develop into prints. The smell of the chemicals he used in the developing process was acrid and metallic and made him want to throw up. He didn't like being in the darkroom alone with his dad with spools of suffering set out in rows, the only light red—like blood. It reminded him of being in church, his dad a priest preparing to intone a Mass. He stood behind him, never allowed to help even if he'd wanted to. Solutions slopped in trays beneath his dad's hands. Faint images emerged, features he barely recognised twisted before his eyes, he was a half-formed ghost. There were over twenty agonies in black and white from which his dad picked out four or five as possible competition winners. He scrutinised each photo for imperfections as it hung on pegs to dry, detached from his subject and with every morsel of humanity drained from him.

Photography was his obsession and that was the way it would always be. His dad wasn't interested in sport like most men. This was another area where Jules clashed with his dad. His mum liked watching boxing, but George berated them for their interest in the game, wanting to know what they found exciting about two men bouncing back and forward in a ring and having a go at each other. Those conversations always led to Jules explaining the game to him, his eyes glazing over as he showed how disinterested he was. Those conversations ended the way they began—as arguments and his mum would slope out of the room to get on with cooking. He tried to tell his dad that boxing was an art, like photography, and a beautiful thing to watch but his dad laughed in his face. His dad was never willing to accept his viewpoint or even try to understand sport of any kind. He wished he had a dad who took him to football matches and watched him play cricket. His interest in sport only served to make George more unpleasant towards him.

'For every moron game you watch on the TV I'll dock your pocket money. You're turning into a little yob.' It was a spiteful comment because his mum liked boxing and wrestling too, but he didn't criticise her for cheering Big Daddy, Giant Haystack and Muhammad Ali.

Pandora and Maggie arrived back from the Girl Guides full of chat about the laundress badge they were working on which involved starches and detergents. Jules and George emerged from the darkroom. Jules always laughed at Pandora in her uniform, which looked quasi-militaristic.

'You look like an air hostess in that silly hat.'

'Shut up baby. Why aren't you in bed yet?'

'Pandora got awarded the musician's badge this week,' Maggie said with pride.

'That will be a lot of use to you,' Jules chided.

'I had to sing the national anthem from memory. And what have you been doing?'

A flush crept up Jules' neck as he relived the lashing. He waited for his dad to answer, chilled by the sinister glint in his dad's eyes that nobody picked up on.

'We've been taking pictures and I want both of you to come for a walk tomorrow in the woods. I've got a great idea for a photo.'

Jules threw a withering look in his dad's direction.

'Don't give me that look,' George scolded, returning to the darkroom to show Maggie the photos. 'It'll do you good.'

Maggie peered at the pictures. 'What on earth are those marks on your back Jules?'

'I asked him that. He doesn't know.'

'What have you been up to? I hope you haven't torn your school jumper.'

'Well if he has, he can pay for a new one,' his dad said.

Jules melted inside at the unfairness of his dad's blatant lie while his mum waited for an explanation. He had to play his dad's dreadful game and come up with a lie of his own. He couldn't think quick enough and knowing how much his dad hated to wait for questions to be answered his cheeks burned in humiliation.

'I, I.'

'How many times have I told you not to stutter. Well come on, we're waiting.'

All eyes were on him. He couldn't bear it and ran upstairs to his bedroom, his mum hot on his tail.

'We only want to know,' she said calmly when they were alone in his room. He considered telling her everything but that was a waste of time. She'd never believe him, and it would only lead to more beatings.

'I took a short cut home yesterday and the brambles scrapped my back. Don't worry, I wasn't wearing my jumper.'

'Why couldn't you have said that. You know what your dad's like. He doesn't like it when you mumble. Just speak up for yourself.' It was alright for her, thought Jules. She wasn't the one suffering.

'He's always taking my money from me.' The words were out, he couldn't stop himself. If this got back to his dad, it didn't bear thinking about.

'I know love.' Her voice fell to a whisper. 'You'll have to spend it faster, don't give him the chance.'

'But I don't want to. I want to save up for a ...' And before he had the chance to tell her that he wanted a new bike she cut him off and with a wave of her hand she left the room.

CHAPTER 7: PANDORA – 2018

'I can't believe you haven't arranged travel insurance. Why would you do that?' Ellie shrieks as the taxi enters the motorway.

'I know, don't go on, just sort it will you? We're not talking Europe, we're talking America. If something happens, I could lose my house to pay for hospital treatment.'

'That's a slight exaggeration Auntie.'

'Just go online and sort it.'

'I don't get it. We're living in a post nine eleven world of failing travel agents and airlines that can't sort out their staff's rota and then there's swine flu, volcanic ash and zika. Travel insurance is a parachute. Essential.'

'And how often do you need a parachute? Anyway, they don't always pay out. I read about a bloke who wasn't covered when someone stole his tent in the middle of the night.'

'You'd think he'd notice it being removed from over his head and under his bum.'

Ellie sorts the insurance as the taxi pulls up outside the airport. It's busy with cars weaving around and suitcase strugglers. Some people have cases roughly the size of their bodies.

In terms of traveller types, I'm the one who doesn't understand how an airport works, or even how I arrived at the airport. They are a means to getting somewhere and the sooner I can pass through their environs the better. Forget the fancy cooked breakfast, the duty-free purchases and any enjoyment of the frenetic ambience of the crazy airport scene, I just want to be on that plane and away, escaping my mundane life. Airports are horrifying places that strip us of our dignity. Ellie, on the other hand is all of these travellers. Passing through an airport is part of the fun of going on holiday. There are various rituals that must be observed. After she has goaded me through the check-ing-in procedure, showing off because she understands the new self-service kiosks, which miraculously accept her passport but hesitate over mine–– we work our way through security to the Promised Land beyond, a place where, given the chance Ellie would live, washing her undies in the basins, drinking sugary cocktails at extortionate prices and flopping out against a bin when she is tired.

'Watch your belongings as they go along the conveyor.'

'Auntie stop being paranoid. Everything will be fine.'

'I'm just telling you to watch your stuff.'

'Why, what do you think's going to happen?'

'I'm telling you, stuff gets nicked all the time.'

'No it doesn't. The airport security guards would notice.'

Ellie removes her shoes and belt, while I dither, waiting until the last minute before taking off my shoes and belt. I refuse to separate my items. They can go in one tray, to hell with the rules, my stuff is staying together. A juggernaut of trays collides into mine as it begins its ascent to the place where I can no longer see it.

'You obviously know more than me,' I say, my eyes pinned to the tray. I mustn't let it escape my view. 'You're forgetting I went out with a lawyer. He dealt with tons of cases, excuse the pun, of theft from conveyors.'

'Another of the many men you've dated lately.'

I put my shoes back on, gather my belongings and get in peoples' way with my dithering. I feel as if I've just been through an apocalyptic nightmare of worry that I'll be stripped of my worldly goods before the holiday's begun. And is this what it's going to be like with Ellie, endless power struggles and disagreements? I don't remember her being this challenging and wonder if I'm about to find out that she's changed from the girl who used to idolise me. There was a time when I could do nothing wrong, when she looked up to me and was wowed by my knowledge, but now, it seems I can do little right.

In Ellie's Promised Land we must have a full breakfast at the airport because it's written on Moses' tablet. Never mind the fact that we never normally breakfast out, it has to be done at the airport and Ellie is excited about it.

After breakfast she declares, 'And now I need to go in search of items for my bespoke inflight snack bag.' A cloud of laughter follows.

'Excuse me?'

'I love my snack bag. I divide it into sections, sweet and savoury and ration myself throughout the journey.' She's got it all sussed. As long as I've got a gin and tonic on board, I'll be sorted. We head to Yo Sushi where Ellie buys extortionate raw fish and chilli rice crackers and sweets in WH Smith.

'My snack bag is to die for. I just love a good snack bag,' she screeches in delight and I enjoy her pre-flight enthusiasm as we make our way to the seating area to await our gate announcement.

'Need to charge my phone now.' She looks for a free chair and accompanying socket. Ellie has an itemised agenda and God help anybody who interferes with it. With the snack pack purchased her phone is priority. We've trawled the aisles of the duty-free, but she's saving most of her money for Sephora.

I fix my gaze on a group of scrawny teenage boys with oversized shoes and curly hair. Every flight has its weirdos. That's a given. Last time I flew I sat next to a woman dressed in Barbie pink with curlers and a hair net and who applied lipstick every five minutes. Sometimes though I wonder if it's my turn to be that weirdo. Like the time that I spent the entire journey farting. I didn't think it was a problem, I couldn't smell it. The blast of air from nozzles above the seats carried it away but after several hours of trumpeting the woman in the seat next to me made a violent display of hand waving and puffing. I got the message that I was stinking her personal space. I put my head in my book and tried not to look her way. But I'm damned if I should feel guilty. Everybody knows that flying makes you windy. It's due to the cabin pressure dropping. A plane once had to make an emergency landing at Vienna after a fight broke out because one passenger couldn't stop farting.

'You messing up on the travel insurance has drained my battery. I've no juice.' She weaves around each row of seats, but the socket hogs have got there first with their iPads, iPhones, Kindles, electric razors, electric toothbrushes and somebody is even charging a foot massager.

When the gate is announced Ellie's excitement mounts.

I follow her pert bubble bottom dressed in a bright pink casual, pajama type suit purchased from a website the minute it was released.

'I'm excited for the shitty, salty meal that nobody actually likes but it's fun to peel off. I'll plug my headphones in, watch endless films and wait for the football score. Auntie just think,' she clutches my arm as we stride towards the moving walkway, 'when we step off the plane England might be the winners of the quarter-finals.' As if I care about football, but this is the World Cup and everybody, man, woman, beast on lead and baby in cot are supposed to take an interest in the World Cup. I hope England lose against Sweden. If Sweden win as we fly across the Atlantic will the entire flight burst into chorus with mindless chants and praise for Gareth Southgate? Hopefully there will be isolated whoops far away from our seats. But if Sweden do win there's one good thing to come from the match. Ikea might be mobbed by stampeding fans, jumping on beds and hurling meatballs at the staff. I'd like to mob Ikea with the football thugs, it'd be pay-back time for the crappy settee I bought a few years ago that had an arm missing.

'I'm going to miss a whole week of Love Island,' Ellie says as we take our seats. 'Do you think you'll download the app' to vote for your favourite couple? There were eighty thousand applicants this year.'

'I don't watch that kind of mindless drivel, Petal.'

I can understand why lots of people would want to escape from reality, it's a distraction, an antidote to anxiety-inducing rolling news about horrific events such as the Grenfell Tower fire, the Novichok poisoning and the Thai boys stuck in the cave. It stops us worrying and shuts the brain off. Sometimes I wonder if I should stop trying to make my brain work. Brexit's left my brain addled. MPs have bickered for two years now over the arrangements for our exit from the EU. The nation has entered a war with itself and confusion is legion. Hard Brexit, soft Brexit, no Brexit, who cares anymore Brexit, it's gone on for too long, it's doing my head in. It's like the English Civil War all over again and Theresa May is Cromwell. Next, she'll be imposing we celebrate Brexmas rather than Christmas.

There was a time when I could keep up with the news, my brain was sharp and on the ball–– but not anymore. A hazy fog has descended and taken root in the dark crevices of my grey matter. The details of a Soft Brexit or Hard Brexit become sloppy omelette, scrambled egg as the news filters through my pea brain. Never mind putting sheets in the freezer to cool them down, why don't I just climb into the freezer instead?

On the plane we shuffle past first-class passengers holding champagne flutes and sneering at us cattle class. I'm behind a backpack bandit who blithely hits me in the face as he comes to a halt, hauls his load into the overhead locker, taking up the entire space so that I have to squeeze my bag into a tiny area, there are no apologies from him.

'Headset or eye shades ladies?' the air host calls, slinking along, his name badge covered by the rainbow colours of his Pride rosette.

'Male air hosts always seem to be gay,' I observe as the man passes.

'Yeah, so, and what's your point?' Ellie snaps, pulling her tray down for her bespoke snack pack. She's the politically correct thought police, the liberal left wing, the mini evil Hitler incarnate. But we refer to her kind as the millennial generation, or echo boomers, because they were born to baby boomers. They demand the highest standard of correctness, but the reality is that their opinions are as bland as potatoes. I'm going to have to insert the filter in my brain to monitor the stream of consciousness and a gag across my mouth. This will be hard. I'm an old fogey in her eyes. I've turned into my mother, donned my rose-tinted glasses and I look back on the past with nostalgia with statements like, 'It wasn't like that in my day.' Growing up in the seventies was a golden age. There was none of this politically correct madness. Nobody worried about TV programmes like The Magic Roundabout and Mary Mungo and her Midge and I rather liked it when my boss flirted with me and admired my bottom. I don't know what's happened to Ellie. She's been put through the PC mangle. Somewhere under this hostile exterior is the old Ellie. I have to find her.

'I'm just saying.' I raise my hands in mock defeat. 'Jeez, am I not allowed to say?'

'Leave the poor bloke alone. He's probably wearing his badge because it's London Pride this weekend.'

'I'm just making an observation, alright? Just conversation, unless you've got something better to talk about.'

She puts her headphones down and leans in, as if about to make a profound statement.

'Women have had their time. We got the vote a hundred years ago. We're tackling sexual violence, rounding up all the predators and weirdos, it's their time now...' She raises her fist in the host's direction as a mark of solidarity. 'To stand up for what they believe in.'

'No, it's not, they've had their day too. It's all about gender realignment nowadays.'

'What the hell's that?'

Sorry, I'm getting muddled up with Brexit. They keep talking about customs realignment, trade realignments. I think reassignment is the word I'm looking for.'

'We're all on the spectrum Auntie. Didn't you know that? What gender spectrum would you say you're on?'

'I'm just a female. For fuck's sake Ellie. We got up at four and you're spouting a load of politically correct nonsense. I'm too tired for this.'

'Yes, but you're freed from the binary of boy and girl. We all are now.' She squeezes my arm and beams at me, enjoying the fact that I'm confused and stressed by the conversation. 'Gender identity is a shifting landscape. There are more boxes these days than just ticking one of two.' She giggles.

'Whatever.'

'Let's see, you could refer to yourself as genderqueer, pangender, polygender, demi-boy, demi-girl, luna gender.'

'Alright, stop right there. I get the gist. I'm going to close my eyes now and catch up on sleep. No interrupting.'

'Before you go to sleep, did you know that President Macron wants to get rid of the term race? He says it's meaningless and has declared that race does not exist. We are all just humans. He's removing the word from the French Constitution.'

'I doubt America will do the same. The American Constitution states that all men are created equal. Has that made a difference to how they've treated blacks over the centuries? Anyway, making the word taboo won't change anything for those experiencing racism.'

'Keep your voice down. There might be Trump supporters on the plane.'

As soon as I shut my eyes an announcement is made. One of the plane's water tanks hasn't been drained properly and an engineer needs to inspect it. I don't remember getting detailed information about technical problems when I flew years ago. Is this a modern phenomenon? The same phenomenon we see in hospitals and schools. It's the type of information they give parents to help them decide whether to turn off baby's life support machines. It's all about information. Keeping us all informed, even when we don't need to know the terrifying details and we aren't expert enough to make decisions anyway. There is little point in being informed if you don't have the knowledge to deal with the information. I'd rather not know about burst water tanks or whatever. I overhear two morons in adjoining seats discussing the tank problem as if they are aerospace engineers. They're talking loudly as if to brag and baffle fellow passengers with their understanding of aerodynamics. There are only two things I need to know. Roughly how long will the flight be delayed and what's happening about food? And if the flight is delayed for several hours will we get compensation? I do like a bit of compo.'

We get off the plane an hour after boarding with a twelve-pound voucher to spend in the food court and instructions to return by eleven-thirty.

'A twelve-pound voucher,' Ellie says with all the excitement of a child let loose in Build A Bear.

'Steady on, it's only twelve quid. It's not life-changing.'

'Yes, but it means I can go back to Yo Sushi and buy the Katsu Curry, the Vegetable Tempura and the assorted Nigiri Maki.'

'I don't know how you know all the names. You do know it's uncooked fish, don't you? It's probably toxic. You're not going to eat it with chopsticks, I hope? That would be messy on a plane and I don't approve of the destruction of bamboo forests for throwaway utensils. That said, with all the bamboo in my garden I could set to work making chopsticks.'

'Get a grip Auntie.'

'You don't have to keep calling me Auntie. You can call me Pandora. It is my name after all.'

'I'd rather just call you Auntie. I'm used to it. There was a bitch at university called Pandora.'

Many of the passengers join me in the Pret A Manger queue. The check shirt brigade and hearing-aid-beige trousers held up with a clunky belt clan are out in force. It's obvious who the Americans are. They wear inappropriate footwear with smart slacks. There are guys with motivational fitness t-shirts that put the rest of us to shame because we aren't interested in fitness, we just want to slob and munch. A boy in front has loaded his arms with cans of coke, and a fat lady is selecting the entire row of cookies and pastries with her vouchers. We know that as soon the flight takes off, we're getting a tray meal, so this is our opportunity for goodies and treats.

'And how are you?' the little jerk behind the till asks. How do you think I am, I want to ask. My flight's been delayed which is great. But instead I smile, he's only doing his job.

'Put the change in your charity box.'

'It's a voucher madam, there is no change.' Damn, I could have bought an apple with the remaining money, but there's a long queue behind.

THE ASCENT IS SHAKY. We fly up and away from the land of Brexit turmoil. Below there are hazy picture book clouds and the fields of William Blake's green and pleasant land are scorched and yellow after weeks of sun and no rain. I have an aerial view of poky houses with no gardens, cars clogging our roads, intensive agriculture ruining the land and ugly suburban views. I prefer America with its open spaces, national parks and well-planned cities.

My love of America began when I was young, listening to Alistair Cooke's weekly talk broadcast on Radio Four, *Letter From America*. He had a beautiful way with words, warm, eloquent, a grandad figure who brought American history, culture and politics to life. Like all good storytellers he gave you the impression he was talking to you and nobody else, and he was the master at enabling you to make sense of complex events. He conveyed the suffering and the triumphs of the American nation so well.

The plane's engines rest mid-air before firing and sending my stomach into freefall like a ride at Thorpe Park. My head-phones are in and I'm about to watch the film *The Female Brain* when there's an announcement.

'Our family invite you to sit back and enjoy the six hours and thirty-minute flight to Boston,' says the pilot.

I turn to Ellie. 'Family? What the fuck. Since when did an airline become a family?'

The drinks trolley comes round and I have a gin and tonic. The gin comes in a small bottle. I pour it all into the tonic on rocks but it's so strong that I can't drink it.

I've been thinking a great deal about Jules' news. It's his responsibility to tell Ellie what's going on in his life. I can't believe he's expecting me to tell her. It's unfair. I'll be dealing with the fallout and Ellie has a volatile side to her character. She won't take it well, I know she won't. But if he's not going to tell her I'll have to. I'm not sure when I should do it. I don't want to ruin the holiday by telling her this early, but if I tell her halfway through the week it will ruin the rest of our time together. And if I tell her on the last day, that's all she will remember of our week together. She'll think I've timed it so that I can escape when we get back, leaving her to pick up the emotional pieces. Whenever I tell her, it can never be an ideal time. I consider calling Jules to convince him he must tell her himself. He's been a dreadful father. I know it wasn't easy for him. Vicky died when Ellie was tiny. He couldn't cope so I raised Ellie myself. His interest in her has waned over the years. I can't work out why. It's appalling. Some people don't deserve kids. Some can pop them out like Pez dispensers and some people, like me would have loved the chance to be a parent, but I didn't get to have that privilege. I think a lot of it has to do with the fact that Ellie is the carbon copy of Vicky. It spooks him to look at her.

When the food has been cleared away, I decide to broach the tricky subject of her dad and see where the conversation leads.

'Seen your dad lately?'

'We met for my birthday.'

'Really?'

'He asked me what I wanted for my birthday. I said eyelash extensions and for him to come down and take me out for a meal.'

'Your eyelashes don't look any different.'

'I haven't had it done yet. My flatmate bought me a voucher for it, so I asked Dad for a Kindle instead and he said he's got an old one in his drawer at home. Stupid cheapskate. So basically, he hasn't had to pay anything for my birthday.'

He's probably short of money, as usual, but I don't tell her this. It's the story of my brother's life.

'Where did you eat?'

'Well that's another thing. What is wrong with Dad?' She pauses. 'He doesn't eat fish. Who the hell doesn't eat fish?'

'I went out with a man who sucked the head of his fish at

the end of the meal. You should have suggested goat's meat. He loves goat meat. Granny and Grandpa kept goats and they were taken to the slaughter house one day in the Mini and came back packaged up for the freezer. Your father loved it. I didn't eat meat for years after that. They tried to convince me it was lamb or beef, but I knew it was Gerty the goat. Goat has a nasty twang to it.'

'That's revolting, and by the way I've heard that story a million times.'

'Sorry. I only have a certain number of stories stowed away up there.' I tap my head.

'I told father it's only prawns or salmon. What's so difficult about eating fish?'

'Grandpa used to go fishing. He'd bring back his catch. It put your father off fish.'

Ellie tuts.

'That is pathetic. Not as if Grandpa caught any prawns on the River Medway is it? Or salmon? Rolled up in a bit of rice you'd hardly know it was fish.'

'You and your sushi.'

I glance at the floor where her snack bag sits. '

You eaten your sushi?'

'No, it was a bad decision to buy sushi. A total waste of a voucher.'

'Why's that then?'

'Because it's been sat there too long. I don't want to get salmonella, do I?'

'What did your father talk about when you met up with him?'

'Nothing. Dad has zero conversation. He quite literally is the most boring person I know. His life is so sad. It revolves around meeting women on Tinder and drinking beer in the dive down the road. I don't know what my mum saw in him.'

Although I fell out with my brother and we had a massive bust-up I'm wounded by her harsh comments.

'He's got a new phone - a crappy one.'

'At least he's not a murdering psycho, or a dark lord on a mission to destroy the galaxy, or worse––spear you like Ivan The Terrible. Appreciate him, not for what he is, but for what he's not. That's my advice for the day.'

'What are you on about?'

'Which would you rather have, your dad or Donald Trump for a dad?'

'Donald Trump, obviously, because he's rich.'

'You're not materialistic then, in any way, shape or form?'

'Dad can be embarrassing. He had a drunken cheeseburger episode when I was round there once,' she laughs.

'Not only would Trump be an embarrassment to the world, but he'd be a super creepy dad. Remember the weird comments he made about his daughter Ivanka? And your dad has a better hairstyle.'

'What hairstyle? He's lost most of his hair.'

Sensing my unease, she switches the topic of conversation to my life. From her deep breath, I know that my life, like her dads, is under attack.

'And how about the men in your life Auntie?'

Ellie and I don't see each other much. My life is ever changing. It's hard for her to keep up. My life shouldn't be like this now, I should be celebrating my twenty-fifth wedding anniversary with Richard, but after the struggle of trying to conceive he lost interest in me and he went off with a younger woman he met at work. It was a hard time. It's taken the best part of ten years to get over. Swanning off with a younger woman was the ultimate insult.

'How many losers are there at the moment?' Ellie adds. I feel the sting of her dig. The last one was nice but a waster, frittering all his money on gadgets for his car.

'Actually, I've been headhunted for a date. Someone on Facebook with a caravan.'

She laughs. 'You're about the right age to go caravanning.'

I nudge her shoulder. 'Problem is he'll be emptying the poo and wee tank after the trip. Not sure I'm up to the loss of dignity.'

'Gross.'

'It's been a bad year for men, starting with that guy I met last Christmas. He was a complete weirdo. I sent him a Christmas card with glitter on it. He told me I was trying to harm him because the glitter had apparently ended up in his pants and given him a boil on his bum.'

'You do meet some nutters.'

'And one guy invited me to his house for a dinner party. His idea of cooking was to slap a few chicken breasts in the microwave with a gravy boat of Uncle Ben's Sweet and Sour Sauce on the table. And for dessert we had Christmas pudding and custard even though it wasn't Christmas. Half way through dessert he let his budgie fly around the room and feathers landed in my bowl.'

I'm in full moaning mode now. I'm off my lead and away I go.

'There are several men I've got my eye on, on various dating apps.'

You're like a utility customer where men are concerned, Auntie, constantly switching to a new tariff because the last one underperforms. You always think you can get a better deal elsewhere. A man is for life, not just for Christmas.'

She's so wrong. There's only one man I ever wanted—the man I married. But he turned out to be a cheat and a liar. Right up until the night I found out Richard was cheating I thought he was in love with me. We had a wonderful life, apart from the agony of going through fertility treatment, and the final diagnosis that I couldn't carry to full term. I tried to work through the pain and I had Ellie. A ray of sunshine she became my world. If it hadn't have been for Ellie my life would have crawled by like a pointless medley. It was all I could do to manage the basic functions of life. It was as if somebody had pre-programmed me to get on with it.

'What about you, Els, still dating the gorgeous Brett?' She's got the pickings of any guy she wants. They're all slim, fit, tanned, hunky beasts. In the candy store of men, she can have the lot, from the lemon fizz to the strawberry cream. At fifty the hard toffee is all I'm offered.

'There was no spark between Brett and me. He's nice but dull.'

'What is he? An electricity pylon? In my day we didn't worry about sparks and chemistry and nonsense like that. We just got on with it.'

Cheering comes from a nearby seat and the air hostess— the older woman with the large bum—hands me a Magnum but I'm too full, from the twelve-pound meal voucher, the big breakfast Ellie bought me and the pasta duet in a Pomodoro sauce, not to mention the two desserts I've had. The very strong gin and tonic sits untouched on my table. England have won the match. I'm glad we're not at home.

'The trouble with you Auntie, when it comes to relation-ships,' Ellie tears the wrapper of her Magnum, 'is that you fail to read the small print.'

She thinks she knows it all and she's only twenty-two. Yes, I've made mistakes with men. But it's not always easy to see the road crash before it happens.

'Anyone new on the scene?' I ask her.

'There is actually.' She gives a snigger that indicates this isn't her usual sort of relationship. I'm intrigued.

'Go on... tell your old auntie all about him.'

'Later on. He's just some guy I met a few weeks ago.'

'What does he do?'

'He works in banking.'

The plane descends over the jewelled sea, the land meanders and laces around harbours, peninsulas and tiny islands. Speed boats carve wake lines, trails of white froth and bubbles like a James Bond movie. As the plane nudges further down a heavily forested expanse of different shades of grey opens up. There are few roads. And then a smattering of buildings come into view, yellow in colour, mostly. I catch my first glimpse of Massachusett's famous weather-boarded houses dotted along the coast.

CHAPTER 8: JULES -1979

J ealous because his friends had money to smoke and go to the village disco, at fourteen Jules took a paper round. He still didn't have a bike of his own. There was no option but to use his mum's bike that had been sitting in the shed for years, unused and dusty. He didn't mind that it was a girls' bike. Nobody was going to notice. It was still a bike. He was just grateful to be earning his own money. This time his dad couldn't take it. This was his first step on the employment ladder and he was proud of himself. He compiled a list of things he wanted to buy with the money and planned to find a better hiding place, even if it meant going into the woods and burying a tin, that's what he intended to do.

His friends introduced him to Old Gerry, the newsagent in the village.

'Have you got any rounds going Mr Heinz?' he asked. They called him Old Gerry behind his back with a Nazi salute and a goose step, because of his nationality. He was a thin man with no beer belly to keep his scruffy trousers up, but he was always hoisting them between customers who came into his shop.

'Alright,' said Old Gerry. 'But no thieving or you're out.' He glanced up the street to a boy on a bike and pointed with his dark yellow fingers where a thousand cigarettes blended with the printing ink of every newspaper from the Times to The Daily Mail and said, 'Not like that wrong-un.'

Old Gerry liked Jules. After two days he said he was a good honest boy and it boosted his confidence after the negative remarks his dad made. He was a tough boss though and sacked lads all the time, but Jules learned that if you didn't cheek the pensioners or steal the paper money the job was secure.

He enjoyed his first week. He liked the throwing part of the job best. The papers were too large for the letterbox and the customers expected to wake up and find their paper on the doorstep. Throwing was what Jules did best. Cricket balls. Snowballs. Mud at his sister. And now newspapers.

But the thing that worried him the most was collecting the money from customers on a Friday night. The idea of going up to a house and ringing the doorbell and peering up at a stranger was making his insides churn. His parents knew that his first Friday collection was a heavy weight pushing down on him. His mum was reassuring and told him not to worry. 'I'll go collecting with you,' she offered but he didn't want to look like a sissy with his mum in tow.

'It's okay,' his dad interjected. 'I'll go with the lad when I get home from work.'

'Will you darling? That's a relief. I don't like the idea of him going on his own, it's his first time. He's bound to be nervous in front of adults he doesn't know.'

'I won't be. I can manage on my own.' The last thing he wanted was his dad to join him. The paper round was an escape from home life, it was his and he intended to meet his friends in the park afterwards. They knew an older boy, called Jaws— because he wasn't somebody you messed with— who bought a packet of Mayfair and they chipped in and passed them round the group. Jaws bought a small bottle of vodka with him which tasted of paint stripper. Jules was looking forward to being a proper member of their gang at last, although he didn't care much for the vodka.

'We know you're worried about going on your own.'

'I'm not.'

'Dad will go with you and that's that.'

Friday came and George arrived home early. In all the time he'd worked in Reading he never got back before six, but it was as if he was making a special exception on this occasion.

'What a lucky boy you are,' his mum said. 'Dad's made a special effort to get home for your round. Isn't that nice of him?'

Jules gritted his teeth. Agreeing with her, while his dad watched was like swallowing Caster Oil.

'The boss wasn't happy. He told me to do extra hours on Monday.'

'That was mean of him love. Well I hope you appreciate this favour Jules.'

'Oh, I'll make sure he does Maggie,' and Jules knew from the twinkle in his eye that this was not going to be good. His heart sank. He'd got up at five every morning to do his round. He couldn't meet his friends in the park because of his bastard dad. He'd got used to calling him bastard in his head. It was how he coped.

They came to the first house in a terrace of Victorian cottages. A man in blue dungarees answered the door. From the kitchen at the back came the clatter of crockery and Jules was worried that he'd interrupted their tea. The man went to get some money from his wife.

'Give the poor lad a bit extra, they earn diddly squat.'

The man returned and handed Jules double what he was owed.

Before Jules had a chance to put it in his trouser pocket his dad said in a kindly voice, 'No, thank you, keep your money. He needs to get used to low wages.'

The disappointed expression on Jules' face encouraged the man to persist.

'It's okay, it's a tip, the lad deserves it.'

'No we absolutely insist, it's his first week,' he chuckled and turning to go down the path added, 'We don't want to spoil the lad. See you next week.' Next week, Jules thought. His heart sank. Surely he wasn't going to join him again. A knot of resentment twisted in his stomach.

Jules had forgotten Old Gerry's instructions and by the third house he remembered. 'When you collect the money ask them if they want the Sunday paper too,' he'd told him. 'You might have to pitch it to them. The Sunday paper represents an opportunity. That's how you sell it to them. There's something for every generation; ideas for holidays, film and theatre reviews, sport, book reviews and a gardening supplement. Come back with a few orders,' Old Gerry winked, 'and I might increase your pay in a few weeks' time.'

The third house was a friend of his dads.

'George, how are you? How's business?'

Jules felt a surge of teeth grinding irritation as they chatted for ages. He checked his watch. If he could leave his dad here, he could finish the road on his own. But they were far too involved in the conversation for him to interrupt.

'I'll finish this road while you chat,' he suggested, turning to go.

His dad pulled him back and he endured another ten minutes of boring chat.

'Don't interrupt and don't be so impatient.'

'I mustn't keep you. Hang on a minute while I get the money.'

In his best business-like voice Jules asked, 'Could I interest you in taking a Sunday paper as well?'

'You don't want to waste your money on a Sunday paper,' his dad said nudging Jules.

'Look at it as an opportunity, Mr ... ah. You can learn so much...' His words trailed into a forest of laughter coming from his dad and the customer. Jules felt as small and ineffective as a tortoise.

'There's a page on holidays,' he said in a hollow tone. Further words lay tangled in his throat. He was intimidated with his dad beside him. It was useless. He couldn't do the job. He wanted to quit and run home to his bedroom.

'You sound as if you're reading from a script, you idiot. Come on we better be off, nice catching up with you Bert, Mr ah...' his dad mocked, with a playful swipe around Jules' head.

As they walked the final street Jules felt a measure of relief. George stood at the end of the path to each of the houses in the last street, giving a nod to the customer as the door opened but leaving Jules to collect the money. Jules thought his dad was bored or tired and wanted to get home for his tea, although he hadn't said anything to that effect. Maybe it was going to be okay after all. The pressure was off and there weren't going to be any more demands or ridicule. Jules relaxed into easy chat for the first time that evening. His dad waited at the gate while Jules knocked at the last house.

'Oh, it's you,' the lady said with a scowl on her face. 'I've been waiting for you.'

He handed her the bill, his hand shaking, hoping that she wouldn't complain to the boss. This was all he needed.

'I'm wise to you lad. You helped yourself to the coupons.'

She left him staring into the void of her hallway while she nipped to the kitchen, a moment later returning with a tea caddy in her hand. As she opened it, he saw the coupons stuffed inside. The papers usually had money off coupons for laundry powder or tea bags. He had no idea why she was accusing him of stealing them.

His dad joined him at the door.

'Is there a problem? What's my son done now?'

Jules hated the assumption that he was in the wrong and felt the familiar feeling of powerlessness crushing down on him.

'I haven't done anything but apparently the coupons were missing.'

'I can only apologise madam, on behalf of my son.'

He turned to Jules, simmering fury building in his eyes he demanded, 'Empty your pockets boy. You'll give the lady some of your earnings by way of compensation. As Jules counted out his pennies, he saw a smile dance around the corners of his dad's mouth. His dad was getting a kick out of his suffering and he was frightened about what would come later.

As they walked home a chill snaked through his veins as he thought about the beating as soon as they were alone in the house. Silent tears ran down his face, but he brushed them away, not wanting George to see how upset he was. He had to stay strong, knowing how much his dad enjoyed hurting him.

CHAPTER 9: PANDORA – 2018

We join the Disney queue snaking around the retractable queue barriers at Boston Logan Airport. Through security, to the luggage claim area, a lift, an escalator and a short bus journey to the car rental firm.

'I was told by the travel company that everything is included,' I point out to the rental staff. I do hate it when rental firms add on extras.

'Mechanical failure is covered, but not breakdown cover.'

Settling in the car, I take out the map of Massachusetts and unfold it.

'We don't need a map. We've got the sat-nav,' Ellie says.

'Whatever would you have done before sat-nav was invented? It's a good idea to use a map as well as the sat-nav.'

'Why?'

'It just is. You're frightened of maps. Go on admit it.'

'No I am not.'

'You'd better get used to them then because Snapchat's just brought out a map feature.'

'Don't pretend to know about Snapchat Auntie. You probably heard that on Radio Four.'

I scrutinise the map, making a note of the road we'll be taking.

'Just punch the address into the sat-nav.'

'I like to know where we're going.'

'But we're wasting time.'

'Maps are interesting.'

'About as interesting as watching paint dry.'

'Well that's where you're wrong. Place names are fascinating. So many of these are English names, that's because the early settlers were from England. I bet Americans outside of this state struggle to pronounce some of them, but we're used to them. For once I don't feel like an awkward, embarrassing tourist.'

Ellie leans towards the map, giving me the benefit of the doubt.

'Take Gloucester.' I point to it on the map. 'I wonder how some of these Yanks pronounce it. Glue- kas- ta and Leicester. Oh my God bet they can't pronounce that. So many e's. That's a tricky one if you don't know. And Worcester. Tricky too. And Leominster.'

'There are a few we can't pronounce though.' She points on the map. 'Cochituate. That's a silly name. Sounds like the food colouring, cochineal. And Billerica. Shouldn't that be Billericay? Like in Essex.'

'Imagine a Chinese person trying to pronounce Massachusetts.'

'Mass chu set tissue, achoo.'

'Mass a chu chu train.'

'Mass a chew chew on a fortune cookie.'

We manoeuvre out of the car park, ignoring the arrows on the ground because the car is new, and I've suddenly turned into a scary ninety-year old driver. I'm working out how to open the windows, while Ellie fiddles with the car stereo. As we drive down a ramp a car approaches us from the other direction. He raises his arms in the air and shouts something. We can't go that way. I ram the gear lever into reverse and drive back up the ramp, hot and flustered and determined not to crash into a concrete pillar.

We arrive at a petrol station. I assume the tank needs filling but can't tell which is the gauge on the dashboard.

'It should have digits. Are the digits to the top? If so then it's full. Auntie how long have you been driving?'

'Thirty more years than you have, you little madam. And how the hell should I know? It's not the same as my car. This is all weird.'

'Alright, calm down. Just fill it up. It's bound to be empty.' Ellie sighs and flicks down the mirror to reapply makeup.

'All you ever think about is your face,' I screech. 'I need your help.'

'I don't know. I don't drive do I? Dad's too mean to pay for lessons.'

'You could pay for lessons yourself.'

'What with? I earn a pittance.'

I'm at the pump half listening to her but flummoxed as to which nozzle to pick up. It's confusing. The woman at the rental firm said to use regular but what the hell does regular mean? The most popular? These Americans love to use the word regular. I used to be able to walk in a McDonalds at home and ask for a medium coke but nowadays it's called regular. I refuse. I will always stubbornly ask for a medium fries and medium coke.

Ellie gets out of the car, screams at me and yanks one of the nozzles from the pump.

'The woman said regular.' I am feeling stupid, as if I don't belong to this world. 'Not diesel.'

'But the nozzle for regular, which I assume means

unleaded, although nobody has yet explained that to me is black and a black nozzle is usually diesel so I'm not filling it with diesel.'

'It's the black one, use the black.'

The machine won't accept our credit card and we go into the booth for help. A tiny wizened lady scorched by sun and age is surrounded by fifty types of lottery cards and an array of cigarette packets—none of them have warnings on the packets like they do in the UK. The place is an Aladdin's Cave, with cool stuff that we don't have at home.

'They've probably tampered with the machines again,' she says. 'They're always tampering. I don't know what they do.' She takes my card and inserts it into a machine and we return to fill the tank. It's a mad system having to pay before you fill because you don't know how much you'll need.

I insert the nozzle into the tank and it clicks. 'The stupid thing keeps clicking.'

'That's because it's probably full.'

'It won't be full.'

'You didn't check the gauge.'

'Couldn't see the gauge.'

'It's probably a faulty nozzle.'

She leans across and throws me a look that says are you really this batty Auntie?

Another click. 'Yes, it's full, it has to be.'

I put the nozzle back, defeated and feeling like a church mouse, I wait for Ellie's talons to seize upon my mistake, but she leaves me be.

With the sat-nav set we sweep out of the garage. I am confident about driving. The journey South to Plymouth is only an hour away. It's a piece of cake. But I'm about to discover the nightmare that is Boston's road system. Boston's central artery through the heart of the city was re-routed underground at a cost running into billions. The project was developed in response to traffic congestion on Boston's tangled streets which were built long before the car. With ever increasing traffic volumes the roads were gridlocked and local businesses clamoured for relief. The underpass system is known today unofficially as the Big Dig. It's the most expensive highway in America. It was joked about by Boston comedians for years because it took so long to build and was dubbed the kitchen project that went on and on.

Americans coming to Britain must hate our winding country lanes and poor visibility due to getting stuck behind tractors and bikes and the massive potholes spreading like acne. I love driving in America and prefer it to England. The roads aren't as busy. I've driven in several major cities across the country with few problems, but within ten minutes on Boston's underground system I'm wound up and nearly in tears. I enter the underpass. There are too many lanes. It's a bright sunny day. The dark confuses my eyes. I reach for my bag, replace my sunglasses with normal glasses and I don't know which lane I need to be in. The sat-nav has lost its signal. The exits are on both sides and there's no warning that they're coming up, they're suddenly there. It's too late I've missed our exit. We're on the wrong road and as we emerge from the tunnel there are even more lanes to choose from. Sweat is beading on my brow as I negotiate more lanes, missing exits and getting more lost. Every road is identical. The place is samey. It reminds me of Crawley or Milton Keynes.

CHAPTER 10: JULES – 2018

I t was Monday morning. Jules stepped out of London Bridge underground station and pushed through the crowd of commuters. Every morning he passed unknown faces and familiar ones too with changing outfits and hairstyles. On Borough High Street he crossed the traffic passing a Jehovah's Witness stand selling their WatchTower newspaper on his way to Borough Market and his office beyond, where he'd worked for thirty years for an insurance company.

Summer flowers bloomed in buckets at the flower stand but a mixed bouquet tied with a ribbon wasn't going to win Mandy over. He'd tried that before, hand delivered from Interflora—and on occasion nicked from the local cemetery. He doubted a meal out would be much good either, but he'd promised her, and this was his last chance.

A man called out 'God will save you.' He shook his head and hurried on. The God Squad had tried many times to turn his situation around. Christians Against Poverty gave him debt advice sessions, but he told them categorically, 'Please don't try and convert me, I don't believe in God.'

They worked out a plan for him, but he let it fall behind

and fail. He had his own plan. A plan that had taken him years to craft - wrong investments, that's all that had scuppered it up till now- the plan itself was sound. People could laugh and pity him but he was an investor. He just had to learn to be a better investor.

Borough Market heaved with people despite it being early. Traders unpacked boxes, the air was sweet with Greek baklavas, honey coated almonds and Turkish Delight. He was only tempted by the sweet treats on display if they were offered on a plate as a free sample.

On the tenth floor there was a commotion in his office. Normally there was a Monday malaise, his colleagues sat at their desks, dark eyed from too much alcohol over the weekend and yawning into their pick-me-up black coffees. But today the office was a hive of chatter and raised voices. Jules picked up a tone of hostility in the air.

'What's up?' He asked, slinging his rucksack on his desk and flicking the computer on.

'Haven't you heard? said the office snitch, a peroxide blonde woman in her twenties.

'Heard what?'

'Management have decided that cut backs are overdue and they aren't going to subsidise our travel to work anymore,' replied the office connector, a guy in his forties who was good at hooking people up to create productive teams. Jules didn't like him. He represented everything Jules disliked about office life.

Subsidised travel was the main perk of the job. It was the only reason Jules stuck it. He loathed London, loathed offices and loathed the people. He loved the view over the Thames though. It was a view he'd miss.

The train season ticket was a huge chunk of money that he'd have to find himself. 'How do you know that?' he asked Mr Over-Bloody-Achiever, the last guy to leave the office each night, the one who never said no to extra work and volunteered to bring doughnuts to every sodding meeting.

'An email.'

'A fucking email?' Jules was stunned. Did they have no respect for their workforce?

'Sadly, it's how the world works these days.'

'Chill everybody, there's fuck all we can do about it, it's what El Presidente has declared.' The office clown gave a Nazi salute, he was always making jokes about serious situations.

Jules stared at his computer, his mind frozen and unable to plan his day ahead. So many calls to make and deadlines hurtling down the pipeline and they were all coming at him at once. It was added stress he could do without. He rubbed his forehead, picked up the stress ball he kept in his drawer and squeezed it. He couldn't trust himself to set aside money for a ticket each month. He could ask payroll to buy weekly tickets with his wages. No–– that would involve his boss finding out about his problem. He could ask a colleague to take control of his bank account and buy the season ticket for him. But nobody here knew. To his knowledge nobody suspected. He had to keep it that way. He could ask Mandy. No, shit no. They'd been through all of this before. It didn't work. He needed control of his money. Otherwise it would be like being a child again, with his dad in control. In any case he'd changed. That's what he'd told Mandy on the phone, now he just had to make it real.

Jules had seen this coming, but had buried his head in the sand, his usual coping strategy.

'It's a heck of a lot of money to cough up, for some of us. Well that's my savings blown. The missus won't be happy. She wanted a holiday in Tenerife,' said another colleague.

A holiday in Tenerife each year. The man had no aspirations. Jules planned to travel the world, eating locusts and alligator, climbing the Rockies, walking through paddy fields. He planned to do the lot. After he had the big win.

'We were just planning a commiseration Chinese and drink after work. Going to join us Jules? The social organiser usually came to work smelling of beer.

Jules was well aware that it was pay day tomorrow. That was one thing he never forgot. They were paid monthly, and he usually sat up waiting for the money to hit his account. He had no internet though, because he'd gone without internet for several weeks, unable to pay for a top up. He would have to get up around two to stand outside the Nat West for the WiFi in order to access his account before he could do a top up.

'God knows how I'll pay the mortgage,' complained the guy who owned more than a hundred silk ties from Savile Row. Mortgages were a burden, a rope around the neck and it was grindingly dull listening to guy-with-one-hundred- and-one-ties drone on about protecting his bricks and mortar. Jules was glad that he didn't have the weight of a mortgage. There had to be an easier way to acquire a property. He thought of his inheritance. Divided between the two of them and after tax it wasn't enough. That was the problem, he didn't have enough to buy a house, have nice holidays and never have to sit on a sodding train to The Big Smoke again.

'No, sorry I can't join you.'

'What's your excuse this time?'

'Palace are playing.'

'No, they're not. That's tomorrow.'

'Oh yeah.'

'Mate, you'll have to come up with a better excuse than that.'

'No money, sorry guys.'

'You still owe me fifty quid from the last time we went out.'

'I'm really sorry, pay day tomorrow, I'll bring it in the morning.'

Shit. Now he'd given himself another stress. But this was a work colleague, not a friend, girlfriend or family member. He'd have to pay him back. He couldn't not. He rubbed his forehead again, trying to come up with a plan. They were hours away from their wages hitting their accounts.

'So, join us, don't be a boring fart.'

It wasn't that Jules was a boring fart. Fifty quid was a lot of money for a night out. He could do a lot with fifty quid. He could double it. Treble it—or more likely lose it. Losing it wasn't an option. The losses were erased from his mind. All he could focus on were the wins, like the time he'd won a thousand quid from a twenty-five pound bet and bought an iPad with his winnings. It could be done. His new system was going to work. From twenty-five pounds he could get three hundred thousand on an accumulator. Enough to sort out the mess he was in. This job didn't pay enough. He didn't want to be like these tossers, getting up at the crack of dawn, mingling with a pile of sweaty bodies on a packed train to eek a living selling insurance policies for the rest of his life. He dreamed of sitting on a Caribbean beach with a Pina Colada in one hand and The Daily Mail in the other, the stories within reminding him that Britain was going down the swanny after Brexit, but it wouldn't matter to him because he'd be well out of it.

THE TRAIN SCREECHED AND SCRAPED, pausing on London Bridge before leaving the glow of lights, trundling along the track, through grimy South London, past endless Victorian semis with long gardens strewn with kids' toys. Jules was relieved that he'd got out of the work's do. It was Monday. What the hell were they thinking of? Monday was for vegging, not in front of the TV, because he couldn't afford a TV but messing around on Facebook and Instagram, chilling he called it. Not that he could actually chill this evening, in the absence of any internet but he could doss round at Simon's because Simon's girlfriend never visited on a Monday evening.

He wasn't in the mood for work banter. Most of it consisted of unimaginative insults and random words picked up from TV shows blended with stuff to do with the insurance world. Office Snitch usually wound Office Clown up for being late for work, even though he was never late, because she had the hots for him and found it funny, and Office Clown always called one-hundred-and-one-ties-from Savile Row an irritating and pretentious prick.

The last time he'd eaten a Chinese he'd been ill with the squits. He was down to one toilet roll and was using it sparingly. He couldn't risk getting the squits. He'd done his maths for the month ahead and there was no allowance for toilet rolls. That was one thing he couldn't pilfer from work. Not after Theresa May had branded toilet paper thieves as enemies of the state, insisting their crimes were an act of treason. He'd read her statement in the Daily Mash. It had to be fake, a prime minister didn't say things like that, but the words echoed through his mind. Without the season ticket perk, stealing toilet paper was the closest he got to an annual bonus from that pig of an insurance company. Maybe he'd have to consider it.

It was two in the morning. He couldn't sleep wondering if his wages were in the bank. A full moon shone through the grubby lace curtains illuminating his room. He sat up, dressed in tracky bottoms and t-shirt, grabbed his keys and phone and went to the bank where he could use their WiFi. With two thousand pounds in his account he topped up his phone, transferred his five hundred pounds rent money to his landlord and walked back to his bedsit. At least this month the rent was paid. He hadn't paid the last three months which had led to an eviction notice. He had to convince the landlord to let him stay, otherwise he would be out on his ear. How was he going get up to date? There was one simple answer to that. The same way he was going to pay everybody else he owed and there was Mandy to think of. The meal out. Money for the baby, a new pram, cot, whatever she needed, he had to prove himself, man up and be the dad she was expecting. He needed a big chunk of money. His wages were a pittance. With fifteen hundred pounds left in his account it just wasn't enough. His head swelled with worries and on his chest of drawers sat mountains of paperwork, mainly demands for money.

Jules sat up in bed and opened his online betting account. From the comfort of his bed he could place bets on any game, anywhere in the world, twenty-four hours a day, seven days a week. Things had changed since the internet and they were changing all the time. There were endless opportunities to gamble. There was nowhere to hide. It lured him in with its clever methods, whether it was a shop selling scratch cards, the office sweep stake for the Grand National or a banner at a football match, there was no escape.

He wasn't restricted to going down the betting shop as he had been in the past although he still liked going to the bookies. It was his social life. He'd made friends there. He loved the characters he met there. Scrumpy was a chap he'd got to know through betting. Jules found it amusing that he kept all his losing slips, he saved them and asked the cashier if she could double check the winners, just to piss her off.

In the betting shop he had a nickname. *I knew it was going to be that number Jules.* Jules played the fixed betting odds terminals, abbreviated to FOBT's, the crack cocaine of the 2018 betting shop. He liked playing the Roulette games on the machine. Thirty-seven numbers of heaven and heartache, where he would often be seen to put a hundred pounds on a single spin of the wheel, and the ball would land on a number he hadn't covered. He always came out with, 'I knew it was going to be that bastard.' Then heaven came for Jules one day when he was down to his last tenner and he put it all on zero. After what seemed like an eternity to him, the little white ball made it round and dropped into the green zero. Jules' fist pumped the air as his balance zoomed up to three hundred and sixty pounds from nothing. As he let out a cry of delight, the rest of the betting shop turned away from the screens showing the latest race for a second to see what all the excitement was about.

Jules had been known to stay for hours at a time, getting his Roulette fix. Going through wads of cash and losing many more times than he won. His friend in the bookies went over to have a chat about the latest number that he'd missed off, and what he could have won.

Jules remembered the night he was down to his last thousand pounds of a one hundred and fifty-thousand pound inheritance, and he was hoping for a big win to sort out all his problems. Jules thought to himself, shit, what's going to happen now?

The betting shop even served tea and coffee and it was the warmest shop on the high street on a cold day when he couldn't afford to heat his bedsit. Entering the bookies was like walking through the wardrobe into Narnia. There was an air of excitement and expectation because he never knew the wealth and enchantment he'd walk out with.

When it was closed, he could do everything on his phone, at any time of the day or night. There were times though when he wished it wasn't so easy, when his gambling was out of control and he had no willpower to stop the money haemorrhaging from his account. It wasn't easy when pops-ups for betting sites were always appearing. He could choose martial arts, football, cycling, volleyball...the list was endless and as a new customer they offered around thirty pounds worth of free bets, he was always downloading new app's to take advantage of them.

He poured a whisky and propped the pillows up behind him. He wasn't a drinker, this was the only time he drank spirits and even then, only a tiny glass. It was a ritual of his to sip whisky between placing bets, it was all part of the experience. He enjoyed the amber glow warming his throat as he made his selections.

He particularly enjoyed betting on horses. He checked Betfair and The Racing Post website to analyse the current odds on each horse and he looked for any horses that were unlikely to win and were worth laying bets against to lose.

He went onto Google to see if there were any sites that he hadn't already signed up to. It was like renewing car insurance. The bookmakers were listed in a similar way, with the benefits and bonuses of joining each one and the number of reviews they had. Many offered thirty pounds of free bets for ten pounds. Everything these days was about reviews. Whether it was buying a book, booking a hotel and or placing a bet. Reviews gave the product validation and trust, betting was no different.

He scrolled through the choices on his Betway Sport account and selected football, Augsburg v Weder Bremen, snooker Kurt Maflin v mark Allen and a greyhound race at Crayford. He chose the best odds available. There were forty-seven live events currently happening and twenty-six about to begin. He placed his bets and then clicked on live casino which took him to top slots and he opted for a game of Millionaire Genie because the maximum win was eight-hundred thousand. That was one big pot of money. That would buy a nice house, car and holidays and he'd never have to see those petty-minded fuckers in the office again.

By the time he got ready for work half of his money was gone. He put it down to greed. His carefully planned system was going to make him a million. He had the figures laid out in an A4 book. If he could just stop this greed. Stop when he was doing well. He was winning on several games; his money had doubled. He could have stopped, but no, he needed more. His mission was to turn a thousand into five thousand and five thousand into ten thousand and so on. He could do it. Next time he'd try harder. He'd have more control to stop at the right point. But what was the right point? He didn't know.

He had to win this time.

Panic set in.

On the train he placed another bet. Lost. Rubbed his forehead. By the time he reached East Croydon he was down by another hundred. And by the time he got off the train at London Bridge he was down by another hundred.

He was chasing his losses. His luck was on the turn, it had to be. One more bet would do it. He hovered outside M&S Simply Food, half an eye on the sandwich selection. His stomach groaned for a beef and red onion bloomer but he had lost track of what he had in his bank account. He moved away and out of the station to join the throng of commuters heading down Borough High Street. He didn't want to waste money on fancy food. There were usually leftover sandwiches in the office kitchen from board meetings the previous day. He was used to dried corners and curling lettuce.

Panic deepened. Next week his monthly train ticket ran out. On Thursday he was taking Mandy out. And she could knock back the wine. And he still had three months' rent to pay to stop that bastard kicking him out. His head felt like an omelette.

Think you idiot, he told himself as he paced, tiredness sweeping over him from being up half the night. A plan was needed. Should he gamble the remaining money in his account? If he won it could be enough for a year's season ticket and enough to support the baby for a year, at least. And winning Mandy back had to be a priority because he could move back in with her and save on rent.

As soon as he got into work, he checked his bank account. He was down to just thirty quid. Shit. The train fare. When the ticket ran out, he wouldn't be able to renew it. He was going to lose his job. And thirty quid couldn't buy Mandy a meal, let alone anything for the baby. Think you bastard. He drummed his hand on his forehead. He was locked in a bubble world, time and place held no significance. He was oblivious to his surroundings.

A tap on the shoulder and the bubble popped.

'Mate, you were zoned out there. Couldn't get your attention.'

It was Ronny from the sixth floor. Ronny worked in HR and was the fountain of all knowledge on everything from pensions to payroll, training to company benefits. Ronny usually brought either good or bad news.

'You're wanted upstairs. Pam Elliott wants to see you.'

'Shit, am I in trouble?'

'Why?' Ronny laughed. 'Should you be?'

His stomach tightened. This was all he needed. Pam bloody Elliott, the bosses' boss. What on earth did she want? He followed Ronny to the lift, the office hum falling to silence. Jules knew he must be in trouble, being summoned to the sixth floor but couldn't think what he'd done. Butterflies danced in his stomach as they ascended the lift. This job was all he had. He couldn't lose it.

Ronny guided him into Pam Elliott's office. The tasteful colour coordinated decor was complimented by floor to ceiling windows with sweeping views over the Thames, reminding him that she was on big money. As he took his seat a thought flashed through his mind. He wouldn't swap her world for all the tea in China, with its mountain of stress —he didn't need that shit. She probably still had a mortgage like every other arse that worked here. This morning's losses were part of a process he had to go through and in a bizarre way the losses drove him along and gave him that added high, the determination and spark. They didn't matter. He had control. He'd get the money back sooner or later and more. He crossed his legs, a tinge of excitement flooded his blood.

'Jules, hi, thank you for coming up.' She stretched out her hand to shake his. Bit formal he thought. Nerves coursed his veins as he wondered what was to come. 'As you know this company has recently gone through a transformation. We were taken over by a larger insurance company months ago.'

'Things are in flux.' Shit here we go, his suspicions were correct, he was about to lose his job. 'Jobs have changed, people have left.' Nice build up, full marks he thought. The praise was coming next then she'd drop the bomb. 'And you've been a great asset to us.'

Really? Nice try he thought, now give me the kick in the bollocks.

'Growth opportunities are fluid for your position.' She was beating around the bush. 'We love your passion to obtain more clients.' Stringing it out, it didn't wash with Jules. Just get on with it, his head screamed.

'We can't afford to lose you.' Had he heard correctly? She paused, frowned. 'You look surprised Jules.'

'I wasn't sure...'

'I'm going to give you a new job title so that you can grow and expand your expertise.' She beamed at him as if waiting for his thanks.

Now he was confused. What did this mumbo jumbo mean?

'We are workforce optimising.'

'Right,' he said, stretching the word with hesitance. He wanted to ask about the golden M word.

She shuffled the papers on her desk. It looked to be a

nervous action to fill the space that would have been a discussion about a higher salary.

'We'll send you on more courses, you can hone your skills. It'll look great on your CV.'

Jules' heart sank. That was all he needed. More courses. More online tests. His most immediate concern was renewing his train fare and unless a pay rise was on the cards, he wasn't interested in some fancy new job title.

'Could I ask something please?'

She glanced at the time on her phone. He hated that about people in power. They made time if they wanted to speak–– but grew impatient if their underling had questions.

'Yes.'

'We had an email about train fare. The thing is it's all a bit sudden and I can't really afford...'

'Take the next couple of weeks off,' she snapped. 'You need to use your leave before the year end otherwise you'll lose it.'

Each year Ronny reminded him about taking leave, but Jules didn't like taking time off. Time on his hands, to think, to stew, to drop into the betting shop. He was grateful for work because it meant that between the hours of nine and five-thirty he was out of harm's way. He could never afford to go away, like the other people in the office. That wasn't an option. The last time he went on a plane was his honeymoon and that was over twenty years ago. He longed for a holiday. He had a passport, they were useful for other reasons when proof of identity was needed. In theory he could go anywhere in the world. He thought about Pandora and Ellie in Boston and wondered what America was like. Boston wouldn't be his first choice, he considered. When I win a big chunk of money, he told himself I'll go to Las Vegas.

'You should be able to cancel your train ticket and buy another in a couple of weeks. That'll save a bit,' Ronny added.

Ronny thought he was being helpful, but his idea only

added to his problems. Pam's office felt too warm and claustro-phobic as waves of sickness crashed. He couldn't wait to get out of it. This was too big a temptation. God damn it. They'd given him a new scenario to think of. He visualised himself at the ticket booth, knowing that he'd cancel the ticket and pocket the money with the hope of turning it into several hundred or even several thousand. He rubbed his forehead and stood up to go.

CHAPTER 11: PANDORA – 2018

We reach Plymouth late afternoon. I'm glad to be out of Boston. If we had stayed in a hotel near Boston harbour we would have paid several hundred a night. Airbnb is a great alternative to staying in hotels. It's more personal, you get a feel for how the locals live and it's cheaper and better value for money. It wins with me, every time.

The stress lifts. This is pleasant town America, where behind the delightful weather-boarded houses and neat gardens there are happy families leading happy lives. I want to believe this, it's what I imagine. It looks a laid-back sort of town and when I come to places like this, I forget that the gun is legal. It looks peaceful and safe, closeted from the horrors of the outside world, the ideal place to raise a family. Jenny Wren House, our Airbnb is in a peaceful road and like so many houses in this area it's adorable and makes me think of the gingerbread house in Hansel and Gretel. It has a white picket fence, a cute mailbox and most of all I love the apricot coloured shutters and front door.

'My partner wanted to start a B&B, she was my soulmate, sadly she died of cancer. I carried on doing B&B and changed the name of the house in her memory. It's a great way of life,' Jim the owner tells us.

Our rooms are decorated in a style I haven't seen in Britain. It's a bit Victorian and a bit Shaker. The wallpaper in my room is deep pink with tiny maroon flowers. The headboard is mahogany and there are various different pieces of wooden furniture. The light switches are fiddly, and I can't open the sash window. I plunge onto the memory foam bed and sweep my arms and legs like a snow angel. It's so comfy, much better than my mattress at home.

We walk down to the seafront and restaurants. Stars and stripes hang from most of the houses, there are several roads around green areas. It's a tidy, well-kept town and there's live music in one of the parks, families are sitting around having picnics. As we approach the shore the sky is fringed with pink and the sun is melting into the sea. There are small huts on a jetty and several restaurants serving freshly caught fish. The names are delightful - there's the Cabby Shack and Cupcake Charlie's but we are drawn to the Lobster Hut beside the shore with views over the bay.

There's a wonderful sound of shells being cracked at every table and empty shells are stacked on plates as customers chatter and dip mucky fingers into lemon water.

'I'll wait for the food Auntie, you find a table. I'm going to check out the fit guys on Tinder, while I wait.' I head towards the red plastic seats by the window and gaze out at the sand dunes flanking the bay.

Ellie brings over our lobster in buns with chips. The lobster is delicious, chunky and succulent.

'Why are you on Tinder?'

'Don't have a go,' she sighs. 'It's just a laugh. I've put a profile up. English girl in the area for a few days, anybody want to take me on a tour? Several have messaged and say the same thing, that they're born and raised in Plymouth. So cute don't you think?'

'You're not really going to meet someone though, surely?'

'I might.'

'What about me?'

'You can go off and do what you want.'

'Cheers. That's nice of you.' I tut. I don't believe for one moment that she will do it. She just enjoys the chase. She won't have the guts to go through with it.

'Show me the guy you're chatting to.'

It's a side-view shot.

'You can't decide on the basis of half of his face.'

The other half might be covered in bad boy zits, boils and scars.'

We collapse in laughter.

Ellie is on a gap year before she starts teacher training. She's working as a housekeeper in a big house near Bath. The couple have three children, a full-time live-in nanny, two gardeners, a wardrobe assistant and several cars including a Bentley, worth the price of my house. They have a swimming pool and a tennis court. It sounds like a step into the Edwardian age and I find it hard to comprehend that some people are so wealthy. No wonder so many people voted for Brexit. It was a cry of pain and resentment from the have nots, those who were left behind economically, who looked to city financiers with bitterness. People like this have had it good for too long while many across the country have lived from hand to mouth. My blood boils as I think about their wealth. As we talk about Ellie's employment, I figure there isn't going to be a better time to break Jules's news, but it doesn't feel right. I don't want her holiday to be ruined by what's going on with her dad.

Ellie dips a chip in ketchup and paints a trail around her plate.

'Auntie. Can I ask you a question?'

'Fire away.'

'We've never talked about my mum's death.'

I reel back in shock. I wasn't expecting this.

'You were young when it happened.'

'But what exactly happened? Dad said it was an accident. But when I've asked him what kind of an accident, he goes all weird, he clams up or changes the subject. It makes me feel awkward for asking.'

'She fell down the stairs.'

My urge is to change the subject, like Jules does. A quote by Mark Twain springs to my mind. If you tell the truth you don't have to remember anything. The problem is it's the lie that I remember and the easy, casual way my brother lied to the police and then, hours later, under pressure from me, his private confession. I find it hard to distinguish the truth from the lie. The lie has wormed itself into my consciousness. I must remain calm, it's a long time ago. What can they do? The case is closed. Ellie mustn't know what really happened.

'But you don't just fall down stairs.' She sounds exasperated. Right at this moment I feel like killing my wretched brother. He's given me a lifetime of grief.

I fix my gaze on a man cracking a claw shell over his polystyrene plate and for a few moments my mind drifts to thinking about lobsters. Maybe it's a coping mechanism, to focus on something different. Years ago lobsters were a poor man's meal. Because of their over-abundance it was an easy way for people with no money to get their protein and it was known as the cockroach of the ocean. In Massachusetts they used to call it trash food, a bottom feeding ocean dweller, fit for the poor and prisoners. The word comes from the old English loppe, meaning spider. With over harvesting of the oceans it's gone from being poor man's food to a delicacy. An animated lobster would probably be wearing a top hat because it's fancy food these days. It was first served in American restaurants in the mid nineteenth century. The railway changed things. It was served on trains because inland passengers didn't know what it was. They didn't know that it was referred to as trash food and so chefs were claiming it was a rare delicacy. I should divert Ellie and tell her all of this useless information but at some point, she will return to her mother's death. There is no avoiding the subject.

'Els, people fall down stairs all the time. Stairs are the place where most deaths happen in the home.'

Ellie shudders. 'I'll buy a bungalow then. I don't want to end up the same way as Mum.'

I look out to sea. There are people on a decking area but despite it being the summer it's too chilly to eat outside.

I turn back to Ellie. It pains me to lie, but what can I do? There's so much she doesn't know.

'She was wearing stilettos. Hit her head on the wall at the bottom.'

'When I've looked at photos of Mum she's never in stilettos.'

'Most women have a pair tucked at the back of their wardrobes. Sometimes they're a frivolous buy, bought on a whim, they are the tools of the devil.'

'I don't know why Dad didn't tell me that, about her wearing stilettos. Why couldn't he have just said?'

'I think that's right.'

'What?'

'That she was wearing stilettos which caused her to fall.'

Ellie's facial muscles freeze and her skin colour takes on a hazy grey hue. Her eyes widen.

'What do you mean?' She snaps, pushing her plate away as if it's a barrier to the truth. 'You think that's right? Surely you know for certain? There must have been an inquest.'

What am I saying? I was there. It's as clear in my head as if it happened yesterday. She must think I'm bonkers. I don't mean to dither. I must stick to the story, but this is hard. I don't want to lie to Ellie. My heart aches for her. I never imagined having this conversation and can't look her in the eyes, because if I do, she will read my hesitation.

For the first time in a long while the lie does not sit easy.

CHAPTER 12: PANDORA – 2018

We sit in a booth and eat a stack of pancakes with fresh fruit piled high for breakfast at the Water-fire Tavern in Plymouth. Delicious raspberry sugared butter melts on the top. It's a dark restaurant with wood panelling and there are no windows. On the breakfast menu are a variety of eclectic items to whet the tastebuds from cookie pies, steak and chips to Indian pudding.

'Excuse me,' I ask the waitress, scrolling my mind for tactful words, 'Do you have news on your TV about the Thai boys stuck in the caves?'

Ellie fixes me with a look that says, what the fuck are you asking that for? I sink into myself with embarrassment under her gaze.

'We're from England and whenever I come to America you don't seem to have much news about things going on outside of your own country. So, I was just wondering...'

'Why yes, I know about those boys in the cave. Have they been rescued yet?'

The waitress chats and returns to her work station and the other waitresses discuss the missing boys in the Thai caves.

'Auntie, what did you ask that for? You're so embarrassing. You should have seen her face. It was so rude of you.'

'Alright, keep your hair on. I was only asking. It's just they can be culturally centric. Last time we were here, don't you remember the news? All about a tarantula and hardly anything about the riots in London.'

She's not listening. She's glued to her screen, swiping back and forth.

'Some of these guys are well fit, so American looking and some are so nerdy.' She turns the screen for me to see. 'This one says he's looking for help with the Sunday crossword.'

'We could go on a double date. Ask them if their dads are single.' I'm half joking but it's an idea.

Her eyes go wide and practically pop out in surprise.

'Auntie, you really are weird.'

'Only a suggestion. After all, you don't know who these blokes are.'

'I'm twenty-two, I know what I'm doing.'

WE SETTLE into the journey as we head towards the Plimoth Plantation lapsing into silence as we take in the scenery. There's lush patchy woodland thick with white pines, beech, spotted alder and greenbriar, boggy and flooded salt marshes with reed beds and mud flats. During the early days of the colonies this area was known for shipbuilding and whaling. Today the area is important for fishing.

Plimoth Plantation is a modern-day re-creation of the original Plymouth settlement of colonists who travelled on the Mayflower ship from Plymouth, in England, in 1620.

I'm relieved that Ellie hasn't wanted to resume last night's conversation about her mother's death, but I'm not fooled into thinking the matter is closed. My heart jolts when she opens her mouth to speak, I'm half expecting another tricky question, but the great thing about holidays is that they are a good distraction, soup for the soul and with new experiences and different scenery they create new memories to obscure the old.

'This museum we're going to is about the first Europeans who settled in America. But how did the natives— the Red Indians—arrive in America?'

'There's been a lot of research but generally we think they came across the Bering Straits from north-east Asia, over Alaska and just kept moving down the country.'

'But if this was thousands of years ago, they wouldn't have had boats?'

'Yeah, some civilisations did, even then—for instance, boats were used in ancient Eqypt.'

'So, when Columbus arrived in 1492 what were the natives like?'

'He arrived in 1492 and first encounters were friendly according to his diary. They wanted to share what they had. They ran to greet them off the ship with food and they were keen to exchange things like parrots and balls of cotton. Columbus showed them a sword and they took it by the edge and cut themselves. They were peaceful people and their spears were made of cane. They worked the land and could spin and weave. They wore gold jewellery and Columbus took them as prisoners and insisted they show him the source of the gold. He persuaded the King and Queen of Spain to fund his expedition promising he'd find gold and spices. Gold was the new mark of wealth and it could buy anything.

'Hang on. I don't understand. I thought the first boat from Europe arrived in 1620, the Mayflower, but what happened between 1492 and 1620?

'In 1585 a Richard Grenville landed and English settlements kept growing. Jamestown was named after King James. At one point the Indians tried to wipe out the English. They massacred lots of people. From then on it was war. These gentle people had never encountered aggression, their lands were sacred to them and they learned to fight and protect their spirit lands. Settling in America wasn't easy for the European pioneers, lack of food, the harsh winters and disease made life hard and only the strongest survived, but people in Britain were taken in by the promotional literature advertising a paradise across the sea. Most were ordinary sailors, footloose bachelors, poor farmers, slum people, the odd gentleman and some convicts. They had no idea what it would be like or the first rule of settlement - to be self-sustaining. If you were desperate to get to the New World all you had to do was steal a rabbit or swipe a cloak, do a six-month stretch and be swept away on a convict ship.'

'There's your answer then, if you want to immigrate. Steal a rabbit,' Ellie laughs. 'Personally, I'd rather a job opportunity in Europe but you Brexiteers have put a stop to that.'

She doesn't miss a trick with her constant reminders of the way I voted back in the summer of 2016.

'And when the Mayflower arrived,' Ellie adds, 'With the Puritans, what were they like with the Indians?'

'Oh, probably just as horrible as Columbus and the early settlers.'

'But they were religious people, just stupid hypocrites then.'

'They too were settling on land inhabited by tribes of Indians. John Winthrop, the governor said the Indians had no civil right to be there and, would you believe it he used a quote from the Bible to defend ownership of Indian land. And he justified use of force and setting fire to their wigwams, by quoting another verse from the Bible. They were treated like animals because they were viewed as animals, racism in its most basic form.'

'So, who actually were the Puritans?'

'They were a group of people persecuted for their religion.'

'What sort of religion?'

'You remember Henry VIII tried to reform the church. Thanks to a man called Luther. They thought the Catholic Church was corrupt and outdated. Some people remained faithful to the Catholic Church. Arguments broke out and different factions broke away and the Puritans were one of these groups. They were devout Protestants and wanted simple services. They didn't agree with Christmas and other festivals and even banned kissing under the mistletoe.'

Ellie yawns. 'I didn't know I'd come on holiday to get a history lesson.'

'You did ask.'

'Some of the Puritans went to Holland to start with, but after several years they grew unhappy and didn't want their children being born Dutch. They returned to England, eventually setting sail on the Mayflower for America, or I should say the New World. That's how it was sold to people that came over. They were entering a New World, with new and better opportunities, and most importantly for them the chance to practice their religion freely. Sadly, after surviving the crossing many of them didn't survive the first winter. The ship didn't arrive where it was supposed to be, by the way. It was supposed to land in Virginia but beached on the peninsula of Cape Cod. That must have been extremely hard. They had no friends to greet them or houses ready for them to move into. They were on their own and had to start a settlement from scratch. They sent a smaller boat out to find a sheltered harbour and arrived in Plymouth.'

I glance over at Ellie but she's asleep with her mouth open. The poor girl looks zonked. I've bored her to sleep.

CHAPTER 13: JULES – 1979

The paper round only lasted a few weeks. What was the point of continuing when his dad took most of the money he earned?

'You're fourteen. I was helping towards the household budget at your age. About time you did the same.'

'Go easy on the lad,' his mum said. 'He works hard getting up early. We don't want to destroy his work ethic.'

'You're too soft on that boy. Sooner he learns what everything costs the better. And don't pay him to do chores round the house. He lives here too. He should help out.'

And so Jules quit the paper round and spent the next couple of years cadging off friends for fags and never had any money to buy records or go to village discos. His social life consisted of meeting his friends by the river. In the summer they'd take a picnic and swim in the river or play postman's knock in the hay. In the autumn they scrumped apples from the orchards and in the winter when it snowed, they tobogganed down the hill.

Jules got used to not having any money. Lack of money in a bizarre way meant freedom. Money only brought problems, never joy or opportunities. Money was a burden, it was linked to cruelty and suffering and came with a goodbye label. Time spent away from his dad, enjoying himself with friends was more valuable than money. And with this growing philosophy he began to dread leaving school, his first job and earning money that his dad would snatch away.

Jules stayed out of the house, out of his dad's way at the weekends which meant he slipped back on homework and his grades suffered. In the summer of 1981, he failed his O levels and that summer his sister passed her A levels with amazing grades and obtained a place at university. She was the darling of the family and this was yet another way for them to sneakily slip money her way. Whenever the golden child did anything worthy of praise it was as if the earth moved off its plates, but whenever Jules did something of note there was a forced smile, from his dad. His mum praised him, but her actions were usually dampened by George's response.

'Let's throw a party to celebrate,' they said. 'She's the first one in the family to go to university.'

They threw a garden party to celebrate and invited family and Pandora's friends. Pimms and lemonade and copious amounts of food was served, and everybody sat around the lake, basking in the August heat. George gloated to everybody about Pandora being the first in the family to go to university. Jules slipped away, down to the village to hang out with his friends in the bus stop. He had nothing to celebrate other than his dad's doom-mongering prophesies for his future. How he longed for his dad to be the dad he knew he could be. Those moments were fleeting but happy ones. The dad who taught him to swim in their friends' swimming pool when he was eight, proud to see his son swim for the first time.

Shortly after the party a letter arrived for Pandora. Everybody was eating breakfast around the kitchen table.

'What's up sweetie? You don't look too happy,' George raised an enquiring eyebrow in Pandora's direction and put the toast he was holding on his plate.

'They're not giving me a grant for university.'

'We pretty much guessed that.'

'What am I going to do?'

'Don't worry about it. It's my fault for earning above the threshold. Work out what you need, and I'll pay it,' he said casually. 'You can't not go.'

Jules wondered if they'd do the same for him if he was bright enough to go to university. He doubted it.

'We've only got one child to support. Dunce over there,' he waved his toast at Jules, 'Who'd rather spend all his time in the flaming bus stop than revising for exams, certainly won't be going to university.'

'He might follow in his sister's footsteps,' his mum interrupted, winking at Jules with an amused expression on her face. At least somebody found his dad's comments funny. Jules felt crappy. He just wanted to be his own person. His sister's footsteps were the last thing he thought about. He had his own pathway to follow. His pathway had no markers, but he was determined to leave a trail. He didn't know yet what his future held, but the thought of working and his dad taking all his money left him feeling completely deflated as well as angry.

'And what about beer money?' Pandora asked. Spoilt little brat, Jules muttered to himself.

'You kids want it all these days,' his mum said with a tut and then added, 'Suppose she can't miss out socially.'

Jules gritted his teeth. There was so much he wanted to add to the conversation, but it wasn't worth it. Whatever Pandora wanted, Pandora got, and if he dared to complain about the unfairness his dad would find a way to punish him. Lately he'd taken to refusing him lifts into town and generally making his life as inconvenient as he could. He seemed to get a kick out of causing misery.

'No, I don't want to be Billy No Mates.'

'I'll add something on for social stuff, as long as you find a little job when you get there. You could work in a bar one evening a week.'

'And what if I can't get a job? There'll be tons of students thinking the same idea. And I don't want to stress myself out by working when I should be studying.'

George sighed and picked up The Daily Mail. Jules knew she'd won the battle by the resigned expression on his dad's face. Why did Pandora always find it so easy to win him round?

THERE WERE NO LONGER any secret trash talks about Jules. George didn't hide what he thought, and it was as if Jules wasn't even in the room as he added, 'No ambition, no interest in anything, I've practically given up on him. What's the point in creating misery all round?'

His dad's remarks were a source of amusement to his mum and if he ever complained about the derogatory remarks his mum laughed and said Jules was being 'way too sensitive.' It was easier to stay silent and pretend that he wasn't affected by the comments.

With six U graded O Levels Jules couldn't stay on at school to take A levels. He wanted to leave school and go and work in a shop or on a market stall. Anything rather than stay on to do exam retakes. But his parents insisted he resit his exams because, in their words 'you have no future without qualifications.' He knew they were right. It did make sense and it put off the inevitable––going out to work and having his pay packet taken from him. He couldn't go through the pain of losing his wages again and being beaten if he hid the money from his dad. School work was hard. His mum couldn't help with Maths and Science and she didn't have patience when it came to helping with homework. Pandora had never needed help. She seemed to breeze through her exams with little effort or stress.

CHAPTER 14: PANDORA – 2018

We arrive at Plimoth Plantation and Ellie wakes. It's spelled Plimoth rather than Plymouth because four hundred years ago there were no rules for spelling and writers spelled phonetically. The name of the town is spelled a number of ways in colonial documents. William Bradford who came over on the Mayflower served as governor of the colony for thirty years and wrote a history of the passage over here and the setting up of the colony. We get much of our information about early life in the colony from his writing and he used the spelling Plimoth. Today though Plimoth distinguishes the museum from the town of Plymouth.

One hundred and two Pilgrims arrived in America on the Mayflower. They're known as Pilgrims because it's a reference to pilgrims in the Bible.

After the orientation film which tells us all of this, we stroll along a wooden pathway and as we do there's beautiful bird-song coming from a tree. There's a guy with a long lenses taking photographs of it and he whispers to us that it's a ruby-throated hummingbird seen regularly along the eastern band.

We wander on and the first outdoor living history exhibit

we encounter is the Wampanoag Homesite where we learn how the seventeenth century indigenous people lived. The staff wear traditional native clothing, but they are not role-playing. The Wampanoag, which means easterners, were made up of several tribes in the seventeenth century and lived in Massachusetts and Rhode Island. There were around forty thousand of them although figures vary depending on the source. They farmed corn, beans and squash. Today there are about four thousand in Massachusetts and about three hundred living on a reservation on Martha's Vineyard, which is like a small country; it has its own laws, police and government but it must also obey American law too. It even has its own constitution which begins: "This constitution is created under the divine guidance of our Creator and the wisdom of our ancestors to establish and proclaim to the world that we, the People Of The First Light are a sovereign nation." And incredibly the Mashpee Wanpanoag tribe are building a huge casino resort in southeast Massachusetts, First Light Resort and Casino, as they plan to break into the lucrative gambling sector, but there's much opposition to the plans.

We learn that European traders in the early 1600s brought yellow fever which killed many natives. And around the time the Mayflower arrived the Wampanoag suffered an epidemic, possibly smallpox or a bacterial infection. The illness wiped out many of its people, making it easier for the English colonists to establish their settlements in Massachusetts. Many Wampanoag men were sold into slavery in Bermuda or the West Indies and some women and children were enslaved by the colonists. Relations between the Wampanoag and the British were good to begin with, but the British were keen to take over their land and they got them drunk so that they signed over their land.

We arrive at a bark covered house and an Indian woman is sitting preparing food.

'Are you descended from the Indians?' I ask.

Ellie scowls at me as if to say, well of course she is.

'We're natives yes.' I haven't considered how I will describe these people. When I was little my mum referred to them as Red Indians and it was a term that stuck. But I guess over time this description is seen as derogatory. They are natives. They were here first. And so native is probably the correct description.

One of the natives tells us that there's a widely held belief that the term Indian was coined by Columbus to describe the natives because he thought he was landing his ships in India. But back then India didn't exist. It was called Hindustan. It's more likely that Columbus referred to them as Los Ninos in Dios, meaning children of God, because they were innocent and peaceful people. So maybe the term Indian could be considered a compliment.

'What was your life like?' I ask.

'We were seasonal people living in the forests and valleys during the winter and during the spring and summer, we moved to the rivers, ponds and sea to plant crops, fish and hunt in the woods. Nowadays we don't live as our ancestors did.'

We find out that Thanksgiving was a tradition adopted by the Pilgrims from the Wampanoag who brought the Pilgrims corn and turkey that first winter.

From the Wampanoag homesite we head to the craft centre to watch bees from an enclosed area and then on to the most exciting part of the day - the reconstruction of a seventeenth century Puritan village where the staff are role playing real Pilgrims who came across on the Mayflower. It's the year 1627 and seven years have passed since the arrival of the Mayflower. They've depicted 1627 because it's well documented and it represents the period just before the Colonists began moving away from Plymouth to settle in other areas.

We stand in the meeting house which crowns the hillside

and view the layout of the village, with the sparkling blue sea and Cape Cod beyond. There's a road running down the hill, between two lines of houses.

We make our way down a rocky dirt track to the collection of thatched wooden clapboarded houses. Chickens scratch in the dirt and the staff are in period costume. I've seen Pilgrims portrayed as wearing only black and white clothing with large golden buckles on their shoes and hats, in books and in paintings. That's because black was for best and they were painted in their best clothes. We learn that this is historically incorrect and the staff are dressed in different colours, although they are sombre; russet, mustard yellow, dark green and grey. The women wear smocks, aprons and petticoats underneath their smocks and thick stockings to cover their legs. We chat to a man in a ruffled collar, puffed white shirt, with doublet and breeches.

'Your outfit must be hot in the summer. Is it made of wool?' I ask.

'Aye, I take my doublet off in the heat, but it keeps me warm in the winter and woollen clothing doesn't get wet easily. We wear cloaks in the winter.'

I pull my phone out of my bag to take his picture.

'Do you mind if I point my modern device thingy at you?'

A confused expression sweeps his face, he's playing the role well and smiles his agreement.

As we walk away Ellie whispers, 'He was cute, I'll find him on Tinder later you see.'

We head towards one of the houses where a woman is beating a rug against a wooden fence. 'It's hard to imagine the Pilgrims arriving here and having to build homes in the middle of winter. Conditions were so harsh that half of them died that first winter. They brought tools with them from England and hardware and they chopped down trees and reeds from the marshes.'

'Well they wouldn't be bringing software.'

'Tell you what,' I say, 'I wouldn't be any good working here. I need my cakes and puddings. They lived on foraged berries and nuts.'

We laugh at the contrast in diets between those early settlers and modern Americans. As much as they've tried to recreate the times it's not easy.

We enter a house, which is dark and most of the daily activities take place in one room. The windows close with shutters and the floors are hard packed earth.

A woman with a large bottom is grinding corn in a bowl. I've never heard of any woman developing a big bottom and big boobs from eating acorns and broiled herrings, but here we have living proof.

The woman's name is Elizabeth Hopkins and her baby boy was born on the Mayflower. She called him Oceanus. Her friend, Susanna gave birth to Peregrine when they docked on Cape Cod.'

'They're unusual names.'

'We use names that express our values and the importance of our religion. My neighbour named his children Experience, Waitstill, Preserved, Hopestill, Thanks, Desire, Unity and Supply.'

'I can't imagine what we'd use if names reflected our values. Let me see–– there'd be Global, Equality, Political-correctness, (Nessie for short), Infidelity, Environmental, (Vi for short) and Green.

'Makes me think of some of the celebrity names. Gwynneth Paltrow and Chris Martin's choice of Apple or Paula Yates and Michael Hutchence calling their daughter Heavenly Hiraani Tiger Lily.'

'Sounds more like a horse race at Kempton.'

'Some of us lost our babies during the first winter.'

'Were you sad when they died?'

'Auntie, what a dumb question.'

My question comes across as blunt and I don't mean it to be, but I'm imagining they are numb to pain, in order to cope with so much death.

'Of course, I was upset. Have you ever lost a baby?'

Her questions sting because although I haven't lost a baby, I have experienced the pain of not being able to have a child.

'I'm sorry, I didn't mean to offend you. How do you cope with so much loss?'

Ellie pulls my arm. 'Let's just get out of here, shall we?'

'The Lord giveth and the Lord taketh away.'

'So, your faith in God comforts you?'

'The Lord looks after us and has a plan for us.'

'What relief do you have for labour pains?'

'We have herbs.'

'Is that it?' I think about the jar of basil on my kitchen rack. 'Give me an epidural any day.'

Labour pains are the sins of Eve and are to be expected.'

'I don't think I'd let a man near me if I lived in your time, knowing there was no pain relief. Did any of your women die in childbirth?'

'About one in eight. Mary Norris Allerton did. She was my gossip.'

'What does that mean?'

'I think it must mean friend, Auntie. Probably old English.'

A group of Puritan women sit on the grass outside the house and talk to us as we pass.

'Where are you from?' they ask.

'England.'

'You bring news from England?'

I try to remember what happened around 1627 and surprise myself.

'Charles II fled to France and returned to England to joyous celebrations.'

I'm sure that can't be right. Charles II fled England during the Civil War in the 1640s, having been defeated by Cromwell's forces. Will they ignore the discrepancy?'

'You were there? You celebrated?'

'Oh yes.' In my mind I'm focusing on the joyous celebrations after the EU Referendum, not the return of Charles II. 'It was interesting. Plenty of flag waving and cheering.'

A man is chiselling a plank of wood to make a gate post.

'I saw the adverts all over London, pinned to fences asking people to make a fresh start and come to the New World. My churchwarden wrote a testimonial to my good character. I came for the adventure and new opportunities.'

'I would have been first on that ship,' Ellie laughs.

'You're only thinking of Disney and Hollywood,' I jibe.

'What possessed you to uproot and plant yourself in another country?'

'Oh my God Auntie, what sort of language is that? He's not a tree. He came on a bloody ship.'

'I'm just getting into this role-playing lark.'

'There was an economic downturn in England. A lot of us young men had to put off getting married and starting a family. And many colonists were dying of disease, violence and hunger. The colony needed to be replenished.'

'How old are you?'

'Twenty, missus.'

'Well from where I come from men don't worry about getting married until at least thirty and more often they don't bother at all. And if there's an economic downturn they join the dole queue.'

'They queue for a doll? That would be no substitute for a woman.'

'Not that kind of doll.'

'He came here knowing he might die of disease or violence. That's a bit like us advertising for people to be shipped over to

Syria. Come to Syria and have your head blown off. The city of
Damascus needs re-building. Would you be first on the boat?' I
say to Ellie, as if the man is a statue rather than a person we are
talking to.

'Yeah but he probably didn't know about the disease.'

'They had newspapers in London.'

'Maybe he couldn't read.'

'He could read, otherwise he wouldn't have seen the advert.'

'Things were bad in Jamestown in the years afore we got
here. During the winter of 1609 the living started to look at the
dead with hunger. They say that people dug up graves and ate
the flesh of the dead and drank their blood and feasted on their
brains.'

'And you thought you'd have liked to come over on the
Mayflower Ellie?'

'Second thoughts maybe not. I'd have been a later immi-
grant. I'd have arrived during the Roaring Twenties and met a
rich businessman.'

A woman steps forward.

'And I came here to find an honest man to marry.'

Ellie and I stare at each other. 'An honest man. What's one
of those?'

'Probably easier to find a man on Tinder than come all this
way.'

The man addressed the woman. 'Women do nothing on
this colony, except devour the food of the land without doing
any day's deeds.'

'Huh,' I laugh. 'Men. They were no better back then. Chau-
vinistic pigs.'

'Pigs. Yes, we do keep a few pigs and goats as well.'

'Yes, well I can see that.'

To the woman I ask, 'Did you have your choice of husband
or were you exchanged for something, like tobacco?'

'We have the man we fondly bestowed.'

'So do we, but half our people divorce.'

LEAVING the plantation we head back towards our Airbnb, looking for somewhere to eat on route.

I sigh. 'I keep waiting for a roadside diner or anything that's not a food chain. I swear that's about the third Dunkin Donut we've passed. I'm surprised I've not seen a McDonalds since we arrived.'

'Maybe they aren't so popular these days.'

'You can't live on doughnuts.'

'Why would there be a drive-thru doughnut takeaway?'

'Maybe they serve other things and not just doughnuts.'

'I could just do with a healthy salad.'

'I could murder a juicy steak.'

'Shame they don't have drive-thru sushi.'

Ahead is another Dunkin Donuts. Hungry and frustrated I give in to the Dunkin giant that seems to loom over Massachusetts and on impulse I indicate and swerve into the car park to Ellie's childlike squeals of delight.

'I suppose we'd better see what it's like.'

'America runs on Dunkin,' she laughs. 'Apparently the east coast loves Dunkin but the west coast prefers Starbucks.'

'They're all chains. I'm glad food chains aren't doing so well in Britain. Apparently a third of our chains are making a loss. There are restaurant closures of Prezzo and Jamie's Italian launched a rescue package a while back.'

'You can blame Brexit for that Auntie.'

'The weak pound doesn't help but wages are going up, rents are high and there's too many on the high street. They can't compete.'

Inside we are met by a blast of cold air. To my surprise Dunkin doesn't just serve the type of doughnuts I'm expecting.

There are bagels and muffins, croissant and Danish. There's an array of coffees on the board from pumpkin white chocolate latte, frozen coffee Coolatte to hot chocolate. It's tea I'm looking for. Just plain English tea. There's vanilla chai but I can't see tea. I'm English. I panic if I can't find tea on the menu. To my relief they serve tea and it's a good wholesome proper English cuppa, apart from the ghastly polystyrene it's served in. I sink my teeth into a heavenly glazed apple Danish. It's so good it's gone in seconds and I return to the counter, to order two more. Bloated and with Ellie at my heels calling me a fatty, I waddle out of the door, like an Oompa Loompa in *Charlie and The Chocolate Factory.*

'We're not going back in there.'

'But you had three of them. You're going to be sick now. You should have had the egg and cheese muffin.'

'Given the chance I'd eat those Apple Danish every day.'

As we get into the car a pick-up truck with huge tyres coughs to life, the driver is attempting to drink coffee, stuff a doughnut into his mouth and steer the wheels round in a screeching two- point turn, before peeling out onto the main road.

Ellie sticks two fingers out of the window. 'Arsehole. What the hell is it with these drivers? Why do they need to drive such massive vehicles, I just don't get it? He's probably used half a tank just to get a doughnut. He should be arrested for wasting the earth's vital resources.'

'Watch it, he might have a gun and come back to get you.'

Ellie's rattled. 'If we were in London it might be a knife or an acid attack, here it's all guns. There's violence everywhere. But why do they all drive such ridiculously huge cars? We're meant to be cutting emissions and finding ways to save the planet. They're leaving the problem to the rest of the world to sort out.'

'It must be nice to be high up and feel all superior though.' I'm imagining applying lipstick at traffic lights.

She raises an enquiring eyebrow as if I'm bonkers.

'But if the temperature rises just one more degree,' she wags a finger in my face and I flinch, 'the earth will be tipped into a hothouse state. The seas and forests can't absorb any more CO_2, vast areas will be uninhabitable and natural systems will spew out CO_2. We need to do something.'

'Well you've got to admit it could be useful to drive one.'

'Auntie, what the heck? You would not need one of those.' She stretches out each word for effect.

'Yeah but they do. For heavy snow.'

'Well they should just drive it in snow... not all year.'

'They travel greater distances than us.'

'Well they should use the train instead. We do.'

I settle into the drive, her voice a lilt of fury.

'And another thing Auntie, those trucks only do twenty-eight miles per gallon. One of the blokes I was chatting to couldn't believe we can get seventy-eight miles to the gallon. How obscene is that? They don't get it.'

Petrol's cheap here.'

'That's not the point. Anyway, it should be more expensive, to pay for the damage they're doing to the environment.' She's a fiery ball of fury, shrieking at me as if I'm personally responsible for the state of the country.

There's a beat of silence as I throw her an enough said look and we laugh. It's spontaneous. Laughter that bubbles from nowhere, like water from a brook. It's as if the tension, not just from this conversation but bound up in much all our dialogue we've had, is released in one steady stream of mirth and sugar-fuelled laughter, which goes on for several minutes as we each come to terms with the fact that we see things differently. I've been so caught up in Jules' problems and my own life I haven't noticed this change in her. She's grown up. She has opinions. She's emerged from a chrysalis and is her own person.

And then I'm reminded that inside she is still a child.

'Wow, a yellow school bus.'

'There was a couple a few years back who converted an old yellow school bus into a home and travelled round the country. It's got a kitchen, bedroom, bathroom and even a dog bed. How groovy is that?'

'Auntie, can I ask you something?'

This sounds ominous. 'Yes.'

'It's very strange that Dad moved into a one bedroom flat. I don't understand why he'd do that.'

I don't like lying. It's not in my nature. I'm conscious that lies cost relationships. Maybe Ellie would prefer to hear the painful truth than a comforting lie. She deserves to hear the truth. She's old enough and I shouldn't have to defend my brother, but I do. And Ellie, in my mind is still young and needs protecting. I want to wrap a blanket around her, but I realise I can't. The truth will come out, one day.

'I suppose it was just him, rattling around in that big house, with you and your mum gone and it meant less cleaning.'

She pulls a face that says you've got to be joking, it wasn't that big.

'It's easier for him to be in a flat.'

'But he's earning good money. He's in insurance for Christ sake. It's pathetic. He's got nothing to show for his money.'

'I don't know. He keeps his affairs under wraps. It's not my business.' My answer satisfies my conscience. 'Maybe one day he'll surprise you and give you a flat.' Why the hell did I say that? I'm digging a hole for myself that I'll have to account for when the shit hits the fan. Do not say anymore Pandora.

'Hey, a pickup with something in it.'

I step on the accelerator for a closer inspection. It's the first pickup we've passed with something in the back. The car judders forward. Ahead of us the traffic lights turn red, but the pick-up has zipped through the lights. When they go green, I floor the accelerator, speeding to catch up and swerving recklessly around another truck, as we catch a glimpse of toilets piled in the back of the truck. As we laugh I almost hit a car . We exchange abusive gestures and furious bursts of car horns but mine are little more than a pantomime because I know it's my fault— well almost. The toilets distracted me.

CHAPTER 15: JULES - 1981

Jules joined the academic studies department at the local further education college for a two- year course to study for O levels.

'I don't know what good it'll do,' George said to Maggie over dinner. 'If he couldn't get the grades the first time around, what hope is there now?'

Jules snapped. 'I hate it when you talk about me as if I'm not in the room.' Taller than his dad he'd started to challenge his nasty remarks. After all what could he do, they were just words, so he tried to block them by singing in his head. His dad couldn't beat him and if he dared try, Jules knew that he'd turn on his dad and end up in trouble with the police. It wasn't worth it. He learned to keep out of his way. He couldn't take money away either because Jules didn't have any. A new strength was taking hold of him and he was proud of himself.

He could only be bothered with Maths, English and Science and knuckled down to those three subjects. Failing again wasn't an option. Exams were a necessary evil. He wasn't going to entertain staying on to do A levels as his parents wanted him to do. Why couldn't they see that he wasn't academic and stop nagging him?

To pay his keep his parents insisted he do chores, something that Pandora had got out of when she was studying for exams. It was as if his dad was making things deliberately hard for him. The bitter winter made it cold upstairs because they had taken to only heating one room with a portable Calor gas heater because Dad complained about the enormous oil bill. But the gas made the air damp which irritated Jules' asthma and nose. Now George was working from home and Jules missed him being away all week and he couldn't bear to be in the same room as his dad if he could avoid it. His mum was always on edge now that he was around, and she was under his spell. He'd never noticed it before but maybe their marriage wasn't quite the perfect picture that he'd imagined it to be when he was younger.

In the evenings rubbing his gloved hands with piles of blankets on his knees he sat at his desk, while he sipped a hot Bovril. In the daytime he used the college library where the radiators pumped out a glorious heat.

The first snow of the winter arrived bringing several inches of snow, the temperature dropping to below freezing caused by strong winds from Siberia. Worried about the pipes freezing over, George was forced to turn the central heating on and Jules was still expected to get up at five to milk the two goats. The pond was mostly frozen which made it difficult to feed the ducks and geese.

He'd just finished milking the goats and had to be ready for college when his dad appeared..

'Go out with an axe and break the ice from the edge to the centre of the pond, so that the ducks can reach their food which I've put out on a metal trough,' George ordered. Putting the wadders on Jules inched out into the darkness. He was afraid that he'd lose his balance and fall into the freezing water.

He knew that it was a pointless task. The food would only get eaten by the magpies and crows before the ducks got a look in.

The following day a couple of the ducks were missing.

'You useless boy, the foxes have got the ducks because you hardly broke the ice.'

'I was afraid of falling into the water.'

'It'd be the best place for you, you can't do anything right. If you fail your exams I doubt the local farmer will employ you. You'd let the foxes run amok around his farm.'

That evening Jules couldn't focus on his studies, despite his first mock exam the next day. His dad didn't seem to care. As long as his precious animals were fed, nothing else mattered. All he was worried about were the ducks and geese falling prey to the fox so Jules had to go out in the darkness to put a lantern out to deter the foxes.

WITH THE HARSH WINTER LIFTED, Spring came tapping at the door. The Summer arrived and with it the final exams.

'How did the exam go?' His mother asked over their lamb chop dinner.

'It was fine. I answered most of the questions.'

'Well that's good dear.'

With half an eye on the newspaper at the side of his plate, his dad carried on chewing. It was ghastly to watch and Jules hated the way he ate his food, stopping to insert a finger to pry out bits stuck between his teeth.

'Have you read this?' He pushed the paper towards Maggie. 'Bank rate's risen and despite denials from the chancellor, it looks as if it will probably rise again.

Jules felt like a shadow around his dad and longed for the day when he could leave home. On the day of his Maths O Level, he peered through the kitchen window to see if the moles had tossed another pile of mud during the night and if they had he would have to clear the mud before he could sit down for his boiled egg.

'All ready for the exam?' His mum asked.

'I think so.'

'Did you know,' his dad said, 'that the English and French break their boiled eggs differently? The English slice off the top with a knife but the French peel them.'

Moments like this, when Jules was included in his dad's conversation felt special, despite the fact that his dad was talking about boiled eggs rather than asking how his Maths was coming along.

'She didn't say what the Germans do?' his mum enquired.

'I don't think so. Maybe I should have asked her.'

And that was the day he sat his Maths exam which he thought went pretty well but what was the point in sharing his thoughts with his dad, only to be slammed down.

'Jesus you'd better bloody pass this time,' his dad snarled over mince beef.

His dad was more interested in his newspaper.

'The papers are full of the Falklands.'

Jules thought about asking where the Falklands Islands were, but thought better of it.

'The Ministry of Defence say we've knocked out eleven Argentinian aircraft that were standing on the airfield. Nott says that Britain will never surrender sovereignty of the island. The chances of a ceasefire look slim.'

Jules wondered whether there would ever be a ceasefire between him and his dad. Just when a thaw was happening the ice between them froze over again.

CHAPTER 16: PANDORA - 2018

Heading out early to another day of glorious sun, we check the map for the site of the Mayflower mounds. We plan to eat breakfast en route but an hour into the journey and all we've passed are more Dunkin Donuts. My heart sinks as it would be nice to have some variety. All I can hope for is a surprise diner, to appear like a mirage on the landscape of my hungry belly. Just when I think I will collapse with pangs of hunger a collection of buildings sweeps into view and there's an IHop restaurant in an Austrian chalet type building. Ellie tells me it stands for International House of Pancakes. With a name like that it sounds as if it has the Royal seal of approval stamped across its door. But the abbreviation reminds me of a child's indoor play zone, the type you find in warehouses with trampolines and climbing frames.

We slide into a booth and pore over the menu, salivating at the delicious choice and range of pancakes and French toast. The place is a cocktail bar of pancakes. At one end of the table are huge bottles of maple syrup, chocolate and strawberry sauces. The pancakes, when they arrive don't disappoint. They come lathered in spray cream and I imagine somebody arguing with me and it smacking in my face as payback. We waddle to the exit, the void inside us filled and in a better frame of mind.

Next we head for Provincetown, the town on the narrow finger of land at the tip of Cape Cod. On the map, it looks like the barb on a hook. It doesn't look to be a particularly green area. Possibly the early settlers felled the trees and they were never replaced. The Mayflower arrived in what is now Provincetown Harbour, after thirty-six days at sea. Provincetown has gone unmentioned in this chapter of American history. The road to Cape Cod is fringed with pitch pines and scrub oak, growing like weeds and obscuring the views. We cross the Sagamore Bridge which connects Cape Cod to the mainland of Massachusetts. The bridge arches dramatically in the middle as the landscape melts away and is replaced by tall reed beds and marshy land, carried out to mud flats merging in the blue sky. Road signs guide us onward to places with homely English names and dramatic histories; Falmouth, Harwich, Barnstable, Chatham. Thankfully they aren't a collection of our silly or rude place names, like Brown Willy, in Cornwall, or Crapstone in Devon or Crackpot in Yorkshire. They've selected our respectable names and added their own magical delights - Woods Hole, Mashpee, Brewster and Osterville.

We pass a shop frontage festooned with lobster pots, fisherman's nets and wicker objects and houses with the requisite Cedar shake, shingles forming the roofs and clapboard sidings. The shingle roofing has bleached the colour to a dull grey over time. There are no gardens, just lawns scattered with pine needles, sand and moss.

There's something pulling us towards Provincetown. It's busy and cars are parked either side of the road leaving little room for traffic to pass. It's hard to drive and have time to look at the beautiful Cape Cod homes. Of all the houses I've seen across the States the Cape Cod, early colonist style homes seen here in New England are the most iconic of all the styles. We gasp at each one. They are the apple pie of the architectural world, neat and nostalgic, white clapboarding and shuttered and look like undecorated gingerbread houses. For the early settler, they were easy to put up and the style has barely changed over time. They sit behind white, freshly painted picket fences and a splash of colour - hydrangeas at this time of year - adorn the gardens. A croquet set is laid out on the emerald lawn of one home. It's easy to imagine the lives within the walls - happy children and doting parents straight out of a nineteen fifties movie. I imagine women in polka dot swing skirts and men in beige slacks and greased back hair.

We park and join a throng of tourists, mainly families heading to the beach, sand buckets swinging from the arms of ice cream eating children. We walk between two wooden houses and onto the beach where circling gulls cry out. The wind is gentle and clean, sharp with salt of distant spray. A spritz of sunlight catches the sea scattering diamonds and making me reach for sunglasses. We trudge towards a flotilla of boats rocking gently in the water by a jetty. The sand is so light that it drifts about the houses lining the beach like snow in a driving storm and forming peaks like the Sahara. The beach slopes gently into the water, bearded by kelp and seagrass. There are canoes, tethered to rope bobbing in the water.

I glance at a man watching his dog swim in the sea.

'He's having fun. Are there sharks out there?'

'Sometimes sharks are spotted and a warning goes out.'

'What about whales?'

A hundred or so years ago the waters around here were full of whales. It was possible to harpoon them from shore. The surviving whales now live some distance out to sea.'

'Can we go whale-watching?' Ellie asks me.

'I don't fancy that. It's an intrusion on their privacy. They ought to be left alone.'

'You should go,' the man says. 'Get on a boat. It takes several hours though and much of your time is spent churning your way through empty water to get to the place where whales feed. They're migratory—they winter to the south and come here in the summer. You are most likely to see humpbacks. They are one of the most remarkable creatures you'll ever see. They're huge.'

'It sounds scary.'

'That aren't bothered by the boats, they're docile creatures.'

The sand is heavy and hard to walk through, so we give up and clamber towards some steps and onto the road leading into town.

Provincetown looks like any other seaside resort. There are ice cream parlours and tourist shops selling an array of souvenirs; the type of things that end up at boot fairs. I don't take any notice of the people wandering by. Standing on the corner of the street are two burly men, their bodies covered in matching patterns of ink. Their noses, ears and lips are pierced. I've got to take a photo and they are happy for me to take their picture. It's one of those rare moments.

'Wow, what a great shot. So glad I didn't miss that opportunity. Such a rare sight. Makes a change from taking pictures of landscapes.'

Light sand whirls around the corners of buildings. Further along the road and we're in the thick of a mecca of quirky shops and there are more art galleries than I've ever seen in one place. The shops all look smaller than life size, the way buildings on Main Street in Disneyland are. Rainbow, multi-coloured flags fly from every shop.

'These flags make a change from the stars and stripes.'

We've encountered a profusion of American flags billowing grandly on steel flag poles, planted absurdly in gardens, hanging from windows and mailboxes. Why does everybody fly the flag? What are they celebrating or is it just an act of jingoism?

'Imagine the reaction if we put a Union Jack outside our house? We'd be accused of being racists, bigots, isolationists and members of the English Defence League. Why only fly them when the World Cup is on? Why are we so afraid of the flag for God's sake? I don't know how we got to be like this.'

I'm working myself into a frenzied knot. If Americans can display their flag proudly, why can't we? They treat the stars and stripes with special reverence.

'It's just something they do and they don't question it. It symbolises everything they've achieved, like freedom and independence.' Ellie suggests.

'Why have they got these rainbow flags?' I ask.

'They've probably just had Gay Pride.'

'It might not be the Pride flag.'

'Of course, it is Auntie. Don't be dumb.'

'Excuse me, before you start being rude and obnoxious, sometimes it's used as a symbol of native people. And sometimes as a peace flag. And this is where the Mayflower landed. So that makes sense.'

Ellie stops and stares at me as if I've just made the most ludicrous statement ever.

'No, that's ridiculous. It's a Pride flag.'

As we argue in the street we don't notice the people around us.

Ellie stops arguing.

'See, I rest my case. Those two men are holding hands.'

I move my head surreptitiously.

'Yes. And the tattooed men I photographed. They were gay too.'

The families with children melt away and wherever I look my eyes fall upon gay men. It's a frequency illusion, the Baader-Meinhof phenomenon. Until she mentioned the gay men, I hadn't really noticed and now, it would seem gay men are cropping up all over the place. I have developed selective attention. I'm funnelling out everything else around me. A dog with a Pride scarf passes us followed by a taxi with stickers saying 'Pride Ride,' as if it's a Gay safari. There are men holding teacup dogs in handbags and I realise that we are in the minority. There are no women. Only men. Men with handbags. Men with a swagger. Earrings. Nipple rings. Retired guys eating picnics on park benches. Young men with smooth tanned skin, rubbing backs. Tender kisses and lovingly, adoring couples gaze into each other's eyes. Artists painting at easels outside galleries, wave their brushes in an effeminate way. I love it. It's extraordinary. An idiosyncratic enclave, like a hidden gem at the end of the coastline. It's more daring than Brighton, the gay capital of England where you rarely see gays hand in hand unless it's Pride weekend. This makes Brighton look staid and conservative by comparison although there are several openly gay towns across Britain who have long got over the staring. Provincetown is Brighton on steroids, a happy go lucky town, it's like the next surprise land at the top of Enid Blyton's Magic Faraway Tree. I break into a big smile. It's wonderful. The high prices in an estate agent confirm what I am thinking. A cluster of creatives flock to this enclave, their presence has transformed a sleepy fishing harbour, accelerating a process, not of gentrification but of gaytrification.

Further along Commercial Street, there's a small theatre. A drag queen and her entourage are strutting their wares in a puff of glamour, they exaggerate femininity in heels and a gust of makeup. I don't catch her name as she waves to passers-by— it'll be something like Trixie or Venus.

I love the names of the bars, they are as quirky and creative as the folk who live here. The Purple Feather, Shipwreck Lounge and Strangers and Saints lure us in and soon we are sipping cranberry and orange cocktails under a sun as bright as the personalities that have made this their home.

Ellie takes a sip, licks her lips and pins me with a cold, hard stare.

'Keep your voice down.'

'I didn't say anything.'

'Will you stop going on about it being gay. What's your problem?'

'I don't have a problem. I like it here.'

'Honestly Auntie, you're so old fashioned. You're a complete dinosaur.'

'Hey, I didn't say anything.'

'You don't have to. It's written across your face. You're disgusted.'

'No, I'm not.'

Suspicion is etched across her face, plucking to accuse me of some treachery. She eyes me judgingly. I'm not sure what crime I've committed this time.

'I dread to think what your grandad would say to this place. He was very old fashioned. He'd be cracking stupid jokes about us landing in a faggot's lair. He'd probably trot out a Bernard Manning joke. That generation were bigoted.'

She thuds her glass onto the table, cranberry fizzing on the wooden slats.

'Now look what you've done,' she snaps. 'Every drop is precious.'

'Don't get so tetchy then. Lighten up.'

'That wasn't even funny. It was pathetic.'

'I didn't say it was funny. I was just stating what your grandad would say.'

I stifle a snigger.

'Your generation is no better.'

The cranberry and the conversation are making my mouth dry.

'In my day we didn't have the bloody national curriculum. We were taught to think for ourselves, we were unique. We had different learning techniques and teachers didn't ram this political correctness down our throats like a hot dog at a circus. But your lot are churned out of schools, mass-produced, with the same moral code. You're all reading from a party script. Jeez, it's like 1984. And the worst of it is Ellie, you have to toe the party line even sitting here having a drink. Hitler's bloody youth that's what you are.'

'Ladies, sorry to interrupt.' The waitress is by our side leaning down. My heart skips a beat. I hope she's not going to throw us out.

'My shift is about to finish and so I'd like to hand you over to Julie.' Julie steps forward and smiles. Julie is a bloke. She's a fella in every way. I glance down at the bulge just to check. 'She will look after you.'

I wait for them to return to their workstation before leaning into Ellie conspiratorially.

'Did you hear that?'

'Yes. I did.' I wait for her to laugh. For the mask to crack. But it doesn't. I consider telling her about the new app she should download called sense of humour, but it would only make the situation worse. Being on my own, with my own private thoughts has to be better than being with this fake young person. I hate myself for thinking this way and am defeated by the emotions swirling inside me. I want to laugh. I want to cry. I want to be understood. I want to be hugged, to be told it's okay to have a humour and that I'm loved whatever.

'What's your problem? So? She's obviously waiting for a sex change. Get over it. Get used to it. It's none of our business.'

'I didn't say it was our business.' My words are barely audible. I feel as if I've shrunk to the size of a peanut under her cold evil stare.

'Sorry, I forgot, got to toe the line, not allowed to laugh.'

She adopts a matronly tone and I sense another wall of tension rise between us.

'Just grow up. That's all I want you to do. Start acting like an adult for once.'

I feel a flush creep up my face but know that I have nothing to be embarrassed about. God damn it. The little madam. She's not getting the better of me.

I suppress the tremour in my voice, determined to stand up for myself against this hardened millennial.

'Do you know I wouldn't dream of speaking to my parents the way you speak to me. You answer back with such rudeness all the time.'

She splutters on her drink.

'Yeah I know, you think it's funny.'

'You've got no respect for people.'

'Well you've been brainwashed into respecting groups, like a dog programmed to eat biscuits. They call your generation the snowflakers.'

The term snowflaker came from the film, *The Fight Club*. I want to quote Chuck Palahniuk in the film, 'you are not beautiful and unique like a snowflake, you are the same decaying matter as everything else.' Her generation think they are special, but they aren't. What is it with her generation? They are so over sensitive and lacking in resilience. I remind myself that although they haven't fought in any wars, they've fought their own battles; growing up in a technological revolution they've battled the mind, the self and the emotions.

'What's up with you today Auntie? Is it the menopause?'

'Come on let's pay and go. I could do with ice cream.'

'You're going to end up a fattie.'

'There you go again, no respect.'

'You're just too sensitive.'

Provincetown is more than a gay twink. It's Bohemian, an eccentric's sanctuary, a fishing community, set apart. It's unlike any other place on earth. In a bookshop, I leaf through pages of Michael Cunningham's book on Provincetown. I learn that it's three miles long and just two blocks wide. If a major hurricane hit head-on it would sweep everything away, since Provincetown has no bedrock.

'I fell in love with Provincetown, the way you might meet someone you consider strange, irritating, potentially dangerous but whom, eventually you find yourself marrying,' Cunningham says. In terms of falling in love with places, I'd like to find the ideal place to live and call it home.

CHAPTER 17: JULES – 1981

'What the hell do you call this?'

Jules felt like shit warmed up. He'd done his best, but it wasn't good enough and certainly wasn't in line with his dad's expectations.

'You might as well wipe your arse with these certificates.' August had arrived and with it the exam results. His dad waved his two O-level certificates in front of his face, spittal from his mouth landed on Jules' nose. Okay, he'd hoped for more passes, but he was surprised to achieve a B in Maths. He wasn't expecting that. It was good that he'd passed English. At least they were the two most important O levels rather than subjects like RE or Art. He was just glad that it was all over and now he could get a job, although the thought of his dad taking his wages like he'd taken the paper round money filled him with dread.

The job situation wasn't great, as his dad kept reminding him with an air of disappointment in him. He didn't know what he wanted to do, and the careers advice wasn't helpful. He zoned out every time his parents tried to pin him down to some positive ideas for his future. Exasperated he applied for a job at the local Wimpy restaurant. It wasn't ideal, the pay wasn't great. The hours were irregular, but it would do for now until he could work out a plan.

Predictably his dad's negativity towards his life escalated.

'Pandora's doing well at university. But Jules is a dead loss. Would you believe he's working at the bloody Wimpy, of all places,' he overhead his dad telling the neighbour when she came round for some of their goat's milk. Having his son work in the Wimpy was a great embarrassment.

And his mum wasn't much better. It was as if she was George's lapdog, repeating the phrases she heard him say and adding to the low esteem he felt.

'We're very disappointed,' was a phrase he overheard her say to friends on the phone. How he hated the use of the royal We. She didn't have her own thoughts and had to go around repeating him.

Sometimes Jules was cocky but not often. 'We can't all go to Cambridge University,' he chanced. 'Otherwise, who's going to serve food and clean toilets.' At the mention of cleaning toilets, his dad gave him a disgusted look. This was the ultimate shame. He hadn't considered that his son would be cleaning the Wimpy toilets too.

Jules had happy memories of burger and chips in the Wimpy, mid-week with Pandora and his mum when they were younger, and it was this nostalgia that made him apply for the job. Burger and chips were a treat after so much goat's meat and goat's cheese on homemade rye bread. Goat's cheese made him want to vomit. Just because they kept goats didn't mean they always had to eat goat and nothing else. Jules loved the diner with its red leather booths and tomato-shaped ketchup bottles which were an iconic part of the Wimpy experience. He gained great satisfaction from seeing the customers happy reaction to his service and they helped him to build team skills which would stand him in good stead.

The day he was both dreading and looking forward to arrived. His first pay packet was handed to him in a brown envelope at the end of the shift. This was his first real taste of hard-earned cash. Having money that was all his, to blow on clothes and music or a pint down the pub was a fantastic feeling. He didn't know how much his mum intended to take out for board and keep but he was pretty sure about one thing - his dad would suggest a totally unreasonable figure and his mum, the lapdog would go along with it.

There was nothing for it. He wanted to enjoy his first pay packet but had little chance of that. Changing into his normal clothes after the shift, he left the restaurant with a plan.

He bought a packet of twenty Rothmans and headed for the chippy where he ordered a large cod and chips and ate it by the river. This was something his parents would never do. The river was, according to them full of old Sainsbury's trolleys and stinky rubbish and fish and chips were for plebs in seaside towns like Skegness. Shopping trolleys or not, to Jules it was bliss. He couldn't imagine anything more wonderful. He felt very grown up buying a packet of twenty. He could have bought a packet of ten, but what the hell, they'd last longer. He threw the straggly chip ends to the pigeons, rolled the newspaper into a ball and lobbed it into a bin on his way back into town. He kept his hands in his pockets as he walked along, enjoying the feel of the jangling money. The sky bulged with leaden clouds. The only place to shelter, apart from under the river bridge was the amusement arcade, after the Pick N Mix counter in Woolworths. Eastlands Arcade, read the neon sign above the premises. His parents refused to go into amusement arcades. They weren't in any way part of their culture and this heightened their appeal. They were the forbidden fruit. Arcades, according to his dad were for scum that went on holiday to Blackpool. But his dad had no reason to look down on others. He'd spent childhood holidays in Blackpool but because he owned a cottage with a lake and a Jaquar XJS he'd become a snob.

Jules determined that his dad wasn't getting his money. He'd earned it and he was going to have fun with it. The arcade was a large room, dark but illuminated by the glow of monitors and marquee lights. It came alive with noises both real and synthetic, blips and bleeps, synthesised voices. He'd entered another world, this was his escape. He unzipped his parka against the warmth the machines generated. Music pumped from hidden speakers creating a party feel to the place. The arcade had all sorts of stuff to do, pin balls machines, pool tables, coin, token guzzlers and video games. The scene before him was intoxicating, a hypnotic dance of pixels and flashing lights.

Walking around the arcade and soaking up the scene, a buzz of excitement built in his head as he played space themed games. And then he stopped at another machine, mesmerised. Its appearance drew him in like a moth to light. It stood out among the machines with a unique shape and artwork high-lighted by the glow of green light. The game looked incredible, with a surrealistic digital landscape and two warriors fighting on a platform throwing arrows at each other. He got into the bucket seat, which resembled a car interior and took hold of the steering wheel.

He used up the remainder of his money on trying to win a teddy from a claw machine and on the coin push machines. He didn't want the teddy but the thrill of winning spurred him on. He was intrigued. Was it down to good hand eye coordination or did the games just randomly give out prizes?

When he was out of money, he checked all of the coin trays

for leftovers so that he could play just one more game. But it was to no avail. Disappointment crashed as he left the bright lights and noise, the rain came down in sheets as he dashed for the bus stop. He was well and truly hooked and couldn't wait for his next pay packet.

As he walked through the door, his head filled with the memory of a good evening he remembered that he was out of money.

'You got paid today.' Was this a statement or a question? Jules didn't respond but carried on eating his lasagne and peas.

'You're late. Any reason? Have a good day?' His mum enquired.

The vultures were descending. He needed a good excuse and couldn't think of one.

'I saw a friend after work, we had a drink.'

'In a pub?'

'Yes Dad, a pub.'

Making it known he didn't approve his dad put his knife and fork down and stared at him.

'What?' Jules turned his head towards his mum. Maybe she would explain what the problem was.

'So not only are you working in the Wimpy you're mixing in the pub too?'

'What's wrong with that? I bet Pandora's in the college bar as we speak.'

His dad shook his head and threw his mum an expression of disapproval. Neither spoke.

'We need to discuss how much keep you'll be paying now that you're working.'

He wondered when this was coming. He'd enjoyed the sense of power, spending his wages and having some fun, but now that his pockets were empty, he felt like a cowboy facing bandits without a gun.

Panic shimmied through him. From the expression on his dad's face, he was going to play with his fear.

'I think he should hand over eighty percent of his wages,' he said to Maggie. And turning to Jules, 'For your own good. We'll take your keep and put the rest into an account for when you need a deposit to buy a house...'

Jules gulped. A house. Buying a house, if it happened was a long way down the road. He couldn't plan that far ahead. A deposit to pay a landlord to rent a room in town was a good idea but not buy a place. He was young, he wanted to live and didn't want the burden of a property and what was the point in saving? He wanted to live a bit, have some fun and not worry about the future.

'It's okay, I'll open an account myself.'

'Oh, I don't think so,' his mum laughed. 'You can't be trusted.'

'You don't know that mum.'

'I know that you never had any money. All the times I've paid you to do chores where did the money go?'

His dad stared at his plate and said nothing. He knew damn well what had happened to it. Well, this time there was no money to beat out of him. He felt good about that even though he was skint.

Jules didn't reply. It wasn't worth it.

'So come on,' his mum cajoled. 'Give me the money, I'll take a bit for food and save the rest.' His dad had trained her well. George didn't need to open his mouth. She was controlling the show. She was his puppet.

'I don't have it.'

'Lying shit,' his dad snapped. 'On the table. Now.' His fist hit the table, making the plates judder.

'It's true. I owed some mates. All this time without any money I've had to borrow loads.'

'Bloody hell. You're in debt already,' his dad shook his head.

His mum looked horrified.

'Your dad and I have never borrowed a penny from friends. We wouldn't dream of it.'

'I intend to pay it all back.'

George gave a spectacular tut. 'Yeah right, course you will. And when you don't?'

'I will.'

'Don't expect us to ever,' and he pointed his finger at Jules, 'bail you out. You understand?'

'Did I ask for money? No.'

'I can't imagine your sister ever getting into debt,' his mum added.

Despite his dad's anger, he was pleased with himself for making up an excuse. That would get them off his back for a while.

His dad raised his eyebrows in defeat and surprised Jules by changing the subject and being more pleasant.

'We've all been invited out for tea tomorrow in the village. A couple of lads from your school are going. Be nice won't it? It's been a while since the three of us went anywhere together and by the way, I saw one of your old paper round customers today and he said well done for getting a B in Maths. He actually planted an idea in my head. Maybe your job could lead to something if you applied for the management course, at some point in the future?'

Wow. A shot of warmth flooded his body. Had his dad really seen an old customer or was this his attempt at finally acknowledging his good exam result? He felt buoyed by his dad's unexpected tone of positivity. This was the dad he liked.

AS THE MONTHS ROLLED BY, he found other excuses not to hand over his wages but there were times when he had no option.

Whatever he did, whether he was buying fags, placing the odd bet on the horses, going down the pub or the arcade he was always skint. He needed a better income. He was tired of Wimpy, of kids throwing milkshakes at him behind the bosses back and having his wages docked if he made a mistake on the till. The last straw came when he was asked to get some burger buns from the fridge in the storeroom and saw a mouse and droppings near the bin. It would be nice to earn more money and work in an office. But he needed better qualifications.

It was his lunch break. Sitting in the staff room upstairs eating a burger and browsing through the classified ads in the local paper, something caught his eye. It was a tiny advert, easily overlooked. 'O Level and A Level certificates, £10 each.' He scribbled down the phone number on a napkin and stuffed it into his pocket.

Jules waited until his parents were out before he dialled the number warily.

He could hardly understand the man at the other end of the line, his accent was so thick, Glaswegian Jules guessed. As he inquired about getting some exam certificates in various subjects, he imagined the man to be big and burly, with a straggly beard and scary eyes. One of Glasgow's criminals and in all probability he lived in a tower block in the Gorbals and had a scar down his cheek. Jules felt sick. What if this was a scam? He could get into trouble. It was a big risk to take.

He was about to bottle out and end the call, but the man asked him what grades he wanted. He stuttered, it was too good to be true. 'I don't mind, C's are fine.'

'What about A levels too?'

'I'm only seventeen.'

'I can date them for a year's time.'

It was like ordering a takeaway. 'But wait, before I say yes will the certificates look genuine? There's a background, a sort of watermark. Will they have that?'

'Course they will. Look do you want them or not?'

'Yeah, what do I have to do?'

'Give me your address and I'll pop them in the post. I'll include my address for your cheque.'

Jules' heart was racing and his hand trembled as he put the phone down. But he hadn't at this stage committed himself to anything. The certificates might not arrive, the man sounded dodgy but he hadn't asked for money upfront, which was reassuring.

It was a painful wait but the certificates arrived three weeks later. He'd almost given up waiting and toyed with ringing the man back, but nerves got the better of him. He knew immediately they were fakes. When he compared his Maths and English certificates with these ones the backgrounds were different. They were ever so slightly blurred. Would an employer notice and if they did and investigated what would happen? In theory, the certificates were the answer to his prayers, but it was the niggling worry at the back of his mind that disturbed him. It was wrong. He shouldn't be doing this. He thought of his sister slaving away at Cambridge and his face flushed with embarrassment.

'Fuck her,' he muttered.

Pushing his worries to one side, he ploughed ahead and applied for lots of different office jobs. Even his dad was surprised at how keen he was to better himself.

'You're up late.' George stood in his bedroom doorway. Jules was at his desk. 'Still applying for jobs?'

George didn't comment further, he just nodded and pursed his lips in an expression that told Jules he was pleased. But turning to leave his room he turned and said, 'I'm proud of you lad. I know we've had our ups and downs, but I can see that you want to make something of your life. I'm sorry I was harsh with you at times but having a successful son was important to me.'

Jules fancied working in London, in insurance. It seemed

like a glamorous line of work. He'd seen adverts on the TV for insurance companies. There were good career paths and soon he'd be able to move out.

A letter arrived inviting him for an interview at a firm in London.

CHAPTER 18: PANDORA - 2018

Our Airbnb host shakes his head as we stand on his lawn in the early morning ready to face the day. As the sun is already beating down, we want to zip into an adjoining state, just so that we can tick another one off our bucket list.

'Don't go to Providence. It's a big city and there are dangerous areas. There are better places to visit on Rhode Island. He walks towards his mailbox to check the post. 'Newport. Go to Newport. Mark Twain called it the stud farm of the aristocracy.'

I watch him flick through his post.

'Newport was a fashionable escape for wealthy New Yorkers around the turn of the last century. They built splendid houses, which were mostly summer retreats. It's the summer playground of the ridiculously wealthy. It's a great day out if you like visiting country homes.'

'Wow. Mark Twain always had something inspirational to say.'

'It'll give you a peek into the gilded age. Mark Twain coined that term.'

I squint against the morning light.

'Wait there. I'll print off some stuff for you.'

He goes back into the house leaving us waiting on the lawn.

Ellie is strutting up and down the pavement checking her phone.

'Are we just going to look round a load of boring old houses?'

My heart sinks. And not for the first time I ponder whether I should have come alone to America. I think I could have done it and resolve to build the strength to do it next time.

'Thanks for the vote of enthusiasm.'

'I wanted to go to Providence.'

'No Els, let's get this right. You did not want to go to Providence. You wanted to go to Sephora.'

Her face breaks into a wide expectant smile and she clutches my arm.

'Yes, please Auntie.'

'When we get to Boston. Between all the historic walks, yes we'll find a Sephora. But we're not spending a whole day in. We're only here for a week as it is.'

She's obsessed with Sephora. Let's say makeup, end of. Not that she needs make-up. Her skin is fresh and flawless. The cost of her foundation, covering the non-existent blemishes could fill my tank with petrol. Even when I was her age my skin wasn't that good. It was freckled, dimpled and laced with spots.

'Okay', she says in a sing-song voice. 'I'll go around your boring palaces if you come around Sephora.'

'They aren't boring houses.' She hated visiting National Trust properties when she was younger. 'These are houses built for some of the richest people in the country, the industrial and commercial elite. You've heard of people like Vanderbilt, Astor and Rockefeller surely?'

'Yeah of course. I'm not completely thick.'

We're in the car waiting for our host to return with the

printout. He's taking a long time and I'm tempted to give up and go, but daren't, as that would be rude.

'It was the age of industry, coal, steel, the railway and a handful of men gained vast power and wealth. They created trusts, combining businesses to create conglomerates that pushed up prices and made them kings of their industries. And some ended up in politics which gave them further control.'

'Talking of trusts one of the friends I met on holiday has a trust fund. It's worth two hundred thousand.'

'Her parents must be wealthy.'

'I don't know what they do. All that money in a fund though but she never buys a drink when we go out.'

'Having money doesn't necessarily make you more generous. But these wealthy people had lots of parties and social gatherings. They might not have been generous with their children and girls were treated differently. Boys would inherit rather than the girls.'

'Yeah but they would have paid lots of tax as well.'

'That was part of the problem. They got extremely wealthy partly because there weren't really any taxes. Income tax started in 1900 in America and sales tax in 1930. That's what happens when there's no income tax, few regulations, and few employment laws. The rich got richer and richer, and there wasn't much in place to stop them.'

'What does Trump think about tax?

'I reckon he believes that tax cuts on the wealthy will stimulate the economy and benefit everybody. You might as well believe in the Tooth Fairy or Lockness Monster.'

'If they started taxing fuel think what they could do with the money. They could have an NHS like us.'

'The NHS is a sinking ship.'

'They love their cars too much. I can't see it happening.'

The host brings a wad of paperwork. He's amazing, going

above and beyond. We wouldn't get this level of personal service in a hotel.

As we set out Ellie reads the information and we learn that Newport is the yachting capital of the world. In the summer huge yachts dock in the swanky harbour but in the winter they head down to Florida where it's warmer.

'How much do you think my dad earns,' Ellie asks out of the blue. 'He's always complaining about tax. Do you think he pays the higher rate?'

I know he does. He's got a good job. It pays well but I'm deliberately evasive.

'Probably, I'm not sure.'

'I'm sure he told me once that he pays the higher rate. Funny really because he's got nothing to show for it.'

'He's got his flat.' All I'm doing is alluding to the fact that he owns it. No mortgage company would touch Jules with a barge pole. No woman would either if they had any sense. But he's a good-looking bloke, he looks young for his age and he's trendy. He never has any problem pulling, it's just keeping them that's the issue. When they find out what he's like they either dump him fast or stick around thinking they can change him. My brother won't change. He's a stubborn arse. He won't take other peoples' advice and he won't go for professional help. He's always got an excuse not to.

'Have you actually been to his flat? It's tiny.'

'It's probably an expensive area though.'

'No more expensive than where he was before. I don't understand why he didn't keep the house we had when mum was alive. It looks beautiful from outside. I think it had four bedrooms.'

'He doesn't need a big house, there's only him.'

'What about me? I could have a room and stay over.'

'You don't really need to.'

'What are saying? Doesn't he want me to stay? It would be

handy staying over. It's a tube ride from the theatres and restaurants. I could even take a friend with me.'

'Would you want to?'

'If he moved to a better flat. It's grotty where he is. No idea why he likes it there. Maybe I should persuade him to get somewhere better. He can definitely afford a better flat.'

Jules should be living in a house worth half a million by now, not renting a poky bedsit. I grip the steering wheel, my fingernails digging into the plastic. Thinking about what happened makes my blood boil, the fool. Sometimes I wish he wasn't my brother. And the worst of it is he's ruined Ellie's future.

'Nanny and Grandad were well off. You bought a new house after they died, I can see that you're better off. We wouldn't be doing this trip if you weren't, but how did dad invest his inheritance? He hasn't bought a house or been on holiday. Do you think he bought shares?'

Uncomfortable with the line of questioning, I bristle. She's persistent and isn't going to let it drop. 'Look I don't know Ellie,' I snap. 'It's none of my business. You should ask him.'

'I'm not going to do that. That would be so rude.'

'He's your father.'

'Come on Auntie, tell me, I'm just interested that's all. I get the feeling there's something you're not telling me.'

'You're wondering if he's set up a trust fund for you.'

Ellie stares at me, her face pink and hard. 'You think I'm just a spoilt brat don't you?'

I fix my eyes on the road ahead and don't answer. I don't want to get drawn into this.

She swivels in her chair and pins me with a cold expression of disbelieve.

'I know you do, you don't have to answer that, I can tell what you're thinking.' Her voice is wobbly and the words splinter. She folds her arms in mock protest.

My resolve to remain calm and silent breaks. A flush creeps up my neck.

'Since you graduated, if you don't mind my saying...' I gulp, taking stock of what I'm about to say as I try to be sensitive and tactful. 'You've become a bit obsessed with money.' I wince, wishing I could swallow the words.

Her eyes anchor on me. 'Obsessed with money? Hark who's talking.' She huffs. 'You're always talking about your investments. Which is what made me wonder why father doesn't.'

'He's more private than I am.' I'm not sure if this is true, but it's a good excuse.

She sighs. 'You could be right. When I talk about my ISA he goes weird. You'd think he'd be pleased that I'm saving up for a house. Well a car first. But he's got nothing to say. No advice to give. He's nearly fifty. He must have some advice on saving money. He works for a bloody insurance company for God's sake.'

'He's hardly the chancellor, darling.' I say jokingly but she doesn't laugh with me. The expression on her face could curdle milk. 'He's just a cog in a big wheel.'

'You'd think with working in insurance he'd be interested in money.'

Oh, he's interested in money alright, just not in the way you imagine, I want to say but don't.

'He makes stupid grunting noises when he's got nothing to add to the conversation. It's as if he's thick. In fact, sometimes I think he is thick. He hasn't got a clue about what's going on in the world. I don't think he ever listens to the news.'

I indicate and turn off the highway and as I glance at her I catch the expression of loathing on her face. It's as if she hates her father. A worrying tide of thoughts sweeps my mind. How can I change this situation? I don't want her to resent him. I don't like listening to this tirade of father hate.

'Hey that's enough.' My heart emits a dull thud. As much as

my brother angers me, I don't like her talking about him in this way.

Breakfast is a break from the heavy conversation in the car. We arrive at a diner having googled diners in advance and punched in a zip code. It's close to the country houses we'll be visiting in Newport. The windows are steamed up and it's noisy with the clatter of crockery and tinkle of cutlery. The air is sweet with the aroma of pancakes, maple syrup and regret. Regret that things haven't worked out differently between Ellie and Jules.

I watch Ellie carve a graceful pathway through the packed restaurant and the chef making omelettes to the restroom at the back. She's the perfect facsimile of a film star. Glossy blonde curls waterfall her back. She's filled out in the last couple of years, she's less stovepipe and has an enviable hourglass frame. She could wear a bin bag and she'd be glamorous. A picture of her anguished two-year-old eyes surfaces, without warning in my mind. The night that her mother Vicky died. If only I'd arrived sooner that evening, even just ten minutes earlier than I did and maybe I could have mediated and prevented what happened. Vicky would not be dead now and Ellie would have a mother. I feel sick inside with the thought.

As I sip my coffee and cut a line into my pancakes I know that I've done the best I can for her. Maybe this is my way of making things alright by fooling myself. But I don't think I could have done any more. When Jules couldn't cope with an active toddler after Vicky died, I took Ellie in as if she was my own daughter. I've loved her, I've always put her first. If I could re-live my life over again, I would do the same. And I've kept the secret of what happened that night. If I'd confessed to the police Jules would have been locked up. Ellie would have grown up never knowing her father. I shudder to think of all the what-ifs and how I've held things together.

'Wish we could move here,' she announces as she returns to

the table. 'They're so much better off than we are. And so lucky to have so much space. Our roads are jammed and British houses are like rabbit hutches.'

'Tell me about it. But in fairness, you haven't seen the trailer parks and inner-city slums. We're tourists. We're shielded from the poverty and the homeless. This country has a massive homeless problem. Don't be fooled by what you see, because it's only part of the story.'

'It seems as though they're better off. And as for Brexit, we'll be a lot poorer in a few years.'

'Blame it on Brexit. Could be a song title or a movie.'

'I'm just saying,' she says sulkily.

'Look I'm just one vote. I'm sick of all my friends parking the blame of Brexit at my door.'

'Yeah well, you'll see Auntie. You'll be kicking yourself when we crash out without a deal and end up poor.'

'Poverty will never be eradicated. Take this pancake. Let's say America is a country of one hundred people. Just to make things simple. And all wealth, homes, land and other assets is represented by a hundred pancakes. That works out to be one pancake per person, which is what everyone would get if we lived in an equal society and wealth was equally distributed. But that's not the society we live in, in Britain or in America. The top twenty percent own eighty-five percent of the wealth. The gap between the rich and poor is growing.'

'I still don't get it.'

I ramble on about inequality and lead into the enormous wealth of the gilded age when immigrants poured into the country and were paid low wages and worked long hours to make a select few very wealthy.

'Stop.' She hisses, putting her cutlery down and pushing her plate away. She's finished her pancakes and there's a sheen of maple syrup shining on the plate under the spotlights. 'Stop talking.'

'God how rude. I wouldn't dream of...'

'Talking to your mum like that. I know. You've already said.'

I can't bear to look at her. Tears are welling in my eyes. I'm so over sensitive. I wish I could develop a rhino skin.

'I get the picture. But I was wondering about Dad. He should be better off but he's not. He should be going on holiday. And buying new clothes and gadgets. He used to be obsessed by getting the latest iPhones. But now he doesn't tell me what he's bought but more what he's sold. And I'm pretty sure he doesn't have a TV. And he should have a car, but for some reason he sold it.'

'Because he didn't need one.'

'I don't believe that. And if he had one, he could come down to Bath to visit me or just visit friends. Most people need a car.'

It's as if we're playing the children's game of Blindman's Bluff where one person is blindfolded and has to feel their way around the room to a person or object and the only help comes when players call out 'getting warmer,' or 'getting colder.' Ellie is getting warmer. I can guide her to the truth, or I can continue to cover up what's going on.

'Auntie,' she continues, not noticing the bubble of tears in my eyes, 'I lent Dad two hundred pounds the other week.' She sips her coffee.

I want to reassure her that he'll pay her back, but I know he won't. Jules has borrowed money before, on many occasions. Several girlfriends have lent him money and he hasn't paid them back. I really liked the women, it wasn't fair and felt very much as if he was just dating them to use them. My brother is a parasite. A leech. There's no other word for him. And mug that I am I paid them back on his behalf. He was never going to and it was embarrassing. I'm ashamed to call him my brother. It wasn't as if these women were earning much. They were earning a lot less than him. He should have paid them back.

Her eyes are dark and brooding. 'He said he had some problem with the bank...' she continues.

It's at this point that I know I need to tell her the truth or part of it. She needs protecting. She needs warning and this has to stop. He can't carry on the way he has, not if it's affecting his daughter. The selfish git, I want to scream, but keep my mouth buttoned. Inside my stomach knots as I brace myself.

'Ellie, listen to me.' I take her hands and rub them, about to speak. She casts me a resigned look.

'I don't mind. I'll give him another couple of weeks and mention it. It's fine really.'

The words I want to say scramble in my throat and I feel a flush creep up my face. I'm not ready to tell her. I'm struggling. The waitress is at our table with the bill, asking if everything is okay. She saves the day, bringing our conversation to an abrupt end and the chance to tell her, for now at least. As we leave the restaurant, we wonder why we always order pancakes.

'They taste of nothing. Like a bath sponge. Synthetic,' I laugh as I unlock the car door.

'Yeah but we eat them because they look so good. The fact that they taste shit is irrelevant. They're nothing like our pancakes. I prefer our thin and crispy ones covered in lemon and sugar.'

We glide through the centre of Newport, sweeping past the swanky dockside crowded with boats and an ocean that never sleeps. It could tell the tale of so many journeys unfinished and stories incomplete.

'I can tell this is an incredibly wealthy area,' Ellie comments.

'This is where all the wanker banker money disappeared to in the 2008 crash, just in case you were wondering. It's where the bailout money went to.'

'And it must be one of the whitest places in the whole of America. I haven't seen a black face yet.'

We pass a store called Ethnic Concepts.

'Being multicultural is a concept they're working on.'

And there's a pub called The Black Duck Inn.

'That's got to be something mildly racist. I bet nobody here complains about the racist undertones. Being so white.'

We pass a wedding shop.

'That's probably everyday clothing for the rich. It's not very practical on a yacht.'

'Unless you have a yacht this would be a pretty boring place to live.'

We turn into Ochre Point Avenue, where Breakers, the Vanderbilt mansion is. Each house is opulent along the Avenue and where the seriously rich live. They were called summer cottages, but clearly there is little understanding of what the word cottage means because these are the complete opposite of cottages. They are palaces, castles and villas, the type of homes that the Royal Family would own. It feels as if I'm playing a part in The Great Gatsby.

'Wow,' we gasp.

'They've gained the wealth, but have they lost their souls in the process?'

Each house is different, and some have notices saying no photos, please respect our privacy. They are monuments staring seaward, once alive with balls and splendour, horses and carriages carrying partygoers. People who live in houses like this make money as they sleep, they don't go out to work in the normal way, like the rest of us. These homes are white elephants, some are grotesque in design, they'd be great in a horror movie or period drama.

'Explain about the Gilded Age again. I wasn't really listening earlier,' Ellie says as we turn into Breakers carpark.

'Mark Twain coined the phrase. It was a derisive term. It wasn't a golden age but a shiny exterior for something rotten underneath. The surface was gold and glittery, just like these exclusive homes but below the surface what do you have? Rampant poverty, racism and corruption. At the end of the 1800s society was divided, two nations of poor and wealthy, a society the Pilgrims wouldn't have recognised and would have been ashamed of. There was a sense of desperation amidst the growing wealth of the few.

We head for a modern building where we buy our tickets. The price is thirty-five dollars to visit five of the mansions, which is pretty reasonable compared to National Trust prices in the UK. It's ten pounds sixty to visit Chartwell, where Churchill lived, for instance, plus three pounds for parking and this is the price for one property.

Breakers looks like a palace and is Renaissance in architecture. It's a self-guided audio tour, which is so much better than traipsing from room to room with no clue about the house, reading boards on the walls and an old lady in the corner of each room about to nod off, there to answer questions.

The audio tour is fascinating. I love the fun snippets of information as we pass from room to room and learn about the lives of the people who lived in the houses. There's a marble bath and it took several fills just to warm the marble. There are four taps—with one for fresh ocean water. There are thirty-three servant rooms. Mrs Vanderbilt changed her clothes seven times a day. In some ways, it's a bizarre pastime to trundle around mansions and country homes. What exactly do we get out of the experience? A cornucopia of luxury and elegance sweeps us from room to room in a cloud of tourists. Oil paintings, beds, an array of chairs and settees, gold trimmings, sculptures, different woods, balustrades. Some people secretly find these tours dull and tiring but don't admit it because they don't want to come across as unrefined and uncultured. It's the human story behind the furniture that fascinates me.

The garden at Breakers is plain and not elaborate. A wide lawn stretches to the sea with magnificent views along the rugged coastline. The gardens at Rosecliff, in contrast, are more elaborate.

And then the big drama of the day happens. We've arrived at The Elms, set behind wrought iron grilles it is the summer residence of Mr and Mrs Julius Berwind of Philadelphia. Mr Berwind made his fortune in the coal industry. The house is modelled on an eighteenth-century chateau and is like a mini Versailles. These details don't matter because I won't recall them. It's what happens in the house that I'll never forget.

Passing statues, fountains and flower beds we come to a set of stone steps leading to the entrance. We enter the house and breccia marble pillars loom ahead. The staff are in a huddle gossiping by the foyer. They don't notice us and the rucksacks on our backs, they're so engrossed and so I don't think to offer my bag for inspection or ask about the self-guided audio tour. It's great that we're allowed to roam at our leisure in these houses. We even forget to ask about the servant life tour, the tour of the basement and servant quarters. We slip past them. Walking onwards and my eye is drawn to the Venetian paintings, chandeliers and tapestries adorning the walls.

We wander into a dining room with oak panelling and a red stone fireplace. The table and chairs are sectioned off with ropes and four chandeliers hang from each corner of the ceiling. Light mingles with gold warming the room. Ellie is in front of me and as I point to a painting of what I think is a Roman scene she swings around, gazing to the ornate moulded plaster ceiling, oblivious to the French marquetry cabinet with ormolu, tortoiseshell and, brass standing against the wall and the row of turquoise eighteenth-century French porcelain vases with gilt bronze mounts. I catch a glimpse of the country scene painted on one of them, in pinks and greens before the row of porcelain is swiped from the cabinet in an accidental motion of her rucksack, sending them to their doom. Porcelain hits and cracks, shards scatter the wooden floor. Bronze thuds and dents the wood. Time stands still, it's as if I'm watching a movie in slow motion. Faces turn, hands clapped to gaping mouths, gasps of horror, as everybody is freeze-framed. I wish the floor would open and swallow us. A hot flush warms my cheeks and intensifies as each second passes. Members of staff bustle into the room and move towards us, guiding us out and away from the visitors, now gathering in numbers around a semi-circle to watch the spectacle of the clumsy, uncouth English tourists. We must do the walk of shame and suddenly the room seems so much bigger and the door so far away. They are a blur. Pound signs ker-ching in my head as we are led along the corridor into a small room, like lambs to the slaughter to await our fate.

A male member of staff in black trousers and a white shirt indicates to two chairs and feeling sick to the bone I'm glad to take the weight off my feet. A woman stands to the side scowling at us and doing her best to make as uncomfortable as possible. I'm shaking and tears spring to Ellie's eyes as the words sorry tumble from her mouth as if there's a play button stuck on repeat.

'We do ask you to leave your bags at the entrance.'

'I'm so sorry,' I splutter.

'Four vases,' the man says solemnly but casually to the woman as if we've knocked four jars of coffee off the shelf in Tesco. He opens a drawer in the desk and scribbles something on a notepad. He's writing the value of the vases on the pad. I register the noughts and stare in disbelief at the floor, biting my lip in shame. Whatever the figure he's written down we don't have that kind of money. How are we going to pay for four eighteenth-century vases? They aren't just any old vase. They are priceless. And priceless means they can't be replaced so surely any amount of money we hand over isn't going to make a scrap of difference. They can't bill us, it's pointless, I reassure myself. But the man is pushing the paper in Ellie's direction. I reach to grab it, I don't want her to see the damage and have this hanging around her neck. She works hard. She's just starting out in life and doesn't need this. Her lousy father can't assist in any way.

My hands tremble as I clutch the paper, registering the noughts. They swim in front of my eyes. I can't take in the horror of what has happened.

'When we arrived, the staff were busy chatting. They didn't ask to check our bags. They barely noticed us.'

The man shrugs at the woman and she shrugs back. This isn't their problem. They want to pass the blame to us. Quite rightly so. We were careless. We're responsible and so therefore, we must foot the bill but how?

'Do you have travel insurance?'

'Yes, but I'm not sure it would cover this.'

'Oh well, you'd better ring your insurance company and find out.'

'Hang on a minute. Yes, we knocked them over, I'll take the blame for that, but your staff weren't doing their job properly. They didn't greet us, they didn't give us the audio equipment for the tour. They barely registered us coming through the door. Quite frankly they were no better than janitors in a smelly public toilet. I'm not having my niece taking sole responsibility for this.'

The man and the woman frown at each other and are flummoxed as to what to do.

'One minute. Please wait here.'

They leave the room.

Oh my God,' Ellie gasps. 'What the fuck did I do that for? I'm so sorry Auntie. All I've been is trouble. I've acted like a spoilt brat and this is my comeuppance.'

'Stop it. Yes, you can be a brat, I love you all the same but let them work something out. They'll have a far better insurance policy than we do. I mean look at the place. It's worth millions. This sort of thing must happen all the time.'

'You mean there are other clumsy people?'

'Well no. I don't expect it does happen that often, but they should push it through on their insurance. The place will be insured to the hilt.'

'What if they don't and our insurance won't cover it?'

'I'll have to sell the house,' I jest, but I'm pretty sure we'll be fine.

'Or Dad will.'

That's not going to happen.'

'Auntie we need to have a serious chat about Dad. There are things you're not telling me. I'm not a stupid kid anymore. I need to know what's going on.' She's a perceptive kid.

'Not right now. Later,' I say, deftly circumnavigating the family situation.

The man and woman return, their faces are more relaxed this time.

'Okay,' the man says, sitting down. 'This is the first time this has happened. We were a bit in the dark on procedures. Panic over.' He smiles. 'I'll get you to fill in a form with the details of what happened. You don't have to worry about a thing after that. The form will go to our claims department.'

Relief sweeps across Ellie's face. We head into a corridor and passing the dining room the area around the breakage has been cordoned off and somebody is leaning down taking photographs of the shattered vases.

CHAPTER 19: JULES – 1983

Preparing thoroughly for his interview with More Choice Insurance Jules used a book on interview techniques and formulated a hundred typical questions with answers. He practiced in front of the mirror, visited the local library to research the company and found out as much as he could about the job. In addition, he had a plausible answer for why he'd been working at the Wimpy and what he'd gained from the experience.

'You look very smart in your new suit and you've polished your shoes,' his dad commented. From the expression on his face, Jules knew that he was starting to mellow towards him now that he could see him making an effort to improve his life.

Confidence oozed from every pore as he headed to London on the train and he was looking forward to the challenge. His heart sank as he entered the reception to see three other candidates waiting in the seated area, they were all slicker and older than him. He guessed that they were graduates although the advert hadn't specified that a degree was required. To his relief, they were school leavers too, with a handful of O levels.

Determined to make an impression he wasn't at all

surprised when he was offered the job. Being turned away wasn't an option. He couldn't stay with Wimpy for the rest of his life and he'd reached a point where he was more than ready to leave home.

'We just need to take photocopies of your exam certificates. You do have them with you?'

An icy sensation of panic crawled over his skin. He had hoped they wouldn't ask for proof. This was it, he was about to be rumbled. *How could I have been such a fool?* The difference between the genuine certificates and the fake were obvious. Perspiration beaded on the back of his neck as all of his hopes and dreams were slayed in one swift move. A sharp pain stabbed across his temples and as he got up to follow the manager into the corridor a dark veil passed over his eyes. He thought he was about to faint.

'Could I have a glass of water please?'

The manager turned around. Jules caught a whiff of after-shave from the interviewer that made him feel queasy.

'Are you okay? You look pale. Here sit down a minute.' He waved in the direction of a seating area and a water machine. Jules picked up a plastic cup and filled it.

'Thank you for coming and congratulations.' He extended a hand. 'Wait here and my secretary will be along to take the certificates. Drink plenty of water.'

Mild relief danced in his stomach that it was the secretary about to discover his crime rather than the manager. That was something at least.

He heard the clatter of the secretary's stilettos and smelled a cloud of strong perfume before she came into view wearing a red pencil skirt fitted like a second skin and a button up blouse. His stomach knotted. As he scrambled to retrieve the certifi-cates from his rucksack, desperate to get this over with, he'd already sussed her. Shit. He was for the high jump. Judging by her immaculate appearance from hair to shoes, nothing was going to escape her eye. She was a detail person, not slapdash as he'd hoped.

He followed her into the photocopy room, and she took each certificate from a plastic folder and positioned them on the glass plate without so much as a glance. While she waited, she was more concerned with buffing her nails with an emery board, fine long nails that could scratch an itchy back or remove a dog hair from a cardigan. Those nails had saved his bacon.

CHAPTER 20: JULES – 1983

'I f you're working in London all week who's going to milk the goats,' his mum asked over dinner.

'Jules can milk the goats at the weekend and round the sheep up in the evenings when he gets home,' his dad suggested.

He'd just been offered a fantastic job in an insurance firm as a trainee and all they were bothered about was the farm. If his dad didn't spend so long in his darkroom developing photographs and if his mum didn't spend all her time sketching and attending art classes and if they both spent less time in front of daytime TV... He wanted to say all of this but there was no point. Neither of them bothered to praise him and weren't attuned to his emotional needs.

Fighting back tears he told himself that he didn't need their reassurance and approval. But as he got ready for bed, he found it hard to keep up his strength, wanting so much to be admired and applauded. He felt envious of Pandora and wanted to hear a drum roll beat for him too. To be viewed in such a negative way didn't do much for his self-esteem. Maybe he shouldn't have applied for the job. Perhaps he should turn it down because he wasn't good enough. Thoughts wheeled through his mind as he tried to sleep.

Outside his room the sound of footsteps on carpeted floor was followed by a scratchy noise as the door opened and his dad's figure silhouetted the darkness. Jules flinched as fingers of fear shot through him. George never came to his room when he was in bed and he hated the way his dad made him feel. He sat down on the corner of the bed and sighed. Jules inched up the bed to a sitting position.

'You did well today.' Praise was the last thing Jules was expecting. In an odd way, it unnerved him.

'But God knows how you pulled it off.'

That was more like it, the usual backhanded digs.

Jules was surprised to find himself pressed against the wall. He hadn't been aware of inching further away. He was locked in this position and with his dad there he stayed rigid.

His dad's eyes trailed around the room, resting on the folder containing the exam certificates. He picked it up and opened it and as he flicked through the pages his frown deepened.

The coldness of the wall seeped through Jules' body. He pulled the blanket around him protectively, his heart thudding in his throat as he waited for his dad's temper to kick in.

'And what are these?' George asked in an uncannily calm whisper.

Jules wrestled with his answer. His conscience dared him to tell the truth. But the truth hung in the air like a bad smell.

'Where did these come from? And don't lie to me.'

'I bought them. From a bloke in Glasgow.'

'I'm speechless.'

'I'm sorry. I saw the advert. I don't need qualifications. I can do this job, but they wanted eight O levels and no matter how hard I work I'd never get that many in a million years.

George's words took on a belligerent tone. 'So, you thought you'd cheat instead?'

Jules wanted to say that there were more ways to skin a cat, but he'd be accused of being facetious and stir him further.

'I know what I've done is wrong.'

He waited for his dad to tell him to phone the insurance company, confess and pull out. His stomach knotted as he visualised returning to the Wimpy.

His dad's lip twisted. His face was a closed book. Jules couldn't guess his fate.

When his words came, they were unexpected and lifted a suffocating weight from his chest.

'I'll let you in on a little secret.' He winked like Sid James in a *Carry-On* film.

His eyes came to life, twinkling as he prepared to tell Jules about something in his past.

'Your grandad lied about his age in order to enlist and fight in the war. Your great grandad did the same in the First World War. And I...' He paused. 'I've lied about many things in my life. I'm not proud of it. I lied about my income in order to get a mortgage to buy this place. I lied to your mother when we first met. I later confessed, but initially I told her I'd been to university.' He sighed, his eyes far away in a different time and place. 'The fact was,' his voice fell to a whisper, 'I couldn't go to university. My dad died when I was eighteen and my mum needed me at home and in work. Bills had to be paid. Everything fell on my shoulders. University was all I dreamt of. All my friends were lucky enough to go and ended up in professional jobs. I was the odd one out.'

Jules knew his dad's father had died young but didn't know any details. He was astonished. Maybe this explained why he'd treated him so badly. It didn't excuse it, but it was a reason. He was carrying a huge emotional weight on his shoulders. He had to grow up fast and be the man of the house. Things were making sense. Jules wanted to tell him that he'd done alright for himself and that it was never too late to go to university, but he was too stunned to speak. He didn't know any of this. A soothing silence followed as they reflected. It was like a final release, like steam from a piston. A sense of calm settled between them.

His next words were clipped. He stood up and as if the conversation had never happened a portcullis lowered in the space between them shutting further intimacy.

'Of course, you'll do the right thing. On your first day, you must tell the boss what you've done. If they like you they'll keep you, regardless of what you've done.' And with that, he left the room.

Jules was puzzled. He'd seen a side of his dad that was rarely seen and was left wanting to know more. One thing was for certain as he settled to sleep he decided that there was no way he was going to confess about the certificates. Absolutely no way after he'd gone to all that effort. He'd be kicked out before he'd started the job and Jules guessed that his dad already knew that. Was it another of his dirty tricks or was he trying to turn him into an honest man? He wasn't sure.

CHAPTER 21: PANDORA - 2018

With the dramas of the day over we head to Newport harbour. Ellie forgets to prompt me about her father which is great because I'm tired, it's late afternoon and I'm not up to an interrogation. All I want is a drink and a walk along the water's edge.

What do you miss most about being in a relationship?' She asks me as we get out of the car in the harbour area.

'The thing I miss most is spot picking.'

A smile spreads across her face as a wicked laugh escapes. 'Yuk.'

'The trouble is only about half of them would let me pick their spots.'

'You should have watched that film on the plane, *Female Brain*. It explains why women enjoy picking spots. It's all to do with grooming. It's a very animal thing to do.'

The truth is, under the guise of spot picking and despite the pain he caused me, there's so much I miss about my husband, like walking round Sainsbury's, cooking together on a Sunday and watching films. I miss all of the annoying things about living with somebody too. They are insignificant as each of them magnifies and overwhelms me with sadness.

I don't tell her all this because I don't want her to know how sad and meaningless my life is. It's kinder to mask my pain. I don't want her to take pity on me or feel that she needs to spend more time with me to make up for my loneliness. She's got enough burden on her shoulders with the problems to do with her father and hell, I've not even told her his big news yet.

'I had a date the other week as it happens.'

'Get you Auntie.' She flicks my knee. 'What's his name?'

'Caravan Man. Within ten minutes of the date, he asked if I liked caravans. He said it was a deal breaker because he goes caravanning every weekend. Anyway, the sun was shining on his bright red nose and there was a massive blackhead sitting there waiting to be picked. I so wanted to. I couldn't concentrate on the conversation because I was dreaming about popping it.'

In my head, I'm not thinking about Caravan Man. I've wheeled back in time to twenty years ago and the day that Richard told me he was having an affair. It was the most painful day of my life, not counting all the days when the pregnancy tests showed up negative. It was a Sunday afternoon and I was watching a repeat of Heartbeat. Richard was in the pub where he was spending more time. From the lounge, I watched him stagger across the village green, drunk again. He stank of cider and sweat as he plonked himself down on the settee next to me and blurted it out. He was having an affair with somebody in the office and said he'd fallen in love and wanted to be with her. I couldn't process it. After everything we'd been through, all the fertility treatment, dashed hope, the anguish, the heartbreaking hugs late at night—he'd fallen in love with another woman. I thought he was working when he told me he'd be late home, easier, I thought to bury himself in his work than mourn the fact that we would never have a family. God knows that's exactly what I was doing. It helped to focus my energy on something constructive. I'd always been good at my work.

He was discarding me like a broken hoover that couldn't be fixed. This woman would give him a baby and all of the dreams he craved. She was whole, she wasn't mangled inside. Her bits worked, they were well oiled like a high-performance car and Richard went on to have a baby with her a few years later.

My mind refocuses on the conversation with Ellie.

'The guys at university used to watch Doctor Pimple Popper on a Saturday night when they were bored.'

'They should be out partying at their age not getting a thrill from watching puss. Kids these days.'

We park the car opposite the post office—the size of an office block and head to the harbour.

'Be careful as you cross the road Auntie,' Ellie warns as the orange man appears at the pedestrian crossing. 'You'll end up smashed avocado with only a pathetic twenty-two seconds to cross.'

We decide that a visit to Newport, beyond the quayside tourist traps, slinky bars and stalls selling slimy oysters isn't complete without a boat trip along the coastline. The sunset cruise is twenty dollars and we are welcomed aboard a former lobster boat, by a Captain Birdseye lookalike with a Father Christmas beard and long woolly socks. The sun is melting to runny egg over the massive Pell Bridge, which connects Newport, on Aquidneck Island and the town of Jamestown on Conanicut Island. Within minutes the sky is a fruit bowl of colour, warm and inviting against the chill of the wind picking up over the bay. There are two small islands, one with a haunted-looking house and fishermen dipping lines from boats and long jetties, hoping for a catch.

As we nudge out to sea through the pathway of boats Captain Birdseye describes Newport as the Disney of the rich who moor their extravagant yachts here in the summertime and when the autumn approaches, they head down to Florida. By Thanksgiving, the yachts are gone and it becomes a yachting ghost town. Their life is one big party. And incredibly it costs them nine dollars a foot to tie their boat in the harbour—per night. The largest boats pay thousands each night for mornings.

We pass the largest, most exclusive yacht moored in the harbor which is humungous. There are large windows and inside is a massive lounge with settees, table lamps and antique furniture. There's a dining room with around twenty guests eating and drinking champagne. It's another world and an image I won't forget as I turn my gaze away to the sun glinting on the glass in the distance making it look as though it's on fire.

Behind us laughter from a string of bars fades away and is replaced by the noise of our boat slapping the waves. 'A bunch of young guys make passes to young ladies in the bars, that's what Newport is all about,' Captain Birdseye tells us.

The lights are coming on in Trinity Church where George Washington worshipped. Every house and every building sprinkled across the town is about name dropping because this jewel of coastline is where the rich and famous lived and still live. The mansion where the Kennedys had their wedding reception, Eisenhower's home and several other presidents, a French chateau-styled mansion once owned by a wealthy merchant involved in the China trade, a Scottish Castle style mansion set on a rock, once owned by a man who made horse-shoes who'd made his millions during the Civil War. The waterfront condominium of Stuart Duncan, maker of Worcestershire Sauce, his home has twenty chimneys, said to be designed to look like Lea and Perrin's bottles. There are too many names. They trip off his tongue like a well-rehearsed poem.

Like the homes across Massachusetts, even the boats fly the Stars and Stripes.

'Americans never miss an opportunity to display the flag. It's so fascist.'

'No, it's not. I think it's chic. Long may it wave. They're just being proud of their country. That's something Britain has lost over the years.'

'I bet you'd learn to crochet the Stars and Stripes if you lived here Auntie. And wear the flag as a jumper as Robin Williams did.'

CHAPTER 22: JULES – 1983

On the evening of his first day in the new job, Jules lied to his parents over dinner. He smiled to himself. The conversation he'd had with his dad had given him an idea to fabricate his lie.

'You were right. The boss said he would give me a chance. In fact, would you believe it,' Jules helped himself to carrots, warming to his theme, 'he closed the door and told me about his own background in a very candid way. Like you, he said he'd lied to his wife about going to university and his income in order to get a mortgage. What a coincidence eh?'

Jules glanced at his dad and in that moment knew that he'd never come clean to his mum about his early lies as he sat there stony-faced. With an expression of shock frozen across his mum's features she clearly had just learned that she didn't know everything about the man she'd married. Their eyes locked as each waited to speak. Jules enjoyed the minutes that followed as he observed his dad squirm under the fusillade of questions fired across the table, while the meat on their plates went cold. With the emphasis on them rather than him when the meal finished, he sloped off to his room without either of them noticing, as they were too embroiled now in an argument that should have happened years before. He settled at his table to plan the future and all the things he was going to buy with his first wages.

Jules did well in his job, leaving home was uppermost on his mind. His parents, realising how serious he was about leaving slackened off when they saw he was saving for a flat. The days of losing his wages in the arcade were over and for the first time in his life, he put money away each month in a savings account. He was obsessed with saving for a deposit to rent a small flat. He went from spending everything he earned to saving like an old miser to the point that once in the flat he kept it up, writing figures in a notebook, recording how much he'd saved on bargains in the supermarket and not going down the pub. After two years in the job, his wages went up and by the time he was twenty-eight he was on a comfortable thirty-thousand a year. And then Vicky came along. The woman he went on to marry in a whirlwind romance, a year on from meeting one evening while he was out running with his dog, Jasper. Vicky came to visit her mum who lived in a flat across the road. Jasper jumped up at her and his lead got caught on Vicky's mum's rose bush. They picked it off the thorns, careful not to get pricked and ended up chatting for twenty minutes before Jules resumed his run. On the way back he took the lead off at the front door as he always did. Vicky was leaving her mum's and waved at him from across the road. The dog bounded across the road. And then everything happened in slow motion. It was too late to prevent the accident. A car turning from a side road was going too fast. He thought the dog would miss the car, make it to the other side and survive. Jasper was caught by the front wheels, turned on his side and flung under the back wheels. There was only the muffled thud of the dog under the car. It was surreal. Blood drained from Jules as he looked on in horror. He thought he was going to pass out by the roadside. The scene before him was a blur, like adjusting the TV set. Vicky took control, getting the driver's details, lifting the dog from the road. There was no sign of death on the animal, just rest. She covered him with a blanket, his body still expelling heat.

'Can't we resuscitate him?' Jules screamed.

'He was on a mission. Nothing was going to stop him.'

'Once he'd decided to bound over to you,' he accused.

'I'm sorry,' she said through teary eyes. 'It's all my fault.'

'I should have taken his lead off in the flat, but he's never done that before.'

'It happened in a flash. There was nothing we could do.'

Vicky wrapped her arm around Jules to console him. After a moment he drew back, and their eyes met briefly and in that moment a connection was made. Until that moment Vicky was just somebody he'd spoken to in the street.

'Sorry,' Embarrassed her arms flew in the air. 'We hardly know each other.'

'I'm just so shocked.' He was having a hard time taking it in. 'My parents didn't let me have a dog. I haven't had him long. I bought him from a rescue home.'

'Oh God, this is real heartstrings stuff. I am so sorry.'

She guided him into her mum's house to make him a cup of strong tea, her caring character flooding into the room, soothing his pain. He knew that he'd met somebody who was going to be very special to him.

CHAPTER 23: JULES – 1996

'Your feet are freezing,' Jules commented as Vicky wedged her feet between his calves.

'Sorry.'

'You spend your life apologising, like the day we met. Come here, I'll warm you up.'

Jules inched across the bed, his fingers gliding up her side, his hand pulling her closer. 'We can get warm together.'

'You will insist on sleeping in an igloo. I think all of my extremities have frostbite.'

'Maybe we should get a thicker duvet.'

'We don't need a thicker duvet, we just need to put the bloody heating on.'

'We've discussed all this Vicky.'

'But you're earning good money, I don't know why we have to penny pinch. It's becoming obsessive.'

'Have you forgotten why you fell in love with me?' He planted a kiss on her forehead and traced a line around her nipple with his finger. 'You said you admired the way I handle money.'

Her eyelids flickered. His touch was stirring her nipples.

She pushed his finger away. 'Stop trying to distract me. I'm being serious Jules.'

'And so am I.' He smiled, his eyes teasing and lustful. He knew the right buttons to press. 'You've got beautiful nipples. They're very suckable. Mr Kipling did exceedingly well with your cherries.'

He took her nipple in his mouth and nibbled, his cock twitching against her thigh.

She pushed him away.

He sighed. 'What?'

'We need to discuss money.'

He rolled onto his back. He was losing his erection.

'Later. We can get a babysitter and go out for dinner, then you'll have my undivided attention.'

'I'm not discussing our financial affairs in front of a restaurant full of strangers.' She folded her arms indignantly.

'God woman, I despair.'

He enjoyed early morning weekend sex with his wife. They'd been married a few years, but sex was still exciting and with Vicky it still felt fresh and adventurous. Ellie asleep after a disturbed night due to her teething troubles, this was a rare event. Sex was too rushed during the week with an early train to catch and other things on his mind, it was more a fumble in the dark.

When Vicky went on maternity leave they'd divided household chores neatly down gender lines. The car, house upkeep and bills were Jules' department, the cooking, cleaning and looking after the baby were Vicky's. Work had taught her to be a feminist, but marriage made her practical. Jules was good with money if a bit miserly and making cottage pie was more fun than changing spark plugs on a car.

Vicky planned to return to work when Ellie was a year old but as the date approached, they'd talked about her taking a break until Ellie started school. It made sense to Vicky, but Jules wasn't so sure.

'We've been used to two incomes, how the hell will we cope? What if interest rates go up?'

'We just get on with it. Anyway, childcare costs are high. I won't make much and it's hardly worth it.'

When those arguments didn't work Vicky found others.

'I'll spend the whole day worried and I don't want to miss out on the baby's first words and first steps.

'What about me? I'll miss out too.'

'Do we really want to hand our baby over to a stranger?'

'They have police checks and they work to professional standards.'

'Really?' Vicky pulled a face. She didn't agree. 'One of my friends had a nightmare time with a childminder. They were billed for things that didn't happen, the meals were poor quality and the house was a building site.'

When Jules' dad asked Vicky, 'When are you getting back into the swing of things?' it jolted him into a decision. Vicky wasn't going back to work. If anybody else had asked it would have washed over his head but the fact that his dad had butted into their affairs riled him.

But a niggling doubt wormed away at the back of his mind. It was going to be a financial struggle. They were used to two incomes and keeping up with mortgage payments was a worry. Jules was aware of what happened to him in 1989, long before he'd met Vicky. Interest rates shot up to fifteen percent. The memory made him sweat and scratch the backs of his hands. He'd never told Vicky what happened and how he'd struggled, panicked and lost a lot of money due to his own recklessness. The greatest secrets were tucked away in the happiest of marriages. He swore he'd never do that again. But he wasn't so sure that he could trust himself if he found himself in challenging circumstances once again.

The bedroom was no longer a sanctuary but four walls where arguments were made and lost. Jules tried to relax but it was hopeless when she was picky about the way he was managing their affairs.

VICKY SLAPPED a letter on the breakfast table. 'For you,' she said through a mouthful of toast. Ellie was wriggling in her arms. It always amazed Jules how she managed to multi-task, eating toast, breast feeding and picking the mail up from the mat. How was that possible?

Jules felt a twinge of anxiety when he recognised the address on the back of the envelope. It was from the bank. Since Vicky had been on maternity leave, all correspondence to do with their mortgage and household bills came to him. He'd taken over the direct debits and gave her a monthly allowance to cover housekeeping. It was a big responsibility to take on and a worry that wormed itself into his sleep at night and left him agitated. It was the first time that Vicky hadn't contributed. Things were tight. He tore open the letter. He usually binned stuff from the bank without reading it because they were junk, but he'd been expecting this. It was a letter to say that their fixed rate mortgage was coming to an end. The rate would revert to five percent. His eyes trailed over the new monthly direct debit. Shock jolted through his body. It was a lot of money. Jules thrust the letter in his suit pocket. Grabbing his coffee cup from the table, he'd drink it in the car on the way to the station because he didn't want Vicky to see the letter. There was no point in both of them worrying.

'Don't I get a kiss?'

'Sorry love, I'm in a rush. My train's leaving soon. I'll see you later.'

'No, you won't. It's Tuesday. I'll be at tennis when you get home.'

Jules bristled. She was a kept woman, a lady who lunches. His Vicky had always worked, she was a power woman with a career pathway.

'Alright for some,' he snapped, unable to help himself.

She threw him a withering look.

'Mum's looking after Ellie.'

He felt himself buckle. It wasn't easy looking after a baby full time, but nevertheless, he expected a meal on the table when he got home.

'What else are you doing today?'

'I've got a keep fit class this morning. She's going in the creche for a couple of hours.'

The expression on his face shifted from sympathy to annoyance. She was happy to leave Ellie in a creche but not with a childminder. That didn't make sense.

'Come on Jules, you can't expect me to sit at home all day.'

He was about to come back with a snide remark but thought better of it and headed for the door.

Jules usually dozed on the train, but today his mind was on the new mortgage rate which they hadn't predicted. He certainly wouldn't have agreed for Vicky to quit her job, if he'd known how tight things were going to get. There was no going back, and he felt penned in a corner. He couldn't change his mind and tell Vicky to go back to work. He had to man up and face up to his responsibilities because he had a child to support. He had to find a way for this to work. They couldn't lose the house.

As the train approached London Bridge a text came through from his friend Ash, who loved horse racing. Ash loved the thrill of a bet on the horses. He followed the racecourse tips on the radio and from those in the know. He spent a lot of his time plotting how he could strike the occasional big bet through various cunning methods. He often sent Jules his suggestions, but Jules didn't often take up his tips.

'There's a horse racing at Haydock today called My Girl Ellie. She's a thirty-three to one, an outsider. Thought you might be interested as she's got the same name as your daughter.'

Jules got off the train and headed down Borough High Street. His mind had drifted to the horse race and despite the terrible odds he could see My Girl Ellie in the lead, jumping the hurdles and fences and kicking up turf. He had to erase the thought of this horse being a winner because it most definitely was not, but he couldn't because he believed in luck, despite the odds. He could hear the shouting from the audience and see the brightness of the jockey's colours, they would be fluorescent orange with pink spots. If there wasn't a bookies on the next corner, Jules would have crossed the road and carried on to work. Within five minutes he'd have forgotten about the horse race. It was as if William Hill had been planted on that corner, to save him from all of his financial worries. Jules believed that things happened for a reason and he believed in luck. Ash's text wasn't just a coincidence, it had arrived for a reason. My Girl Ellie was a winner. Even outsiders deserved a chance in life. As he pushed open the door, a thrill he remembered from the days of his early working life when he went to amusement arcades jolted through his body as if he was being electrocuted. He felt a surge of emotion as he placed his bet of four hundred pounds. He couldn't afford to lose so much. It was a once in a lifetime, all or nothing situation.

As the day went by Jules enjoyed the thrill of wondering how much he'd win. The thought of winning gave him a buzz, despite the fact that deep down this horse was a loser. He couldn't wait to down tools and head back to the station via William Hill. If nothing else the bet was a distraction to all the other problems looming in his head.

Leaving the throng of commuters rushing to catch trains he entered the sanctuary of the betting shop and was met by stony silence as old potbellied men with biros tucked behind their ears turned towards the stranger in a suit. One man wore a cap and the others were in old cardigans. One of the fellas was handing round a Tupperware box of Bourbon biscuits. Strangers were rare and were eyed with suspicion. Jules made his way through the smoke-filled room to the counter. He had no idea whether the horse had won. As he handed the assistant his paper his heart pounded and blood rushed to his face. When the assistant told him the horse had won the race, winning a staggering thirteen thousand pounds, he couldn't believe it. His ears buzzed, he thought he was about to faint and held on to the counter to steady himself. It felt like a dopamine release and was such an easy way to make money. As he left the shop, feeling on top of the world—he felt exhilaration like he'd never experienced—he was already planning what he would do with the money. First, he'd make an over payment on the mortgage and he wouldn't have to worry about it again for a few months.

He got home and paused on the pavement underneath a streetlight, taking in the scene. He loved their home and was proud of himself for owning a detached house. It was all he'd ever wanted, partly to prove his parents wrong and to show that he could make something of his life. He didn't have a degree like his sister but he was doing okay. He had a beautiful four-bedroom home and a wife and child. His life was complete and after the win, he felt relaxed and less stressed than he had in a long time.

He'd known before they even stepped into the house that this was the one. It was a modern mock Georgian detached house built in the sixties. When they were looking for a home Vicky always keyed in on the negatives before she could see the positives, commenting on the lounge net curtain bunched in the middle that looked, in her words 'like an old woman's underskirts after a visit to the toilet.' It had taken a few days to win her round to putting in an offer and her dithering had nearly lost them the house. 'I doubt those mock Georgian houses are praised in the hallowed halls of the Institute of British Architects,' she'd said. 'I don't want to live in the land of swags and tassels.'

The view over the village green and duck pond won her over though despite her hesitation over the price. 'We don't need to spend that much. The mortgage will cripple us.' But they were both doing well at work, Vicky's salary had jumped, so they sold their terraced semi for a hundred thousand and took on a two hundred -thousand pound mortgage. Jules remembered how terrified he was at the time, he was taking on a big mortgage but it was exciting at the same time. The payments were thirteen hundred a month, up from a comfort-able four hundred. The lender had been satisfied with their combined incomes and was happy to lend them four times their income. This house was their pension. They'd downsize in years to come freeing equity to live on. Jules had it all worked out.

She would be at tennis. That would give him time to decide if he was going to tell her about the win. He had no idea what her reaction would be. She'd probably think he was foolish and want to know why he'd placed the bet. And four hundred pounds was a lot of money. He could hear her scream at him. 'What if you'd bloody lost it? That's food and petrol for the month,' she'd remind him, and she would be right. No, it was best to keep quiet. He was supposed to be the provider, supporting his family and in control.

He couldn't contain himself though. As soon as Ellie was in bed he blurted out, 'I think we could go out at the weekend and buy a new TV, a flat screen.'

'Are you having a laugh?'

'No, I'm being serious.'

'I don't understand.'

'You've wanted a new TV for ages and a camcorder so we can record Ellie. We'll go to Dixons at the weekend.'

'Jules, what's going on? Have you won the lottery? If we can afford all that, then why have we been penny-pinching lately? It doesn't make sense.'

He wasn't expecting the Spanish Inquisition and he should have predicted this. Of course, it didn't add up. Fuck, he thought, how am I going to explain?

'We were late being paid.' The lie tripped off his tongue. 'And they owed me some commission.' He blushed. He wasn't used to lying to her. Now she'd ask how much. Figures whirled in his head. How much was he going to say?

'That's fantastic, well done. And a new TV, oh my God I'm so excited.'

'I might even buy you a Magimix as well and a Dyson.'

Steady on Jules, a voice in his head warned. This is going to look suspicious and she'll come to expect more and more things. But damn it, another voice countered, I love her to bits and she deserves to be treated.

She kissed him on the lips, her eyes glittering with pride. 'How much commission did you make?'

He tapped his nose. It was best not to give a figure.

She cupped his face playfully. 'Why are being so secretive?'

'You'll have to kiss it out of me,' he teased.

'Is that so?'

And before he could say more her hands were on the back of his neck and her tongue down his throat. The touch of her soft hands and gentle kisses feathering his neck were intoxicating. They rushed to undress, in the middle of the lounge. Lost in the heat of passion his leg knocked over a box of Maltesers on the coffee table, sending them flying in every direction. Kneeling in front of him, unzipping his flies, a Malteser crushed under her knee as she freed his penis. Hard and pumping with blood he thought it looked like a purple soldier but it was in her hands and in her warm mouth, exploring her cavities. Sweat beaded his brow as he swept his hands through her hair, bent to stroke her nipples and inched closer so that he was deep inside her mouth.

Sensations rushed through his brain, all the stresses and pressures forgotten as he concentrated on what she was doing. This was the perfect escape from reality. In no time at all his white gravy was dribbling down her mouth and with the thought of her question about the money returning to his mind his penis was shrivelling fast. This had been one of the best days of his life. An incredible win on the horses and amazing sex. As they hauled themselves to bed and recovering his erection, he made love to her slowly under the sheets, knowing that the day's events would anchor in his mind and be repeated.

'So, are you going to tell me how much commission you earned?'

'Oh, not much.'

Her simple question riled him and reminded him of when his dad used to ask about his wages and demand he hand them over. It was irrational because he was married to Vicky and she had a right to know. They were a partnership, but he couldn't help resenting the question. He had to keep the figure to himself. It was like protecting an egg in a nest. Money was fragile. It could disappear as quickly as it came in. It was his money and he'd earned it. This was a mantra he'd repeated as a child so often.

'Enough for a few treats.' He calmed himself. It would be easy to lose control and let his emotions get the better of him. 'But after we've had a spend we've still got to be careful though.'

'Yeah, yeah,' she said as she poured cornflakes. She wasn't having it and didn't believe him.

'I'm serious babe. We've only got one income remember.'

Her phone rang and she picked it up. Ellie was upstairs and was crying in her cot. He went to get her and coming down the stairs he overheard her talking about the things he was going to buy. He guessed she must to talking to her mum. That was all he needed, her mum thinking they were doing well. Now he'd have to keep up the pretence with her too.

'Jules is doing really well at work, he's making loads of money and says he's going to buy me a Dyson, a new TV and a Magimix.'

There was a pause while Vicky listened to her mum at the other end.

'Yes, I know Mum, I'll get him to buy one of those too. Don't you worry.'

She came off the phone as he entered the kitchen, handing Ellie to her and grabbing his jacket from the chair ready to leave.

'What were you saying? Buy what?'

'A new pushchair for Ellie. One of those expensive ones with the big tyres.'

'Can't you buy one in the Friday Ad?'

'No Jules,' she snapped. Last night's passion seemed a lifetime ago. 'I told you before. It'll probably have some child's dried vomit on it.' She stroked Ellie's curls and kissed her cheek. 'Only the best for our Els.'

Next time he won some money— and there would be a next time— he decided it would be best not to tell her. Her mind was a riot with all the purchases she wanted to make.

CHAPTER 24: PANDORA – 2018

Leaving Plymouth we head towards Boston where we will be spending a few days. Stopping for petrol my card is declined at the pump, so we go into the kiosk to pay. I don't notice the little Chinese lady sitting behind a glass screen because behind her is a wall of scratch cards, a hundred times more on display than in Britain. A harmless flutter or a costly addiction I wonder. Just as well my idiot brother isn't here.

'Wow,' Ellie gasps. 'So many. Can we get one?' her eyes alight with excitement.

'It's a waste of money.'

'Don't be boring.'

'We're only buying petrol.'

'Dad used to buy me a card every time we went in Tesco and one for himself.' Sadness sweeps across her face. 'It's silly but they were the best times I spent with Dad. He'd buy me a can of Coke and we'd sit in the park and scratch the numbers off.'

I stare at her in disbelief.

'What?'

I relax my face, not wanting her to pick up on the irritation that's mounting inside. 'Oh, nothing. Did you ever win?'

'Not often. A tenner here and there. Dad didn't buy them to win. He said it was just fun and money for charity.'

'Is that right?' I say with a sceptical tone.

'It felt like our special time. A scratch card, a coke and a play in the park.'

We fall silent and I turn the radio on. The presenter is referring to Trump as a douche. We laugh.

'There's a Trump baby flying over Parliament. Up until a year ago,' the presenter is saying, 'Britain was our number one ally and now they're flying a Trump baby in a diaper, I kid you not, over Parliament.'

Taking shape in the distance is a collection of buildings and we're hopeful this time there will be somewhere to eat that isn't a fast food joint. We glide into another IHOP.

'You're obsessed with pancakes Auntie,' Ellie screeches as we steer into the car park. I'm salivating before we've even got out of the car. I want as many pancake breakfasts as I can get before going home and then the Ryvita and cottage cheese diet will commence.

'I don't see anywhere else to eat.'

'You need to start the day with green tea.' She says slamming her door. 'I keep telling you. It's packed with antioxidants, but you don't listen.'

'I knew about the virtues of green tea long before you were even born, so don't give me that.'

'Well drink it then. You'd feel so much better and you wouldn't get all grumpy.'

'I'll give that a miss, I need a strong coffee to kick start the day.'

'The only thing that's going to kick is your sleep at night. It's not good for you. I'll send you a link.'

I lead the way to the entrance, visions of pancakes and sizzling syrup swirling through my head.

'Name me another food that has its own celebration day? Early Christians were celebrating these gloopy delights.'

'They didn't intend it to be a glutinous feast,' she hisses, grabbing the door before it closes.

'Pancakes are as old as mankind. Even cavemen ate pancakes.'

'Not with syrup though. You cannot eat any more syrup Auntie. You'll lose your teeth and mess up your blood sugar.'

'Oh, lighten up will you, we're on holiday,' I slam back at her, as the friendly waitress leads us to a booth.

'Tofu and spinach. That's what you should be eating for breakfast.'

'Yeah right. Well, I don't see that on the menu. And spinach gets stuck in the teeth.'

'When we get home, I'm going to make you a meal with tofu. It's so good for you. You have no idea.'

'Can't wait.' I'm trying to ignore her and doing my best to focus on the fantastic pictures of pancakes on the glossy menu.

'Have a bowl of fruit instead. I'll let you have your coffee if you eat fruit.'

'I will eat fruit.'

'Good. That was easily sorted. You won't regret it Auntie when the pounds slip off your thighs.'

The waitress appears at our table. 'Fruit with pancakes and maple syrup please.'

'Auntie,' Ellie snaps. And addressing the waitress she asks for a bowl of fruit.

'Stop it. Leave me alone. 'I'll have the pancakes with fruit and syrup.'

Staring at me Ellie barks, 'but we agreed you're not having pancakes.'

'And I'm not a kid, I'll control what I eat thank you very much.'

The waitress beams. 'Ladies, this is the house of pancakes. It's time to indulge. You both have lovely figures. You don't need to diet.'

'She does,' Ellie nudges me looking disgruntled. 'You could have my figure if you put some effort into your diet.'

Before she leaves the table without a word the waitress and I exchange knowing withering looks. We overhear her taking her next order. The customer is asking how they make the pancakes and after numerous questions, the customer asks, 'I'm allergic to dairy, do they have milk in them?'

Ellie leans towards me. 'What a dumb woman. Why couldn't she say that in the first place?'

APPROACHING BOSTON, we see the worst drivers, congestion and road works I think I've ever faced anywhere. Boston sends me into meltdown, there are eight-lane highway tunnels and roads veering off in all directions. I have multiple hissy fits, swerving towards my exit at the last minute, my hands are clammy and I hear violent honking behind me. I mutter half a dozen swear words under my breath. Ellie is as cool as a cucumber and checking her make-up in the wing mirror she catches the eye of good looking guys in adjacent cars - can't understand why I'm so stressed. There are drivers texting, aggressive drivers using their horns, there are road workers drilling into the road and a cement mixture passes spewing black smoke from a small chimney.

'Quick, get a picture of all that smoke,' I yell. 'That's one for Twitter, Mr Donald bloody Trump.'

We're too early to check in to our Airbnb so we head into downtown Boston and park up near the State House which borders the fashionable Beacon Hill neighbourhood. I recognise the houses from pictures on the internet and am keen to wander around this area but Ellie drags me away. 'I'm starving, let's find somewhere to eat first.'

The heat is oppressive and the humidity stifling, making the temperature feel hotter than it is. I feel the sweat build as my heels hammer the sticky tarmac. We head up Beacon Street and across the road is Boston Common with a paddling pool. Groups of children, in holiday clubs, wearing colour themed t-shirts are guided through the park by leaders. I long to join the children paddling in the pool. It's the best place on a day like this.

'See this red brick line along the pavement. That's the Freedom Trail. All we have to do tomorrow is follow the trail and visit the historic buildings and landmarks along the way.'

'It sounds like a lot of effort. Can't we drive around Boston instead?'

'No,' I laugh. 'That's not the idea. It's a walking tour. Anyway, the city's full of crooked, narrow streets.'

'Are you for real?'

'You told me to drink green tea for energy. It isn't doing much for you then?'

'Tea. That's just what I could do with right now, after a glug of water and a burger. After all that's what Boston is known for, it's tea.'

'The tea wasn't grown here. Boston is known for its Tea Party.'

'What was that then? A giant tea party?'

'Oh, dear Ellie I can see that I'm going to have to give you another of my history lessons. I thought you were going to train to be a teacher. You'd better start reading if you want to teach the children anything.'

'Go on then, bore me with all the details.' She fakes a yawn.

'It wasn't a tea party. It's just called that. It was a protest against taxes imposed by the British Government on tea imported into Boston. The tea chests were hauled overboard when they entered the docks by protestors angry about the tax.'

'So the fish swallowed the tea?'

'I think Jamie Oliver created a dish, cod with English breakfast tea.'

'Tax, I wish we didn't have to pay tax.'

'Tax is a fact of life, next to death it's the one sure thing. The British were fighting the Seven Year War to kick the French out of America. There was another unpopular tax called The Stamp Act that caused civil upheaval.'

We stumble across a grotty food hall. The air is filled with grease and sweaty bodies and my growling hunger is replaced by a punched in the gut feeling of despair. It occurs to me, not for the first time that fast food has completely taken over America. We're in the city that heralded the beginnings of liberty and freedom and yet this nation has given up feeding the brain. This is just sustenance and heart attack inducing fat. Revolutionaries need food to ignite ideas and create energy. The likes of Paul Revere, Thomas Hutchinson and Benjamin Franklin would be turning in their graves if they could see what this nation has turned into. Fighting a revolutionary war against Britain set the Americans on a new path, creating their own culture but it has become a culture of bland sameness, that represented something very unique but a step down in terms of cultural sophistication.

'I'm sick to death of fast food,' I mumble, as my teeth sink into a burger.

'Stop moaning Auntie. You led us in here, telling me we needed to save money.'

'I couldn't find anywhere else to eat and that's the truth of it. I want to try one of the State's famous Clam Chowders. Did you know that there's a National Drive-Thru Day? Twenty percent of meals are eaten in the car. How fucking ridiculous is that?'

'Steady on. Your blood will boil over and spill into your burger if you're not careful.'

'Yeah, and here's another ugly fact I read. One-third of vegetables eaten in America comes from the potato.'

'Nothing wrong with the humble potato. The Irish probably brought it over.'

We hurry back to the car before the meter runs out. There's an orange ticket attached to the window. My heart sinks. It's a fifteen-dollar citation for parking in the wrong direction and I have twenty-one days to pay before it goes up. Fast food, oppressive heat, complicated roads and now this... I'm not warming to Boston, but tomorrow is a new day with new adventures to look forward to.

Our AirBnB is near the end of the tube on the Orange line. The car trundles around a maze of roads near the tube station, driving into roadworks and dead ends, reversing back onto the main road, the sat nav is as confused as we are. Finally, we pull up outside the apartment block. Ellie gets out of the car and rings the bell and Sam, our host answers the door and directs me to park on his driveway. I carefully manoeuvre the car into the small space, watching the reversing camera as I go. I don't notice the huge pile of rubble on the drive, it appears as a grey smudge on the screen. I hit the rubble, panic, worried that the tyres will burst. Ellie opens the boot while I bend to examine the tyre, my hand resting near the boot.

Pain seers through me and I yell in agony. My finger is trapped in the boot door and I'm yelling for her to open it. She's jumping up and down screaming as if it's her finger trapped, yelling, 'Oh my God have I chopped your fingers off? Where are the car keys? I think I'm going to be sick.'

It's then that I realise I'm holding the key. I frantically stab at the keypad which releases the door. My finger is bleeding, the skin torn and Sam is guiding me into his apartment to bathe it under cold water.

He hands me a bandage and produces a massive tub of painkillers containing three hundred tablets.

'Wow, what a huge tub,' I gasp through my tears.

'I was recently in England and had a headache. I ended up in Boots and only found small cardboard boxes with twenty tablets in. I guess Boots finds it can charge a lot for a small number of tablets because most people with a headache, aren't too bothered what they pay,' Sam says.

I'm yelping and despite the excruciating pain I answer him. 'The number of tablets sold is controlled and it's in blister packs so that you have to tear each one out. It's to stop people attempting suicide. Statistically, it's proven to have drastically cut suicides. Serious overdoses cause kidney damage.'

'I didn't know that. It sounds like your government has no faith in the people. I guess that's why it's known as the nanny state.'

Ellie and I exchange irritated glances. He has no idea what he's talking about and no common sense, but now is not the time for an argument. My finger is throbbing and I'm pacing the floor.

'Do you want to go to the hospital? Your finger's in a bad way.'

'Oh no. I'm not going to one of your hospitals. I read about an English woman who had a baby in New York while on holiday and the care cost them two hundred thousand dollars because the insurance wouldn't pay out.'

'No way,' Ellie gasps.

'Excuse me,' our host laughs as I continue to pace the kitchen. 'Our hospitals are very good. But the things I hear about your NHS.' He chuckles and winks at me. The conversation is light-hearted, but there's a serious undertone to the chat. 'We've seen people dying in corridors on the news and infections are rife,' he witters on as he packs the bandages away.

'Come on,' Ellie says, goading me away, 'Your finger's fine, let's get going.'

'I think I'd rather lose a finger than my house.'

'You do not need to go to hospital Auntie,' Ellie says, smiling back at the host as we walk through the corridor to the door. The host comes to the door with us and gives us directions to the tube and quotes the cost of the ticket.

The ticket man at the station is a big black guy with a diamond earring.

'Did you notice his fingernails,' Ellie asks when we're out of earshot. 'His small finger had a really long nail. That's for cocaine. And don't pull that face Auntie, drugs are everywhere.'

The passengers on the train could be passengers on any underground system across the world but there are people who look completely out of it, maybe they're on Meth. And every woman, according to Ellie is wearing nail varnish.

We climb the steps out of the subway station and out into Downtown Boston, peering up at Old State House, I'm amazed to see that the entrance to the station has been built into the basement of the building. These days it's a museum about the city's role in the American Revolution. We gaze up to see a clock and a balcony. Below the balcony, there's a circle of paving slabs marking the first bloodshed of the American Revolution. An old homeless guy with a long beard sits with a placard saying 'Seeking Human Kindness' and a pot of money —a reminder that inequality exists in every city, despite ambitious intentions to change society and garner greater fairness.

We cross the road and head towards a row of restaurants and Faneuil Hall. There are street entertainers and stalls selling handbags and clothes—it's a buzzy part of Boston. A street trader selling leather handbags catches us as we pass and he passes us handbags to examine.

'I don't really need a new handbag,' Ellie declares after examining just about every bag he is selling.

'Well stop wasting his time then. It's embarrassing.'

I drag her away. 'No wait. I think I'll get the pink bag.'

'How much?' I ask.

'Twenty-five dollars.'

He puts it in a plastic bag.

I go into a theatrical mode.

'I've lived in this city for years and I know what you sell these bags for, I've seen you selling them, so can we just cut the haggling shit and get on with the sale. Fifteen dollars.'

'Twenty-five dollars.'

'Okay, right this is what I'm going to do. I'll walk away, you call me back with a lower price, I decline it and then I'll walk away again.' Throughout I'm laughing and so is the man. It's like a mating ritual in a David Attenborough film.

A crowd form around us to watch. I catch the violent flare in the man's eyes and feel guilty. Maybe he's sussed that I'm a tourist and is not having any of it. I've had some fun. I don't mind paying the full price because he doesn't earn much from his trade.

'Auntie leave it. I'll get a bag from Primark. It'll be loads cheaper.'

I'm like a dog with a bone. I will win this battle. 'No you won't. I'm getting you this one darling.'

'Come on sweetpea, take the money,' I coax.

'Auntie, you've had too many holidays in Fuengirola. They don't operate like that in classy Boston.'

Ellie strides off, in the direction of her beloved Sephora. I catch the violent flare in the man's eyes as he puts the bag back on the pavement and realise I've lost my battle. Poor guy, I feel dreadful. I hand over twenty-five dollars and take the bag.

I catch up with her and we enter her favourite make-up emporium.

'God you are so embarrassing,' she screams, flapping her arms, as customers weave around us, watching us with interest.

I pick up an orange lipgloss, apply it and take a selfie to help me decide whether to part with twenty dollars for an item I don't need. I frown. My face is puffy and there are dark lines under my eyes. I show Ellie the photo.

'Do I really look like this?'

'Yes, 'fraid you do.'

I hold up two lipsticks. 'Which one suits me?'

'Neither. Lipstick doesn't look right on your lips because you have a pair of scribbles for lips. Big lips are in this year. I wish I had big, voluptuous lips.'

She picks up a pack of false eyelashes and a highlighter palette.

'These eyelashes are so gorgeous.'

'False eyelashes are common. They make you look as if you've got spider's legs attached to your eyelids. You're going to be a teacher soon. Teachers don't wear false eyelashes.'

'No, they wear frumpy glasses, like you Auntie.'

'You're so horrible to me, I'm fucking sick of it.' Tears spring to my eyes and I blink them away. I don't want to appear like a baby in front of her.

'You insulted the eyelashes.'

'They're eyelashes for God's sake.'

'Well, I need them for tomorrow night's date.'

'I noticed your light on at four this morning. You're not still texting guys on Tinder surely?'

'I'm going to meet him after his work.'

'Why? What's the point? You're never going to see him again.'

'Best way to go. No strings, no catching feelings.'

She says this as if feelings are a disease.

As we chat I try on some eyeliner and stand back to admire myself in the mirror.

'No,' she says in a matronly tone, surveying my handiwork. 'Not like that. You put it on your eyelids, not under your eyes.

You look like Granny, oh my God. Granny. So outdated. Here, let me.' She grabs the eyeliner pencil from my hand.

'Leave me alone,' I squawk as a wicked grin lights her face, her mind on overdrive, working out how to transform her auntie into a half beautiful specimen.

She sketches the air with the pencil. 'I'd love to do your eyebrows. You so desperately need to do something with them. There's nothing of them,' She laughs.

I give a morose shake of the head and step away from her.

'Leave my eyebrows alone. They're fine as they are.'

A shop assistant who has been watching us steps forward. That's all I need, her opinion as well and a pile of stuff in a basket that I don't need. Why are we here? Oh yes, because Ellie is obsessed with makeup.

The assistant smiles. 'I just love your accents. You sound like royalty.'

I'm not sure about that. Ellie sounds like a petulant teenager. And I'm *The Idiot Abroad*.

'How's Meghan Markle? I just love her. She's just a regular girl and wears such lovely clothes.'

'I've never met her.' I don't see why I should discuss somebody I've never met, just because they're royalty.

Ellie whispers to me. 'Just go along with it Auntie, for God's sake.'

'Yes she's so beautiful and we watched the royal wedding,' Ellie swoons.

'The royal wedding was shite,' I mutter under my breath.

CHAPTER 25: JULES – 1996

'Where are the dips?' Jules shouted from the lounge.

'We're not having dips,' Vicky shouted back, from the kitchen.

'Why not?' He asked, joining her where she was preparing a three-course meal. It was their turn to host a monthly dinner party for their friends Hilary and Mike. Hilary was an old friend of Vicky's and they'd stayed in touch since meeting at college and Mike and Jules had hit it off. From going to each other's weddings, buying houses to the first baby they'd followed life's journey together. Hilary and Mike had been looking for a new house for a couple of years and were frustrated because they'd had no offers and couldn't find what they were looking for. All the talk about houses had given Jules and Vicky the idea to move and they had beaten Hilary and Mike to it.

The dips would be in the fridge. Vicky said that the timing of the dip was crucial and that she could only put them on the coffee table as the doorbell rang, otherwise he'd wolf them down, leaving a congealed mess of dip and

Tortilla crumbs and nothing for their guests. Jules loved his dips.

'I wonder if they'll notice the new telly,' she said putting the plates into the oven to warm.

'Of course, they will. You can hardly miss it.'

'They aren't very observant.'

'No, let's get this right,' he said waving a breadstick, 'they are observant, but they choose not to notice.'

Vicky gave a knowing smile and shook her head. 'Remember that time when she babysat. That was weird.'

Jules and Vicky had returned from the pub one evening and walking across the common they saw Hilary in their bedroom snooping around.

'Jealousy, you mark my words. It's like when we moved in and gave them the grand guided tour. They went from room to room making no comments. Couldn't bring themselves to say what a nice house it is. Not a word.'

'Not a dicky bird.'

'So bloody rude.'

'I'm not lowering myself to their silly games,' Vicky snapped. 'Come on, get the Dyson out. She's bound to notice that. And the Magimix.'

'I feel sorry for them not finding a new house.'

'God I don't. I wonder what they'll say when we buy a new camera. I can't wait to see their faces.'

'What new camera?'

'You said we were buying a new camera.'

'I don't remember saying that.'

It was several months since the big win and there was nothing left of it. He'd made an overpayment on the mortgage and bought some stuff including new clothes for Vicky because she'd grumbled about being a different size since having Ellie. The buzz of the win had worn off and the overpayment on the mortgage, which had seemed like a great idea at the time had only made a small dent in it. With the fixed rate ended he was feeling the pinch again. In some ways, Hilary and Mike were in an enviable position. At least they didn't have a big mortgage.

'Come on Jules, get with it. I don't want to watch their smug faces next time they pull out their flashy camcorder.' She took her apron off and smoothed her hair ready for the guests. 'We've got to keep up.' She brushed his arm. 'How do I look? I should have had my hair done. I bet she's got new highlights.'

'Your hair looks fine.'

Jules' heart sank. Was this what their life had been reduced to? Keeping up with the Hilary and Mikes of the world.

'And another thing,' she hissed, taking the chicken and green bean salad starters out of the fridge and putting them on the table. 'Next time you get some commission, let's have a holiday. A decent holiday for a change.'

Getting four glasses out of the cupboard Jules sighed. Why had he lied? He was digging himself into a deep pit and couldn't claw himself out. He'd never earned a commission. His job was salary based.

'Don't sigh. I'm serious.'

'Look, can you stop planning what to do with my money.'

'Your money? Since when was it your money?'

Suppressing a shudder Jules took a deep breath as anger replaced his irritation. Blood pricked and thumped in his head.

'You know what I mean.'

She wheeled around, her face hard as stone.

'I knew you'd make me feel like this the minute I finished work.'

'Make you feel like what for Christ's sake?'

'Inadequate because I'm not contributing anything to the household.'

'Stop twisting my words.'

'I'd just like to visit my cousins in Sydney. I'm sick of hearing about all the places Hilary and Mike have been to.

They love to brag. But with her common accent, you'd think she went to Southend each year.' In full pelt, Vicky didn't hear the doorbell. 'It's about time we went abroad. I can't cope with her snooty laughter when you entertain them with tales of leaking tents.'

'The flights cost thousands.'

'You haven't chilled the wine,' She gasped spinning on her heels towards the fridge.

'I think I should answer the door first,' he said on the third ring.

Settling in the lounge with their drinks the conversation turned to events in the village. The closure of one of the pubs, the new notice at the pond not to feed the ducks and speculation about whether bonfire night would be cancelled due to the heavy rain. Vicky was certain that Hilary had noticed the new TV. With a flick of her head, deliberately Vicky thought, she haughtily turned her back to the TV as if it were an unwelcome visitor.

'What do you think of our new TV?' Jules asked. He knew that Vicky wouldn't be so bold as to ask the question. She enjoyed the petty games of one-upmanship. It gave her something to talk about after they'd gone.

Hilary sniffed in the direction of the TV.

'It takes up a lot of room,' she said.

'Nice, but I personally—and don't get me wrong mate—but I'd rather spend the money on a holiday myself, but each to their own.'

'Shall we tell them?' Tickled pink Hilary's shoulders were puffed out, gloating with the chance to announce their latest booking. Knowing this would stoke Vicky's idea of a glamorous holiday, Jules felt his stomach sink.

Sadness swept Vicky's face. He was failing her. He wasn't the husband she wanted him to be. He had a challenge on his hands to make her the happy wife that Hillary was.

'We,' Hilary began, tapping her manicured nails on her wine glass, eyes glittering, 'Are going to Hawaii.' She beamed at Vicky, the cat that got the cream. As she put her glass on the coffee table, announcing that it was time to eat Jules watched Vicky struggle to control her emotions

'That's fantastic,' Vicky said as she swept from the room. 'Can everyone come to the dining room please.' Jules, worried she was going to be teary, joined her in the kitchen to help.

'Hawaii, what the fuck,' came her whispered hiss as she took the pie out of the oven. Her face was full of loathing as she slammed the pie on the worktop.

'Keep your voice down.'

She whipped him with the tea towel.

Everybody sat down to eat. After hearing about Hawaii from the starter to the desert Vicky announced, 'We're thinking of going to Australia next year.'

Shock jolted through Jules and he coughed on his food. What was she playing at? He wanted to correct her but not in front of their friends. He had to keep up a show of happy couples was his motto.

'Not sure we'd want to go to Australia, would we Mike? It's dry, flat, infertile and all the creepy crawlies are deadly and the culture's too western.'

Hilary pulled a face. 'All those old men in white socks and sandals. Why would you want to sit on a plane for hours to see virtually the same culture? Sod that.'

'You must be doing well mate.' Mike raised his glass to chink Jules. 'Bit of a step up from camping in Wales.'

'Yes, Jules is making big money these days. He earned a lot in commission a few months ago.'

'You two can't go abroad. We enjoy your stories of leaking tents too much.' Hillary chuckled. 'Remember the time you wore Aran jumpers in August, it rained all day every day and your tent flew over the edge of the cliff.'

Everybody broke into laughter.

'It was seriously grim. I can't cope with another holiday in Wales,' Vicky laughed, but under the laughter, Jules knew she was serious. She was a woman on a mission and like a dog with a bone, she wasn't going to drop the Australia idea.

IT WAS Monday morning and Jules was dozing on the train, still in recovery mode after the dinner party, his body thawing from the ruinous effects of too much alcohol.

'Any racing tips?' he texted his friend. There weren't many travellers with a phone. Everybody hid behind broadsheets and paperbacks but if somebody took out a phone— because it was such a rare thing everybody stopped what they were reading to gawp which embarrassed Jules. He cringed when he heard somebody on a mobile asking their wife what was for dinner. Mobiles weren't for pointless conversations in his opinion. He wasn't a showy person, but his Motorola gave an element of prestige. The reception was poor, and the text didn't send until the train arrived at London Bridge waiting for a reply. He sauntered down Borough High Street thinking that his friend probably didn't have reception either. He stopped outside William Hill. If he was going to take Vicky and Ellie to Australia he needed another win and he couldn't let her down. Remembering drinking more whiskey after Hillary and Mike had left, he recalled the trail of fire burning his tongue and fading to a warm glow in his stomach. Then the alcohol danced through his body grabbing him by the hand and leading him to promises and commitments that couldn't now be broken and finally dragging him into a well of sleep, plagued by nightmares. In the sober light of day, he couldn't remember all that he'd promised but Australia was top of the list.

He pushed through the door of the betting shop and stared,

through the smoky fog at the boards displaying the day's races. The Racing Post was on the counter and he flicked through the tips, his eyes falling on a horse racing at Goodwood called Australia's Delight. That was the one. It was racing for him. Perfect. Meant to be. Euphoria flooded his veins. His heart thudded. Nipping to the cashpoint, his head a blur, not worrying about how much he'd withdrawn he returned to the counter to place his bet.

It was only on leaving the betting shop, resuming his walk to work that it hit him how much he'd put down. He slipped his card into another cashpoint machine and was horrified to see that he'd withdrawn fifteen hundred pounds. He only had a hundred pounds left in his account and the mortgage would be taken in a couple of days' time and there were other bills due to leave his account -council tax, gas, electricity, a car loan. What the hell have I done? It would be okay though, he'd win and it would be enough to cover a couple of months of bills plus the trip to Australia. He believed in luck which was about preparation meeting opportunity. He'd taken a chance. That was no bad thing. Seeing his horse he'd risen to the occasion. What was the worst thing that could happen? He wasn't sure because he didn't want to think of worst case scenarios. He had a positive streak and this morning a spring in his step.

After work, he hurried to the betting shop and handed his ticket to the assistant. She shook her head.

'Sorry mate, it didn't win.'

'What?' She was wrong.

'Check again.'

He left the shop, his head spinning and his stomach in free fall. As he leant against a wall normal life whizzing past him— cars, lorries and people, all just white noise that he was oblivious to. Nausea swept over him and he thought he was going to throw up into the gutter. He could feel his blood sugar dropping and needed a glass of juice. He couldn't believe it. Despite asking the woman three times he still couldn't believe he'd lost the bet. Now, what am I going to tell Vicky? He'd lied about the win but lying about a loss was a whole new ball game—he didn't want to contemplate what was going to happen to them. Limping to the cashpoint to check his balance, he had one hundred pounds left. He had to get his stake back. He couldn't afford to lose the money. It wasn't an option. But chasing his losses felt like chasing a butterfly. It was an impossible mission, but he had no choice. It was the gamblers' downfall. He'd bet what he couldn't afford to lose and repeating his stupidity with their last one hundred pounds was the only chance he had of recouping their losses. He withdrew eighty pounds and went back to the betting shop. He chose a random horse, racing at Epsom the following day. He'd get the money back and more. He wouldn't need to tell Vicky. This time tomorrow he told himself, the money would be back in his account and she would be none the wiser. He couldn't let her down. After tomorrow's race, he'd have to be straight with her and tell her they couldn't afford to go to Australia—unless he won a huge amount. Why the fuck hadn't he been assertive in the first place, rather than pussyfooting around throwing out half-baked promises? Part of him believed he could take her to Australia to see the cousin she longed to reconnect with. He still believed it was possible.

He was terrified as he approached the counter.

'Sorry love, the horse came second to last.'

'What?'

Jules stared at the woman. It had to be a mistake. He couldn't possibly have gambled his last hundred pounds. Balling a fist he slammed it on the counter.

'Step away from the counter please, otherwise I'll call the manager down.'

'Sorry but you'd be annoyed if you were me.'

'Better luck next time.'

'There won't be a next time,' he snapped, turning to leave the shop, but as he did so he thought he caught a smirk on the assistant's face. Was he paranoid and imagining it? He pushed the door open, a sense of unease prickling the back of his neck as he felt her eyes following him. His brain was playing tricks on him. He'd show the bitch. He'd be back to win. But how was he going to do that, he wondered as he walked onto the station concourse when he had no money. Shit. It dawned on him that they had no savings. Vicky had blown what they had put away when she was pregnant preparing for the baby - decorating the nursery and buying new furniture, equipment and baby clothes. He let her use all the savings. What a fool I've been, a voice in his head screamed as he ran for the train, leaving the platform. He'd have to get a credit card. When they got married Vicky didn't like credit cards because her first husband had got into debt using credit cards and they divorced because of it. Worried this would happen to them Vicky had a credit card that she rarely used but wouldn't let Jules have one in case he got into debt. At the time he had gone along with it but it irked him that she didn't trust him. Fuck it, he would apply for one.

He drifted into an unsettled sleep comforted by the rhythm of the tracks until the train screeched to a stop at grimy East Croydon, the sound was like nails on a chalkboard. The view over grey office blocks always depressed him. But today his spirit was on the floor, he was beaten.

As he train trundled along, the ugly tumour that was East Croydon melted into pleasant fields and reaching the Balcombe Viaduct, a thought hit him like a sledgehammer. He'd take out a loan. Of course, it was simple. A loan would solve all of his problems, while he chased his losses. If he could win more with the money from the loan everything would be alright. Then he'd quit.

It took a few days to sort out a loan. He was edgy, not himself and Vicky picked up on the change in his mood.

It was Saturday morning and Jules felt the insistent bash of Ellie's hand on his face— indiscriminate, her open palm landing on his nose and eyes, forehead and mouth with force, in an attempt to wake him— and he struggled to open his eyes. He frequently woke to find Ellie between them and wished that Vicky was firmer with her and didn't give in to her crying by bringing her in bed with them.

He rolled over to face his daughter. 'What's she doing in here again?' he grumbled, squinting at the clock. It was not even seven. 'I was hoping for a bloody lie in.'

'Grumpy Daddy,' Vicky said, pulling Ellie into a hug. 'You don't normally mind.'

'I don't appreciate having my face bashed and legs in my back.'

'What's up with you? You've been bloody miserable all week.'

'Nothing.' He tugged the duvet, pulling it over his head.

Now that he was awake, he couldn't think about anything except his money worries. Whenever he tried to focus on anything else his thoughts skittered away in the face of overarching anxiety about money.

Vicky pulled the duvet off him.

'Fuck off. I've been working all week, let me sleep.' Jules didn't normally shout or swear and he surprised himself.

'Don't shout and swear in front of Ellie.'

Jules knew that he should apologise but he wasn't in the mood.

'God damn it, don't tell me how to behave,' he shouted.

He knew he was being out of order. It was out of character for him, but she'd started this whole problem, pressurising him to book a holiday to the other side of the world. Nothing was ever enough for her and he'd bought her a TV and a Dyson. It was about time she appreciated everything he did for her. He didn't like the spoilt little girl streak in her, it was as though she had a fundamental right to get what she wanted. Her ethos of self-entitlement was an ugly trait.

The following morning, he woke with an erection and looked at his wife, but Vicky was asleep, her floppy blonde hair curtaining her porcelain face, a rosy hue around her cheeks, she was angelic. Her beauty still turned heads in the street. He was a lucky man, but aware that he was treading thin ice, one wrong move and it might not take much for her to leave. The thought of being on his own again scared him, but most of all he was determined to prove his dad wrong. George had told him at their wedding that it would be a doomed marriage. He had no idea why his dad had said that, it was yet another cruel and unsubstantiated jibe.

He leaned down and gave her a light kiss on her forehead. Vicky stirred, took his hand, turned over and groaned. She caressed his hand and after several moments, with hope rising for morning fun, he slipped his hand between her legs and nuzzled into her neck.

'Mm, as wet as a wet weekend in Bridlington,' he whispered, rubbing her and sliding a finger into her moist passage.

'Stop it,' she said as if he'd electrocuted her. She pushed his hand away and wriggled towards the edge of the bed. He might as well be an electric fence he thought, for all the thrill he gave her these days.

'Don't you want it? You're moister than a monsoon in Monserrat.'

Humour usually relaxed her, but not today.

She wheeled round to face him, her face set like stone.

'You just don't get it do you?'

'Get what?'

'It's sore.'

'It shouldn't be with foreplay.'

'Thanks for the sympathy Jules, I told you the other day

that I've got little cuts up there. I think it's some vaginal infection. It hurts when I pee.'

Jules turned on his back, sighed and stared at the ceiling.

'Oh I get it,' she hissed. 'This is all about you.'

'Jesus what did I say now?'

'You didn't have to. I know what you're thinking.'

'And what would that be?'

'You think I'm frigid.'

'I didn't say that but yeah I suppose it's coming across like that.'

'You think it's deliberate? That I make it up. Well, it's fucking painful.'

'I'm getting up.'

'I'm sorry. It's not my fault.'

'You have other holes.'

'Don't be so crude.'

She threw a pillow at his back.

'ARE we going to the Cafe Rouge for breakfast?' She asked, joining him downstairs with Ellie in her arms. They usually went to the Cafe Rouge on Sunday morning but Jules was watching every penny. He had nothing in his account until he could secure the loan, and if that didn't happen fast the mortgage and other bills would default. His stomach churned with the worry and the lack of sex made him moody. The last thing he needed was a full English breakfast.

'Money's tight.'

He hadn't meant to use that excuse, but the words were out and he couldn't change them.

'Money is so not tight,' she laughed. 'Don't make pathetic excuses Jules. You're just punishing me because you didn't get any this morning. I'm the one suffering, do you think I enjoy having lady pains?'

'I don't have the appetite for a full English this morning.'

'Well have a pain a raisin instead then.'

'Can't we just give it a miss?'

'Oh come on. It's my one treat of the week. You like going there. Just have a coffee. You can pinch my sausage if you get peckish.'

'I'd rather pinch your bottom.'

She put Ellie's coat on and gathered her keys and bag giving him little choice but to trail behind as she headed for the car. He'd have to come up with an excuse as to why he couldn't pay the bill.

Jules ordered two cooked breakfasts. If she was going to have her weekly treat so was he. And when the breakfasts were finished, he ordered pain au raisin and fruit juice. It had been a tough week and now that he was in the restaurant the pleasant ambience relaxed him, making him forget his money worries.

'Oh my God it's Hilary and Mike,' Vicky gasped. 'They never come in here.'

Jules turned his head as their friends came into the restaurant.

'Shall we join you?' Mike called over, grabbing the menu from the waiter and indicating to him that they would sit with their friends. Jules was irritated that they were coming over but what could they do? This was their family time, just him, Vicky and Ellie. He wasn't in the mood for company. They threatened to ruin his day if they talked about holidays. He took a swig of his black coffee, enjoying the surge of caffeine through his veins.

Coffees and croissants were ordered for Hilary and Mike.

'We've got some news for you,' Hilary began, pushing succulent raisins around her plate and beaming across at Vicky.

Oh God, what is it this time, Jules thought. Please be pregnant, a voice in his head willed, rather than announcing another holiday that he'd be expected to compete against. Vicky didn't want a second child, so that was no competition.

'Since we last saw you we've booked a trip to Australia.'

Jules' heart emitted a dull thud. He glanced at Vicky, watching his wife's pain as initial shock was replaced by glazed eyes, a protective veneer to hide her emotions.

It took a moment to register their news.

'Australia? But you said...'

Vicky's voice was hollow and wheezing. Jules felt her pain. He had to do something as this was cruel. He knew how much she longed to visit her cousins in Sydney. What sort of an idiot husband was he that he couldn't give her this one thing?

'You got us thinking...so thank you.'

'What changed your mind?' Jules asked.

'Flights are cheap.'

Jules squirmed. He didn't want to hear this.

'The Great Barrier Reef, the Outback, Sydney Opera House. We want to see it all.'

The waitress came with the bill and after ten minutes Vicky said, 'Come on Jules, pay the bill, we need to get going.'

'I left my card at work, can you stick it on your credit card for now.'

'Oh for God's sake. Why did you leave it at work?'

'I was in a hurry to get the train.'

'That's no excuse. You know how much I hate using credit cards.'

'It's just breakfast, I'll pay it off on Monday.'

'Make sure you do, and anything else we spend this weekend. I'll keep a tab.'

'Stop worrying.'

≈

JULES AND VICKY stood outside Thomas Cook scanning the
offers in the window. After breakfast in the Cafe Rouge, Vicky
moaned all the way back to the car about Hilary and Mike
going to Australia. On and on she went. He was sick of it and
his head felt as if it was about to explode. Unable to stand it any
longer and wanting an end to the discussion he'd agreed to take
a diversion home and call into the travel agent. He was
dangling a carrot before her eyes, knowing they couldn't
afford it.

'We could look online for a cheap deal,' he suggested. But
Vicky had fixed ideas about holidays and would only book
through an agent.

They went inside, a bad move he thought as she flicked
through brochures. Jules stood on the sidelines hoping his lack
of interest would dampen her enthusiasm but when she took
the pile of brochures to a waiting member of staff, he knew this
wasn't happening and his heart sank.

An hour and a half later they left the shop, a three-week
trip booked and paid for on her credit card.

'You can pay it off when the bill arrives.'

'Cheers for that.'

'Don't be so tight.'

'You assume I'll be able to pay it off.'

'Of course, you will.'

'Vicky, just stop a minute.'

He pulled her arm and the pram jerked as he made her
turn to face him.

'It's going to take me several months to pay it off. I won't be
able to pay it all in one hit.'

'You're not serious? Why couldn't you have said? You let me
buy an expensive holiday and now you're telling me we can't
afford it?'

'Well we can, it'll just take a while to pay it off.'

Shit, why did he say that? Vicky's intimidating tone had put him under pressure, making him cave in. He was under attack and hated how this made him feel.

As if he'd rolled the dice and lost, Jules felt defeated. His money problems were out of control, but instead of being assertive with Vicky and putting his foot down like a man all he could do was acquiesce, for an easy life. His head was in the sand, with nobody to dig him out.

Over the next few months, he took out several credit cards and maxed on them all. He placed bets on several horses, chasing his losses and hoping to win. There were a couple of wins over the months, but nothing of significance. He missed two mortgages payments and then contacted the mortgage company to ask for it to be extended and he forged Vicky's signature. He felt wicked for doing it but he had no option. She'd flip if she found out—which was going to happen at some point very soon. He was holding things together by the skin of his teeth but Vicky wasn't interested in official letters and left all the finances to him. When demands hit the doormat she put them on the desk in the study. Jules shoved them in his desk drawer, unopened, hoping they would disappear. Vicky never answered the landline, unless she recognised the caller on the display. Before his money worries, it irritated Jules that she avoided answering calls.

'They're only junk callers,' she'd say.

And he would reply, 'Unless you answer the phone you don't know. It could be an important call.'

The holiday cushioned him from reality. They had a great time, and to fund the spends Jules had taken out another credit card. What happened before and what was to come spelled the beginning of the end. Within minutes of getting back from Australia the shit hit the fan. While he paid the taxi driver Vicky opened the front door, gathering the post from the doormat, as she went, while fussing over Ellie and shouting over her shoulder that if she didn't get a cup of coffee fast she would die.

He struggled up the path with both cases and coming in through the door, his shoulders aching he heard her gasp from the kitchen.

'What the fuck.'

She waved a letter at him. If only he'd gone in ahead of her, but she never opened mail, he hadn't been worried.

Before he reached the kitchen he guessed the letter was from the mortgage company or one of his creditors. She put it aside, ripping into the pile and tearing into envelopes in a frenzy. She was like a child opening Christmas presents, except there wasn't any joy or peace in this scenario.

'They've made a mistake,' she said through eyes of terror. 'Yes, they've made a mistake.' When Jules stood at the kitchen doorway saying nothing, staring ahead at the garden beyond tears sprang from her eyes.

In a cold calm voice, she asked, 'This isn't a mistake is it Jules? Please tell me this is a mistake.' She was in front of him and grabbed his sweater, turning it in her hand.

'I'm sorry, I've fucked up.'

'Why do we owe money Jules?' She was shaking, her face white. 'What's going on?'

Everything tumbled out. In those few moments every thread of happiness woven into the marriage unravelled, every aspect of trust in the relationship analysed until they were spent, nursing their wounds, two souls waiting to heal.

CHAPTER 26: JULES – 2018

The restaurant was almost empty, except for an older couple by the window sharing a bottle of carbonated water with their curries. Jules was relieved as he didn't want their raised voices to be witnessed by a roomful of gawping customers.

The restaurant was new, the waiters over solicitous and the decor too pristine, as if waiting for the atmosphere to arrive. They were shown to a table close to the other couple—on the assumption that people liked the illusion of company when they ate out—but Mandy asked for a table at the far end of the room instead, where they could talk privately.

'What do you think?' He looked around.

'It's fine,' she replied.

They sat opposite each other. The Kingfisher beer was ordered and he felt his stomach churning. Where did he begin? A meal wasn't going to seal a lifetime together, or smooth over the cracks in their broken relationship.

'Cheers.' He raised his bottle to connect with her but she didn't respond. He wanted the spark that had existed between them to reignite and to feel the warmth of their early carefree days together. But that was before his addiction came to light and Mandy got pregnant. Their sell by date was gone and yet here they were, about to become parents for the first time together. A world of sorrow wedged between them, all of his making. He couldn't accept it was the end for them.

She busied herself tidying the cutlery and unfolding the linen napkin, before putting it in her lap.

Making polite but awkward small talk he fisted the stack of poppadums, breaking them into shards to dip into chutney. When the waiter served dollops of korma onto their plates Jules ruminated on what he wanted to say. He decided to launch straight in, rather than beat around the bush.

'I'm sorry Mandy, so bloody sorry. I've let you down badly.'

'Your problems run deep Jules. If I could have the man I met that day at the seaside I would.' Her eyes glittered with tears.

'But I'm still me.' He reached over and touched her hand. 'I haven't changed.'

'Your personality doesn't matter. You could be the nicest guy in the world, you could be Brad Pitt, but the fact remains you're a gambler.'

'I know I've got issues.' He scratched his head, flummoxed at the hurdles before him. He couldn't promise her that he'd change and wished she could see gamblers differently. It was very one dimensional, black and white and fixed.

'I can't trust you Jules, what we had early on has gone. And it's not about money—I don't need a high earner, just somebody who doesn't waste their money. Some of the best times we had were basic. Chips on the beach in a shelter huddling from the rain. The small gifts you used to give me—homemade gluten free bread, a bag of BabyBels. How do I know you'll never steal from me or my family to fund your filthy habit? You've already begged me for a loan. I'm not prepared to take that risk and now I've got a baby to protect.'

Her words sliced into him.

'I wouldn't do that.'

'You'd end up destroying me and it would be like taking on another child.'

He didn't know what to say.

'You could take over my bank account. Control the money, that would stop me.'

'No. You'd resent me doing that. You have to learn how to manage your money yourself, you're a grown man for God's sake.' Her face was angry.

'But it's what plenty of couples do in this situation,' he pleaded. 'I'd have my wages paid into your account.'

He realised, as her shoulders slumped that she didn't want to take on the problems of his addiction. And why should she? He should have been honest, at the outset when they first met, but how could he do that? She wouldn't have touched him with a barge pole.

'And you could stop your wages going into my account at any point. A few clicks on the computer is all it would take.'

He raised his eyebrows. She was right.

'You can't just expect to play happy families, while you're in the grip of your addiction.'

He looked anguished. 'Okay, you don't need to say anymore. I don't deserve to be given another chance.'

'Everybody deserves a second chance.'

His heart soared, she was throwing him a crumb, but from the sad expression on her face, he knew she mean't everybody but him.

'I just can't take on your problems, okay? The thought of you losing our money is frightening beyond words.' She stared at him. 'I can't. It's going to be hard enough bringing up a child.'

He could see the layers of hurt that he had created. The wall between them was solid. Her words weighed heavy on his mind. 'Oh Mandy, I'm not sure how I get that trust back.

But maybe over time and from a distance, I can prove it to you.'

'The trust has never existed. I didn't know you before the addiction. I look at you and I see an addict.'

'I wish we'd met years ago, maybe you could have fixed me.'

'You can only fix yourself.'

He shook his head, dropped his gaze to the floor for a second, then looked right at her, 'I know I've got big issues, but I can promise you loyalty and love. I'm not a rich bloke, I'm skint but I'd always be there for you, would you consider taking me back at some point in the future if I can break my addiction?'

'But you've been addicted for years. If you have therapy then maybe, just maybe in a few years' time if you're completely clean I'd consider it. But right now it would be a disaster waiting to happen.'

The withering expression in her eyes told him all he needed to know. She wasn't going to ever take that risk.

'I can't make any promises.' There seemed no point in pulling the wool over her eyes.

They sat just thinking and feeling.

'Isn't it a bastard,' she said, rubbing his arm, 'Just when you catch a glimmer of happiness like we did, it shatters like glass.'

'I'm sorry.' He was crying as he spoke.

'Oh Jules, they're just words.' The tears were biting at her eyes, too. 'Just words. It takes a lot more effort than saying sorry...' Her voice trailed, tired with the emotions of it all.

When the bill was paid, he didn't see much point in lingering.

He slapped the curry splattered napkin onto the table.

'Look I'd better go, but thanks for hearing me out at least.' Standing to leave he offered a fragile smile. There was no choice but to walk away. Too much damage had been done, he couldn't blame her, only himself.

CHAPTER 27: MANDY – 2017

Mandy's first date with Jules was the best first date she'd ever been on, and Mandy had done a lot of online dating over the years. The memory of most dates fluttered away, like ashes caught in the breeze. She couldn't remember most of their names or where they had been to. It wasn't fancy gifts or fine dining that left a lasting imprint on her mind. Mandy's greatest dates—those with Jules had simpler magic, like eating chips in a windy bus shelter or a picnic on the floor in candlelight. Even running through the town in pouring rain under an umbrella after a pub gig was magical. Those early dates with Jules gave her hope for the future and reassured her that online dating wasn't so bad after all. He was easy to chat to, wasn't pretentious or arrogant and had nothing to prove like so many men she'd dated. He focused on her, asked her questions and seemed genuinely interested in her life. He didn't brag about his job or how much he earned. It was refreshing to meet somebody like Jules.

They'd arranged to meet on Eastbourne seafront at her favourite cafe that sold the best cupcakes in town. She arrived early and found a bench hidden from view by a flower display, a short distance from the cafe. It was a glorious day in late October and felt more like summer than early autumn. As she closed her eyes against the sun she wished she'd worn a t-shirt rather than a jumper, but couldn't take her jumper off because she had an old vest on underneath. But it was a promising start to their date—eleven and it was already warm without a cloud in the sky.

A shadow fell across her closed eyes and she opened them to find Jules standing in front of her smiling. In his profile picture, he had a beard. She didn't like beards but it gave her the impression that he was intelligent and sensible, but hopefully not in a dull way. First impressions were immediate and impactful. If it worked out though, she intended to get him to shave it off. But she was pleased that he hadn't thrown away his razor—the beard was gone and he was clean shaven. He looked years younger than his profile picture.

They walked away from the seafront, weaving around children on scooters and dog walkers and up some steps towards the cafe. In those first five minutes, Mandy was aware of a fluttering, churning excitement in her gut. They fell into an easy conversation about the things they had in common before they even reached the cafe. Inside the steamy cafe they ordered tea and sat outside.

'Did you grow up in Eastbourne?' He asked, switching the topic of conversation.

'My grandparents lived here. I spent a lot of my childhood with them because of problems at home.'

Jules looked puzzled. 'Oh?'

'My dad was an alcoholic and my mother spent years battling the emotional crisis. It was easier to pack me off to my grandparents.'

'That must have been hard to live with.'

'I thought I could fix my dad—like in the films when the character you love is about to die and there's a dramatic scene before the bad guy surrenders. In the end, everyone lives happily ever after. I was definitely starring in the wrong film. My childhood was full of endless disappointment, but even in my darkest moments my dad was still my hero. I still loved him for who he was. I knew it wasn't really him—it was the alcohol. I spent years hoping he'd get better, the hope kept me going, even when the process was so sad. I constantly compared my life to my friend's lives, wondering why my home life wasn't like theirs.'

Jules reached to stroke her hand and by the look in his eyes, she felt as if he understood the pain she'd gone through.

'Is he still alive?'

'No, he died from liver failure.'

'I'm sorry.'

'I've forgiven him, I've had to, otherwise it would screw me up. I think he'd want to be forgiven.'

'Shame we can't choose our parents.'

'You have a daughter?'

'She's at university, I don't see her much.'

'That must be hard, I bet you miss her.'

'Yes, I do. We used to spend so much time together.'

'It sounds as if you're a great dad. I bet she appreciates the times you do spend with her and I bet you spoil her rotten.'

'I try to.'

'Come on, let's walk along the seafront, I know of a lovely cafe at the foot of the cliffs. If we start now, by the time we've chatted more we'll get there in time for lunch.'

'I need to get some money out first. Is there a cashpoint nearby?' Jules asked.

'The town's in the opposite direction. Don't worry about it, I'll pay for lunch and you can get some drinks later.'

'If you're sure.'

∽

AFTER LUNCH, they wandered into town. Jules hadn't reminded Mandy about needing a cashpoint but she hadn't forgotten. While she was happy to pay for lunch she wasn't prepared to buy drinks as well. It niggled her ever so slightly that he'd forgotten that he had no money on him, but the date was going so well that it wasn't an issue.

They paused to look in an estate agent's window.

'I'd love to move down here,' she said, peering at a three-bedroom semi.

'It's good to downsize as you get older.'

'We're a bit young for downsizing,' she laughed. 'What's your place like?'

'I'm living on a friend's sofa at the moment. Long story. I made a really bad investment after my wife died and lost a lot of money. But I'm waiting to get a mortgage, so I won't be sofa surfing for long.'

'A bad investment?'

'Yes, it was an investment broker I found locally, in the Yellow Pages.'

'God, who uses the Yellow Pages these days?'

'I thought it would be more reliable than the internet.'

In the evening they headed towards a pub in the Meads, a quaint village full of charm, in between the town centre and Beachy Head. The connection between them hung like an invisible thread, as they sat on bar stalls, their heads close in deep conversation. Somewhere in mid-sentence, as she chatted, he reached over with a kiss. When they left the pub it was gone eleven. The date had lasted twelve hours and they both knew that they would see each other again. In her mind, she was rearranging her calendar so that she could make time for him. They walked down the hill, adjacent to the sea. A full moon made a milky pathway across the sea, scattering light through the pines. They stopped to look at it. It was one of those breathtaking moments she wouldn't forget and they kissed, lightly on the lips.

IN THE COMING weeks Mandy and Jules met whenever they could. When they didn't see each other, they chatted on Facebook. One evening Jules scrolled right back on Mandy's timeline, clicking like on all her photos.

'Two can play at that game, you bugger,' she said to herself, although part of her liked the fact that he was interested in her life. He had a boring Facebook profile, most of his updates were jokes and links, with nothing about his life. There were no photos of social occasions or birthdays, but she kept her finger on the button as she scrolled back, year by year. And then she stopped. Something caught her eye. It was a picture of dice with a quote about gambling being a loser's game. Underneath the picture, his friends had commented. Her heart emitted a dull thud. What had she got herself into?

'I saw something on your Facebook profile. Do you have something to tell me?' She asked on their next date.

He didn't hesitate before answering her and didn't bluff. 'Yes. I'm addicted to gambling.'

'Shit.'

'You should go. I'm bad news.'

'When were you going to tell me?'

'Tonight.'

'But it's ten o clock already. When were you going to squeeze that one in?'

'We were getting on so well, I didn't want to spoil things.'

'You've lied to me from the start.'

'I haven't and I stopped gambling months ago.'

'How do I know that's not a lie. My dad was always promising he'd stop drinking but he never did.'

'We've had some nice dates, but you're better off quitting while you're ahead.'

'The bad investment you said you made. That was a lie?'

'I was economical with the truth.'

He always lifted her spirits, he was fun to be with and made her value her life in a way she hadn't since her dad died. But at that moment her spirit plummeted to the floor. Their relationship couldn't continue, but it was too late. She'd fallen in love with him and worse than that, she had news for him. She was carrying his baby.

CHAPTER 28: PANDORA – 2018

Thunder and lightning crash and compete with the clatter of the air conditioning unit as I lie wide awake in fruitless pursuit of sleep. As I prop myself up on pillows and read a book, I'm hopeful the storm will calm the humidity and make for an easy day of walking around Boston. On one of the shelves I find the story of how Airbnb began. Two guys in San Francisco were out of work and struggling to pay their rent and were looking for an extra way to earn some cash. They noticed that all the hotels were booked due to a conference and bought a few airbeds, put up a site and advertised their room. The idea succeeded and they saw an opportunity. Once again, I'm back to thinking about my brother. If only he could shift his mindset. Finally drifting off to sleep, I wake as dawn creeps through the curtains.

It's cooler today as we head to the subway station passing houses with flags flying from posts and twee picket fences. But the American dream is changing. Pneumatic drills and jackhammers are breaking up the road near an old building site and are creating a new urban lifestyle. Down in the subway, the trains look old with pockets of rust. Water leaks onto the track from a pipe but nobody notices because the passengers are glued to their phones. 'The doors will reopen, the doors will reopen,' an announcer blasts through a microphone. On the platform, I watch a glamorous blonde lady strut up and down in a wide-brimmed hat, a black cat suit and gold shoes.

We're on the train heading into downtown Boston on the oldest underground system in America, another fact I picked up from Googling in the middle of the night. Like the underground road network, it arrived after a lot of political squabbling.

We sit opposite a girl with dreadlocks who is talking to herself.

'Weird,' I whisper to Ellie.

'She looks normal,' Ellie says.

'She's talking to herself.'

'She probably has wireless headphones in. Why would she laugh for the sake of it Auntie? There are gaps when she's not talking, meaning she's listening to somebody. Duh.'

As I stare at the girl I wonder if she has a mental problem or is she on social media? And I think about how underground trains are like human cages for people to observe each other, like in a zoo. We are a cage full of random people or a laboratory for the study of human behaviour. All races, colours, religions, nationalities, shapes and sizes mingle and jostle, inches apart, everybody in their own bubble, oblivious to their fellow passengers. Nobody smiles, nobody connects, everybody jockeys for their personal space which can't be invaded. We're here together because of shared interest, simply to get from A to B. It's a sad life. If we connected think how fun it would be. But we only engage when something goes wrong, if for instance there's a suicide or a bomb on board. I want to tell Ellie my thoughts because tube train psychology is interesting but now is not the time because the unwritten rule is silence.

I glance around me, trying to piece together the puzzle of

each person's life in the way they are dressed and from how they behave and smell. It's primal. I spot a woman in a horrible outfit. She's wearing thick black socks to mid-calf, slide on footwear and baggy black sports shorts.

'What's that all about?' I whisper to Ellie, nodding in the woman's direction.

'I can see the style she's going for,' whispers Ellie.

'She should brush her hair at least.'

'Stop being so judgemental.'

'Can't help it. We all do it.'

We walk out of the subway, order a coffee in Cafe Nero and head to the rendezvous point for the walking tour of Boston.

A gaggle of tourists are gathered around a guy in his late twenties who is sweeping his arms in the air and explaining that the City Hall Plaza was voted the ugliest building in the world.

'He's the type you should be going for.' I say to Ellie as we approach the group.

'He's quite cute, but I've got my date lined up for tonight.'

'Yeah, yeah.'

'You don't believe me?'

'We'll discuss it later. Let's concentrate on the tour, you might learn something.'

Mr Hunky tour guide in his tan-coloured shorts greets everybody. We are referred to as guys in every other sentence, a gender-neutral, inclusive, collective noun that I detest and find cringy. For once why can't tour operators call us folk or ladies and gentlemen?

'This is my home city,' he begins, in a sing-song voice, after handing out headsets and information packs. 'They say that if you don't know what you want to do, be where you want to be. And that's why I'm here. I never wanted to have a proper job, so here I am, taking you guys around my home city. I'll try not to bore you with comments like I remember when this was... Or when I was a kid...

Ellie leans into me. 'He's cute.'

'You weren't interested five minutes ago.'

'I like his accent.'

'Listen to what he's saying, not how he's saying it.'

'You wanted to come on this tour, I'd rather visit that truck.' She points to a pink van which I assume to be an ice cream van because there are pictures on it that look like ice lollies, but are actually strips of bacon. It's a van selling bacon.

'Massachusetts is the most educated, literate state in America. It's becoming gentrified here.' Mr Hunky says. He's walking backward, taking huge sexy strides in his sand-coloured boots. The ginger hairs on his legs glint in the sunlight. 'We like pedigrees.'

'Glad to hear it. Hope my Tinder guy is a pedigree.'

'By the way, there's a sexually transmitted disease that's on the increase, called MG. I read about it this morning,' I say to Ellie.'

'What's that got to do with me going on a date?'

'Just saying.'

We're the stragglers at the back of the group but the headsets ensure we can hear the talk against all the city noise.

'The American colonies were the least taxed part of the entire British Empire. Then they fought the Seven Year War against France and had to recoup their financial losses. We had the Stamp Act, then the Tea Act. There was a lot of opposition to all this taxation but Benjamin Franklin sided with the loyalists and told the colonists they were being unfair, they should expect tax in order to be defended. Work hard to pay your taxes, Franklin said.'

'Dad's always moaning about tax.'

That's the one bit of money he can't squander, thank fuck, I muse to myself. Luckily he isn't self-employed or he'd never pay any contributions.

Mr Hunky throws in lots of names into his talk about the American Revolution as he saunters the streets of Boston, stopping to explain the importance of different buildings. Thomas Paine arrived here and couldn't believe how much the colonists liked the king. It was a new idea to knock down power. Paine said that the individual gives the government power. James Otis was the wise man who got the revolution going. An orphan, John Hancock, was the richest man in Boston and Samuel Adams was the helmsman of the revolution. He was a tax collector but owed money. He inherited money and blew it. He sounds like my brother. My mind drifts back to that lazy fucker. I need to tell Ellie about the baby, as we'll soon be home and time is running out. I zone back in, the names and their significance are a jumble in my menopausal head, as he tells us that Massachusetts was the most democratic place on earth.

After the walk, we wander around the shops and harbor, stopping late afternoon at a cafe for drinks.

'You need to drink green tea Auntie.'

'So you keep saying,' I sigh putting my cup on the table.

'Oh Auntie,' Ellie sings. 'You know it's the best thing for you. The free radicals will keep you looking young and help your bowels.'

'But it tastes disgusting.'

'That's because you're not brewing it at the right temperature.'

'When are you going to give up Els?' And enunciating each word slowly I tell her, 'I do not like green tea.'

She's not giving up. 'Loads of tea drinkers don't even know that temperature-controlled kettles exist. Get a proper kettle and it'll change your life.'

I take a bite of carrot cake.

'You do like your cake.'

I give her a withering look as she reaches over to pinch my waist.

'I can feel at least an inch. It's not going to go when you eat stuff like that.'

She opens the rice cakes she's bought and takes a sip of her green tea.

'Delicious. You should give it a try.' She passes her cup to me, but I wave it away.

'If the temperature-controlled kettle doesn't give you a good cup you're using the wrong water. You need spring water or filtered water.'

'Oh, for God's sake. I just turn the bleeding tap on,' I shout exasperated.

She taps away on her phone chuckling to herself as I people watch.

It's as if we're celebrities because heads are turning to listen, conversations have stopped. Even the clatter of cutlery on crockery has hushed. There's a deadly expression on the faces of the other customers.

I wipe the table with my napkin, pushing the plate in her direction. I don't intend to do this with force, but I do, and it slips into her lap. Her hands go up and a what-the-fuck escapes her mouth for all to hear. I'm about to storm off but remember the bill so I sit down. I'm tired of defending my brother and can't carry his secrets any longer. Unwelcome emotions scud through my brain as I reach boiling point. I love her, I've raised her, the little madam because her idiot father wasn't capable in the wake of her mother's death, which by the way was probably caused by him. Shit, I can't tell her any of this. I need to control myself.

Reining in my thoughts, I calm my breathing, but I'm burning with fury. If Vicky hadn't died, we wouldn't be sitting here now. She'd be on holiday with Vicky instead of me or Jules and Vicky. But the flip side of the coin tells another truth—how I was, around the time that Vicky died. Barely holding it together, I was an emotional wreck. My husband had left me and I was alone and childless. I'm wracked with guilt. I took Ellie under my wings because it suited me. Because I wanted to be a mother—so badly, that it tore me up and made me neurotic. My state of mind led me to whisk her away the night that I found Vicky dead at the bottom of the stairs. I chew my lip. I didn't do it for Ellie, I did it to satisfy my own selfish needs, but I can't tell her any of this.

She pins me with a cold, hard stare. 'Explain to me why Dad can never be arsed?'

'Give me a break.'

'See you can't.'

'You need to talk to him.'

'I don't want to. I hate him.'

'You don't mean that.'

'Why does he get me to pay when we go out? Why's he borrowed money from me and not paid it back? What sort of father does that?'

'I wasn't aware of that. You should have said.'

She's on a roll and there's more to come.

'And come to think of it, I've never asked you because you've done so much for me, it's not that I'm ungrateful, I am grateful...' She flounders as if she's searching for words that won't offend me and will soften the blow. 'I do appreciate you, I love you, you're like a mum, but...' she pauses, 'But why didn't I live with Dad?'

'He couldn't cope.'

'Initially, it must have been hard for him after Mum died, I get that, but once the dust settled, surely he'd have wanted me. What sort of dad would dump their kid on their sister?'

'I didn't mind. By then Richard had left, I had no children of my own.'

'Butter wouldn't melt in his mouth. He can do no wrong in your eyes.'

'That's not true, you don't know the first thing about my relationship with my brother.'

My head is pounding as I resist the urge to scream at her. Green tea, now her dad... I can't cope. I want to crawl away to the harbour and enjoy a stiff drink, on my own. My mind is in turmoil, it's one of two options, leave the cafe, go to a bar or confess everything here and now. I'm on a cliff edge and am falling into new territory, but I can't stop myself.

'Your father's got a problem,' I announce.

'What sort of problem?'

'To do with money.'

'Why? He's got a good job.'

'I don't know how to tell you this but sooner or later you're bound to find out...'

'Just tell me.'

'He's a compulsive gambler. Has been for years.'

She looks confused as if she's struggling to understand.

'And Mandy's expecting his baby. But they aren't together, because of the gambling.'

'Woah, this is too much to take in.' Her hands fly up.

There's a stunned silence as her mouth falls open and her eyes roll back. Her words come in slow motion.

'What the hell, I don't know what to say.'

Now that it's out I feel better. I bite my lip and realise I'm going to have to answer a string of questions. But the questions don't come and instead, she gathers her bag and phone, a wounded expression on her face.

'I'm going. I can't deal with this.' Her eyes are teary. 'I'll see you later.'

'Where are you going?'

'My date.'

'Sit down. What date? Explain.'

'I've been telling you all week about a guy on Tinder.'

'And does he have a name? What does he do? Where does he live? Please Els, it's not a good idea and your Dad agrees with me.'

'Why the hell have you told him?

'I rang him a couple of days ago to say I was worried.'

'I'm twenty-two and you're not my mother. You can't tell me what to do.'

I flinch, the words searing through me like a flame. She's never used this weapon before, not even when she was a stroppy teenager.

'You're in a foreign city, it's not safe to meet strangers like that.'

'Of course, it's safe. We're not in Raqqa. I know what I'm doing. You've forgotten I worked on a marine project in Mozambique last summer. I'm quite capable,' she sniffs, slinging her bag on her shoulder.

I try a different tack. 'I'm actually thinking of myself...'

'Just like you were thinking of yourself when you took me to live with you? You weren't thinking of Dad at all. I filled a void because you couldn't have kids of your own.'

I struggle to keep my nerve through her spiteful remark— even if it is true. 'I don't want to go back on the tube on my own. You saw the weirdos on the train this morning. Some of them looked like they were on Spice.'

'You're not going to answer my question then?' She snaps.

My words are a strangled croak. I feel like a scapegoat for the wrongdoings of my brother.

'Cancel your date, we can get a drink and talk this through, but we can't if you're going to storm off in a strop.'

'I'm not in a strop.'

She turns to go.

I get up and grab her arm.

'Get off me.'

'Tell me where you're going and what time you'll be back. I'm only thinking of your safety.'

'I'm meeting him around the corner. We'll go to a restaurant.'

We're outside the cafe and she turns to go.

'Wait. Don't go Els. I've got a bad feeling about this.'

She laughs and waves me away. I run after her panicked. It might be the last time I see her, and I don't want tomorrow's headlines to read *Girl Missing*. The words on the imagined headlines sway in front of my eyes.

'What if I discreetly sit in the restaurant with you, on another table, just to make sure everything's okay?'

She shoots a sardonic laugh. 'What, like a chaperone?' I'm crushed by her mockery and back off. I want to cry, I feel so alone.

'Keep your phone on and be back by ten.'

'Ten? I'm not a thirteen- year old. I'm not going to the school disco.'

I wish she was going to a school disco. How simple life was back then when all I had to worry about was her drinking too many Fruit Shoots and eating piles of crisps and whether there would be a parking space when I went to pick her up at nine-thirty.

'Ellie please, just be safe.'

'You're about as sensible and crusty as Angela Merkel.'

I feel as if she's slapped me and for a moment, I'm rooted to the spot unable to move as I watch her walk away and fade into the distance. I'm drained from the weight of our conversation in the cafe and I'm shaking with pent up frustration towards her. For reasons I don't understand Ellie has shaken the delicate structure inside me and rocked the life we had. Our relation-ship feels like a stack of cards about to topple and I have no control over what's happening.

Wandering to the harbour area, as I cross the road a cyclist shouts at me for not looking where I'm going. I find a bench and watch a group of fitness freaks do press-ups on the lawn. At first, I relish the peace with my eyes closed into the warm sun and my arms outstretched across the bench but as the minutes tick by panic returns with all the what ifs that could befall Ellie in this big unknown city. I'm unnerved by the changing dynamic between us—because there has been a change. She doesn't respect my opinions and thinks she knows everything about life. While it's great to have the confidence of youth, she has no wariness about her and is oblivious to all the things that can go wrong. This holiday has highlighted that. It's frustrating because I can't seem to tap into her these days. It's as if we are orbiting two different planets and I need a probe to reach her.

In a rash move, I call her. She declines the call, clearly embarrassed in front of him. Him. I don't even know his name, and God forbid what he looks like, hair, height, age, clothing and all of the other things the police might need to know. I chastise myself for my morbid thoughts. I call again but she's switched her phone off. Stop it, I tell myself. It won't come to that—stupid batty woman. She's a modern girl, she's intelligent and has her wits about her. The Ellie I know wouldn't do anything reckless like going to his flat or getting into his car, but how can I be sure? I don't understand her anymore.

I get up and walk, as walking helps. I pass carts selling freshly squeezed lemonade, the tang hits my nostrils before I get another aroma, this time it's carts of cashews roasting in sugar. I take in the scene along what is called the Emerald Necklace; the connecting parks and green space areas of the city, they are carefully planned and aesthetically pleasing. There are water features for children to play in, deckchairs and even outside greenhouse style workstations where people are using their laptops, in a measure to encourage teams and individuals to take their work outside and connect with the environment. It's a wonderful concept and it encourages people to be more productive. There are even outdoor cycling desks, a unique concept to get fit while you work and take in fresh air too, they have been designed by workplace strategy experts. I smile to myself and think of how job titles have changed in recent years. This city is amazing and as I walk my mind is taken away from Ellie and her wretched date.

When I think about her again, I'm cross with myself for my lackadaisical attitude and dig my nails into my palms in self-punishment. I should have stopped her, whatever was I thinking? She'll be okay an inner voice chides, but I'm still worried. I pull out my phone and call Jules but there's no answer. I called him three days ago to tell him that he needed to tell Ellie himself, about the baby.

'What?' Came his answer.

His manner was rude as if I'd caught him in the middle of something.

'Sorry, it sounds as though now is not a good time.'

'What do you want?' He snapped. I didn't feel encouraged to continue, but an inner will drove me on.

'I'm just a bit worried about Ellie.' I unburdened my worries, not quite believing that for the first time in many years I'd admitted to him that I was floundering. I've always been the capable one who can handle any shit if it's thrown my way. I told him everything about how difficult the holiday had been and that it was getting harder for me to hide his addiction from her.

'Let's get this right....' Until this point, I had the impression that he was only half listening and was distracted by something else. 'She's looking at guys on Tinder and you're just going to let her let go off on a date with someone she's never met, in a foreign country. For fuck's sake Pandora. What are you thinking? You need better control over the girl.'

I'm in full-blown panic now. He was right to warn me, and I ignored him.

'I'm coming over,' He'd told me.

'Don't be stupid. Where are you going to find the money to get over here?'

I need to talk to her.'

'You've had years to do that.'

'I'm going to step up to the plate. Shut up woman I'm coming over.'

'I've heard it all before.'

'You'll let her go on a date and then she'll go missing.'

'Don't be pathetic,' I barked.

'She'll be just another kid splashed across tomorrow's papers. I'm not taking that chance, I'm coming over whether you like it or not.'

'You're mental.'

He'd ended the call without a goodbye and that was the last I'd heard from Jules. I don't believe he would spend several hundred pounds getting here, just to have a conversation he could have when we return home. He doesn't have that sort of money and as three days have now passed without another word from him, I'm not expecting him to come over here. He's probably forgotten about my worries because he doesn't give a shit about his daughter. I know my brother. He doesn't have money to buy the next packet of toilet rolls, that's how bad things are.

CHAPTER 29: JULES – 2018

He was standing at a machine in Ladbrokes when his sister made the call. He was starving and to save breaking off from his game Steve, one of the assistants, had nipped out to get him a cheese roll. The assistants treated punters like gods and would often bring over a cuppa when he needed one. The longer they kept the customers in the shop the more money they lost.

Bloody Pandora. He was at a key moment in the game and hated distractions and he only had half an hour before the bookies closed for the night. At first, he ignored it, but she rang again. As the small white ball skittered over the numbers on the spinning roulette wheel heat rose to his face. She was adding to his stress. Tappity-tap. Tappity tap. The noises heightened the experience and it felt as if he was in a casino. The ball ricocheted off a red even number and landed on a black odd number. In his mind he saw number patterns and the machine made him think of HG Wells' time machine— you never knew which numbers it would throw up. That was the thrill of the game. He'd put his chips on corner bets and multiple numbers and maximised the stakes. He put chips on even numbers in the third dozen numbers. Over the fifteen years or so that he'd played roulette on these machines he'd tried different systems. Split bets, multiple numbers, street bets, corner bets, odds, evens, top line of numbers, bottom line of numbers, he'd tried them all. He'd spend hours trying to fathom out how these machines worked. 'The truth is mate,' Al, an ex-betting shop manager told him, 'you've lost before you've played. It's not a real game of roulette, the machines determine whether you win or lose. It's always random.' Jules found this hard to believe. There was a panel on the side of the machine telling him which numbers had come up in the past, suggesting some kind of pattern. He wanted to believe that Al was wrong.

'You beauty,' he patted the machine as if it were a horse. He was up to one thousand pounds. His finger hovered over the button that would finish the game and let him claim his win, but he paused, unsure whether to continue.

He stared at her name on the phone's display, in a stupor. Had she broken his news? He hadn't spoken to Pandora since they'd arrived in Boston and he was desperate to find out his daughter's reaction. He knew he was a coward, it wasn't up to Pandora to do his dirty work for him, but he wasn't up to doing it himself. He'd been a shit father and it was too late to repair their relationship. Ellie's life was moving on. There was a time when he should have been the standard against which she would judge all men, but he was no role model, he knew that much. He'd broken her heart before any boy had the chance to, by handing her to Pandora to raise. His daughter was his flesh and blood, but over the years the link had broken and the bonds of father-daughter had severed. He couldn't pinpoint when it had happened. He noticed one day how like Vicky she was. It was so hard to separate Vicky from Ellie. They were one person. She was as a living reminder of Vicky, a beautiful, radiant woman he missed, and Ellie was the constant remnant of the ugly truth about what happened at the top of the stairs the evening she tumbled to her death.

About to pump more notes into the machine his phone buzzed again, and he grabbed it impatiently from his trouser pocket and answered. The buzz of the game dissipated but the nervous tension sat at the front of his brain.

In a moment of glaring clarity, he felt an urgency to get to Boston.

'I'll come over,' he said on impulse. He had to make it up to her and be the father she needed. A voice in his head coaxed him to man up. Get over there and sort it out. He stared at the total winnings illuminated before him. It was enough for the flight. The voice of old that had always protected his vulnerable heart from further pain and taught him to hold back, be careful, don't love her too much, you could lose her too— that voice had gone. His emotions were in mortal combat. I can't lose her —but I can't lose this game either.

He ended the call, resolving to get to Boston. He could end the game and walk away with his winnings. But it would only take seconds to press 'Bet' and 'Spin' to repeat the game. If he was going to America, he needed more. He always needed more. A thousand wasn't enough. He needed spending money in Boston and money to impress Ellie. He'd take her out for a lovely meal to make up for the disappointment of her birthday.

His finger hovered over the button to take the winnings.

Adrenaline rushed in his brain. Winnings or repeat, repeat or winnings? The temptation was too great. The machine had him under its spell. Before he could contemplate the possibility of losing and not being able to go to his daughter his finger had jammed repeat bet, his mind sucked in. He watched in silent concentration as the white ball danced around the wheel, adrenaline buzzing through his brain, the ball rattling around the rim. In a zombie state, with balled fists, he was ready to thump the machine if he lost. With all thoughts of withdrawing the money gone, all he wanted was to keep playing, to feel that adrenaline rush. The ball hopped over his numbers, landing on red five. He'd lost. And like a junkie, he couldn't stop. Repeat, bet. Spin. Lost. Repeat, bet, spin, lost. And so it went on. In a terrifyingly short time, he'd burned through the lot. His head was in a fog as he thumped the machine, fighting tears and broken dreams. The game had drained the life out of him and drained the life from his wallet. Like the machines in the cotton mills of eighteenth-century Lancashire these machines were evil, a modern form of slavery. If there was a gambling classification similar to that of drugs these machines, Jules believed would be class A.

Walking back to his bedsit he tried to console himself—other people lost far more. At least he wasn't his mate Terry, who'd lost forty thousand in a single day on one of the machines a couple of years ago. He'd been playing maximum stakes of a hundred pounds every twenty seconds. Or there was Ewen who'd come into the bookies with his life savings in ice cream containers and lost the lot. He'd known gamblers his whole adult life who took big hits. There was always somebody who had lost more than him—always somebody with an addiction much worse than his. He was just one gambler in a town full of them. Jules longed for the government to do something because gambling was destroying lives and he saw it all around him. It was a blight on bedsit land where he'd counted eight registered betting shops in his street. Because the law stated that each shop could only have four machines, betting shops were burgeoning and there was no escape. The government was studying the possibility of reducing the hundred-pound maximum bet limit to two pounds, but this wasn't coming into force until 2019, the following year. That law, if it had come in at the outset, when these idiot machines were invented, at the turn of the millennium could have saved him hundreds of thousands of pounds. But nevertheless, the machines were only a small part of the gambling industry. He would still be able to pour five hundred pounds into the fruit machines in betting shops–– and the online possibilities for gambling were limitless and this was where the growth was. As far as he was aware nothing much was being done about that.

The memories of wins were branded in his mind. Losses left stains, time unshackled the chain of self-blame. He'd once won five hundred pounds and bought a laptop, another time he'd netted seven hundred and bought a car. These were life-changing wins. Losses left stains but it was the wins that were indelible. His mind had a convenient way of erasing his misfortunes. The police tracked him down for lack of car insurance and the laptop had to be sold after a year for hard cash that he didn't have. His mind blotted facts like that away like a spill on a carpet.

What was he going to do? He needed the money for a flight, but nobody would lend him money because he never got around to paying anybody back. He planned to pay them back, of course he did, because he wasn't a complete shit. He promised to pay them when he'd won. Gambling was the only way he was ever going to pay people back. It was going to happen, one day. Not that any of them were clamouring for their money. Maybe they didn't need it back, Jules thought. If he stayed focused it would happen. He owed hundreds to every girlfriend he'd ever dated—except Mandy, he'd never asked her for money. She was stingy, not a generous soul like the others. She always said she didn't lend money, but in this moment of desperation, his hour of need, he would ask her. She was his best hope, his only hope.

CHAPTER 30: JULES – 2018

Gripped by a wave of nausea he knocked on Mandy's door early the following morning.

Mandy was pale, lines that weren't there before were sketched around her eyes and made her face tight. A cotton shirt billowed over her swollen belly, his baby waiting to make its entrance into the world. At forty-two with sleek dark hair swept into a ponytail she was still a stunner. Due to her height and size eight figure, there was something endearingly sweet and innocent about her but the no-nonsense expression she wore belayed that. He quailed to think what she had to face alone and longed, with all his heart to be a better man. He'd tried so many times, but she couldn't take on his problems, why should she? He'd failed her. He couldn't drag her down with him. There was no way out of the prison of his addiction and the only key to the cell was more gambling. It was a vicious circle of despair and destruction.

'What do you want?' She slurred, employing the tone she reserved for cold callers. She peered at him with contempt through hurt eyes as if he was a lump of dog crap she'd found on her shoe. He felt like a lump of dog poo. It was what he deserved, he knew that much.

'Can I come in? Please. I need to ask you something.'

Her mother appeared in the hallway.

'What does he want?'

Her mother folded her arms and glared at Jules. She reminded him of an intimidating bailiff.

'I don't know Mum.'

'He'll be wanting money.'

She turned to her mother. 'No, he won't. He knows I don't have any.' Then back to Jules. 'That's right isn't it?'

'Of course, he wants money why else would he come snivelling round here.'

This conversation wasn't new to Jules. When her mother found out about Jules' problems, she hit the roof. She didn't talk to him directly. It didn't matter how pleasant he was, or how much he loved her daughter, he was scum. All gamblers were scum but that wasn't an unusual attitude. He was used to it. He was a condemned man, charged without trial. She'd formed her opinions and didn't want to hear his story. Like the homeless on the streets of Britain, like the drug dealers and the murderers, gamblers had themselves to blame and anybody that stepped into their lives could end up a victim, fleeced of money, conned and lied to. But Jules had never stolen and was always honest, but it made no difference, he was tarred with the same brush.

'We don't have any more to talk about Jules, you'd better go.'

Before she could close the door, he put his foot on the threshold.

'Get your foot out of my house,' her mother moved forward to wave him away. He didn't budge.

'It's Pandora, she needs me in Boston.'

'Why?'

'Because I need to tell her about the baby. Mand I'm skint. Please. I'll pay you back. I promise.'

'Don't listen to him love. It's probably all lies to get money out of you.' Her mother put a reassuring arm around her daughter and to Jules, she barked, 'Now clear off.'

'Please Mandy. I'm literally begging you.' He hated groveling but he was banking on her support, because there was nobody else he could turn to.

'So, you're still pumping those bloody machines. You told me you were making an effort. Now I find that you're broke as usual. I'm glad I wasn't conned yet again by your words the other night.'

'I'm sorry.'

'So, you keep bloody saying,' she spat in his face. He stepped back, horrified at her anger. 'Wait there,' she said and stormed into the kitchen at the back of the house, with her mother following after her.

'You will not lend that man any money, do you hear me? You need every penny for the baby. He won't be supporting it. That much we know.' She raised her eyes to the ceiling in despair.

Mandy shut the kitchen door but from the doorstep, Jules could hear all sorts of accusations against him. The words she used to describe him came thick and fast, like air rifle pellets in her husky Yorkshire accent. Idiot, loser, waster, sponger, leech, liar, con merchant, parasite and wanker. She had the voice of somebody warm and welcoming, but Jules had never witnessed it. He'd heard her words before from various people, usually girlfriends and their mothers. They swirled into one ugly heady mess. Jules leaned against the wall like a sloppy teenager and dug the tip of his shoe into the soil of the flowerbed making a small hole. He felt a strong urge to kick her chrysanthemums across the lawn but he wasn't a hooligan, he didn't have a temper and did not want that label added to her already very long shopping list.

'Yes, yes Mum, leave it to me, I know what I'm doing.'

Jules realised that he hadn't told her how much he needed. She couldn't possibly have that much in her purse. He'd imagined they'd walk down to the cashpoint together, but the truth was he hadn't believed she'd say yes anyway.

'There, have that.' She thrust a twenty quid note into his hand. Jules stared at it as if it was toy money, all hope of getting to Boston drained away like sunshine turned to rain.

'That's not going to get me to Boston. Please Mand,' he pleaded.

'That's my share of the meal from the other night.'

'I don't want it.' He passed it back to her. 'I told you it was my treat.'

'I don't want you getting false hope. There won't be any more meals out. And there won't be any more handouts, so don't come here asking again.'

'The other night was the least I could do.'

'I thought you needed money? Make up your bloody mind. That's all I've got.'

His hand hovered, unsure what to do. He was pleased with himself for taking her out for a meal, the first in months. He'd considered it a waste of money to fritter on wine and food. Fifty quid could have bought a week's shop for a whole family. That was his hard-earned money. It could have bought a second-hand pram for the baby or a pair of new trainers. The soles were falling off his trainers. He'd felt resentful when the bill had arrived and as for a tip, there'd been no chance of that. He could have taken the fifty quid into the bookies and turned it into more money.

He took the money she gave him and thrust the note into his pocket before she changed her mind. He felt dreadful, like a thief. She needed the money. But he'd pay her back, of course he would. Twenty pounds was better than jack shit. He could easily turn twenty pounds into an airfare—and hopefully more. Hope was returned. He had to get to his daughter, but more than anything he had to get to the betting shop. It was a void that sucked him in.

Her mother, hovering near the kitchen door stepped forward, ready to sweep him away like dirt.

'You've had her money now hop it.'

'It's okay Mum, I can handle him.'

'I don't think you can, that's the problem. You had a baby with him.' She gave a mocking laugh and turned away with a huff.

'Look Jules,' she said when her mother was safely upstairs. 'I don't want you coming here again but you can take the baby for walks in the park.'

He gulped, surprised by this concession.

'I don't want it going to your hovel though.'

'Cheeky cow, I only cleared up the other day.' He was relieved that she was at last prepared to let him have some involvement with the child. It was hard. They'd only known each other for a short time when Mandy discovered she was pregnant. They were thrust into the situation and it wasn't what either of them wanted but she hadn't wanted an abortion either. At that point, she hadn't known about his gambling. He'd hoped to break it to her slowly, but she'd scrolled down his Facebook profile to find out more about his life and found the link to a blog post about his addiction that he'd written under an alias. Jules remembered her confronting him in the pub and the short silence that followed. 'I haven't gambled since the Summer.' It was an easy lie, but as the weeks went on it became obvious to her that he hadn't stopped. This was one addiction that could be hidden but it was hard to hide in a relationship because he simply couldn't afford to go out. It didn't take Mandy long to guess that he was still in the grips of his addiction.

'It's a dump let's face it.'

'I don't intend to live there forever.'

'That's what you always say. You're full of bullshit. Nothing in your life will change until you stop gambling.'

'I can't just stop like that. It's not that simple.'

'That's another thing we'll never agree on. You don't try.'

'I do. I am cutting back.'

'You need help.'

He wasn't in the mood for one of her lectures. 'Look, thanks for the money,' Jules said, digging his hands into his pockets. 'I appreciate that.'

She smirked. 'Hope you sort out your family problems.'

It was a game to her, throwing him crumbs that wouldn't get him to the end of the street, but if he was creative, he could turn it into a flight ticket. He had to get back to the betting office. Time was getting on. He didn't know what more to say. Every conversation he had with Mandy was a merry-go-round. With the issues that clouded what could have been a good relationship, he couldn't have a jolly chat.

CHAPTER 31: PANDORA – 2018

Finding it hard to relax with a drink and my kindle I check the time, silently praying that Ellie will be alright and will be back at the Airbnb at a reasonable time. I phone my brother again, but his phone is still switched off. I hope he's not really going to jet over here, it was a mad idea of his, but now that this has happened, I find myself needing him.

I can't concentrate on the book I'm reading. It's maybe better to get up and walk around. I follow the Freedom Trail because that way it's impossible to get lost. It weaves around to Faneuil House, near the waterfront, a marketplace and meeting hall since 1743. I have a hard time pronouncing Faneuil, I've heard it pronounced in different ways. It's a noisy area and there are street performers and singers. The site of important speeches by eminent orators over the years Faneuil Hall represents the cradle of liberty and is the site of protests and debate. The Stamp Act and the tea crisis were discussed and debated in Faneuil Hall and many stirring issues of the day through to later issues like slavery and women's suffrage. It's also where new citizens to Boston are sworn in. Faneuil Hall is one of several locations in Massachusetts for swearing in the 20,000 new citizens naturalised each year. Crowds of well-wishers are gathered outside to welcome these newly minted Americans. I pass a protest outside the hall near a statue of Samuel Adams and forget the weight of Ellie's absence as I get into a conversation with them.

'We just love your Trump baby,' one of them says laughing. They are referring to the giant inflatable caricature of Trump flying in London as a protest to his visit to England this week.

As I soak up the austere surroundings— white pillars and paintings and Stars and Stripes on the wall— words form in my head, dancing into creative sentences and forming mini-speeches on issues that spring from the deepest crevices of my mind. There's something about the atmosphere here and I know the importance of the hall to the history of American democracy. It makes me want to get up and speak to a huge audience, vomiting random thoughts on every issue in politics and when I've exhausted every topic I'm back to thinking about Ellie.

At Quincy Market, I stroll around shops and walk and walk until my feet ache and blisters form. I pass Boston's gleaming State House dome and find myself on the upper crust red bricked cobbled streets of Beacon Hill where house buyers don't get much change from a couple of million. It's a quiet enclave, you wouldn't know you were in a busy metropolis. Birds are singing and there are no traffic noises or sirens to be heard. As charming as these gas lit, tree-lined walkways are, my mind crawls with visions of what might be happening to Ellie. I try her mobile for the umpteenth time, but it's still switched off. It's eleven O clock. I wish to God we'd agreed a time for her to get back. What time was reasonable and what time does the subway close?

I wander into Walgreens trawling up and down the aisles aimlessly until I reach the drugs and cosmetics and then my interest piques. There are tubs of painkillers containing more than three hundred tablets and a whole manner of remedies and medicines on everything from vaginal infections to diabetes. On the top shelf there are paternity kits and DNA tests—tests that in Britain we would have to order from the internet and yet they can pluck them from a supermarket shelf, for a smidgeon of the price. There's a whole selection of Avenno products but in Britain, they only stock the eczema cream. I'm in awe of so much choice. This is why I love this country.

CHAPTER 32: JULES – 2018

J ules walked past the machines in the bookies, to the boards displaying the day's races. It wasn't his lucky day for slotties, but with the twenty quid in his pocket, he felt a shot of luck course through him for a bet on the horses. Everything hinged on the twenty-pound note. A couple of old men in flat caps were pouring over the Racing Times scrutinising the results or gleaning odds for the afternoon's races. Jules thought it was a shame it wasn't the Grand National or the Royal Ascot. They took place in April and June and he liked those events. Betting shops were different places to the shops of thirty years ago. When there were no races there were always virtual races filling the gap. He didn't want to waste time looking at the odds on all the horses. Impatient, he took his slip to the desk and asked the assistant to stick down some random selections on races taking place. He barely registered the names of the horses and wouldn't have selected names like Monumental Man, Octave and Zumurud or Chikoko Trail if he'd taken more care, but those names were among the choices he made. These were sentient beings, very temperamental ones at that, and sometimes the combination of jockey and horse wasn't compatible. He relied on his gut instinct with choices, or he picked a lucky number.

His mate Bob-the-Bet was in the bookies pumping money into the machines. Bob was a veteran of the betting shop, hence his name and over the years he'd taught him the ropes. He'd also got to know something of Jules' personal history.

'Mate,' he said to Bob slapping him on the back as Bob pulled his ticket from the machine to collect his winnings.

'I've just won two hundred,' Bob beamed.

'Lucky beggar. I lost on that machine earlier.'

Bob's win had planted a thought in his mind. The machine had taken his money and now it was starting to pay out. What should he do? Place the bet on the horses or play the machine. The machine owed him the money it had taken. But before he could decide Bob was back with the cash and ready to pour some of his winnings back into the machine.

'You okay mate?' Bob asked before selecting his numbers.

'Not really mate. My sister's having problems in Boston with my daughter and I've come in here with twenty quid hoping to turn it into an air ticket.'

'Don't play the machines then, you'll only lose.'

That was rich of him.

'You've got to be savvy with your money. Go for the horses. And if you lose what will you do? Got a plan B?

'My options are running out. I've asked Mandy to lend me the money, but she won't.'

He watched Bob play the machine, overwhelmed by an urge to watch him sink his winnings so that he could win them when back after Bob had left the shop, but it felt like fleecing a friend. He couldn't do it.

Jules went to the counter with his betting slip. He hesitated as he handed it over. Had he made a good choice? No, he'd cross one of them off and spend a pound on a scratch card instead. But which horse to eliminate? He went for Monumental Man racing at Brighton. Brighton was a bad luck town because he hated the Brighton and Hove Albion Football Club. He wasn't alone in loathing the Seagulls, plenty of Palace supporters did. He went home to pack, just in case they were winners, hope soared with his new bet, all thoughts of his earlier losses on the machines were erased from his mind. With a belief that his luck had turned, partly because Mandy, the mother of his unborn child had touched the twenty-pound note that had placed his bet, her touch was magical, a dead cert. It was a daft thought, but he was driven by superstition. Another streak of superstition was that he never placed a bet on Crystal Palace, the football team he supported. That was plain bad luck and asking for trouble.

ONCE IN A WHILE, the betting gods tossed Jules a nice winning ticket to keep his faith and keep him betting. Would it be one of those favourable days?

Standing at the screen he watched the first race. His horse was poised perfectly on the outside ready to pounce. Jules' head pounded in anticipation. The jockey wasn't urging the horse and he was standing up in the saddle. The horse was hanging badly in the lane and going wide. He thought the horse might be injured. It was obvious that the jockey didn't want his horse to win. Maybe he was treating it as a prep race, intent on a bigger race further down the horse's career. The horse was so close, it looked as though it could win. Jules rubbed his forehead. It was torture. But he gained ground, he was ahead by inches, a metre, then he fell back. Jules swore and hit his head. He gained again, then dragged again, to the finish line, coming in second. It was close, fuck, bloody close, fuck. He had Betting Tourette's. Sod's bloody law, Jules thought, smacking the chair next to him.

The next race would be better. The horses were lined up at the gate and then they were off. 'It's the second race of the day.' the commentator said.

They went over the first jump. His horse was overtaken by one called Ellie Light. Fuck, he thought. Why didn't I see that name on the list in my haste? They settled into the race. His horse was flanked by Pandora Spritz. Fuck, another one I missed. How on earth had this happened? There were two of his family names in one race. Fate was against him, it was a sign. The horses skipped along tightly grouped. Adrenaline coursed through his body as he waited in anticipation of what was going to happen in those precious minutes. Just as they reached a corner his horse unseated the rider. The rider got to his feet, unharmed, but it was too late to remount. The horse was off without him, he had a race to finish. He gained good ground, galloping ahead, over a hurdle, down a dip, now in the lead, typical with no rider to claim the victory. Jules punched the air. This was it. This was his race. His win. He was off to Boston. Close to the finish, Devil's Dance touched his horse which veered to the left allowing Purple Ribbon to overtake. The others in the race pounded past his horse to the finish. Race over. Lost. Lost again. One race to go.

Bob, who had now lost all of his winnings was standing beside him, consoling himself with a packet of Bourbon biscuits and a flask of tea.

'And they're off,' the commentator said. But it was a false start and the horses dispersed in all directions and were recalled to the start. It was a nail-biting moment, but the race was restarted. Down to the first fence and over. At the next hurdle, his horse gained ground, past Roadson Jules. 'Oh my God,' Jules screamed, 'another name I missed.' Roadson Jules took the lead. Why the hell didn't I choose that one? But as the race progressed his horse galloped on, past one horse, then another, now in the lead, he made a good jump, still ahead, a

couple of lengths in front of the others, making good progress
and through to the finish—he won. Jules jumped and punched
the air. He couldn't believe, he had a winner. Tears of joy
sprung to his eyes. And with his elation came a new and
exciting thought. With his win, he could place another bet. No,
an inner voice screamed, take your winnings and leave.

He turned to Bob and they did a high five.

'Now before you go betting your winnings give me the slip
and I'll collect the money and escort you to the flight shop to
book your flight.

'No mate, I'll be fine.'

'You so won't be. C'mon man do this for your daughter.'

Before Jules could get to the counter Bob took the slip from
his hand and was striding towards the assistant. As much as
they egged each other on, they could also be good like that.
They supported each other when it mattered. Jules was in two
minds, rooted to the spot, enjoying the buzz of the bookies, the
thrill of the game and the warmth and company of the other
punters. Shirley, the assistant smiled at him. He wanted to stay
and watch another race. It was fun, more fun than anything
else in the world and more important than getting that flight.
He'd chat to Ellie when she got home and hope that Pandora
was wrong in her worry about Ellie wanting to go on a date.

'I'll have another bet Shirley.'

'You said you needed to get to America.'

'I do.'

'Bob, give us the money.'

'No.'

Bob thrust the money in his pocket and Jules tried to grab
it, but he had his hand firmly pressed to his pocket and he was
a big guy. In another life, Bob could have been a boxer. He had
been a bouncer at the local nightclub, years ago. He was scary
and on instinct, Jules stepped away.

The sympathetic smile of Shirley touched his conscience. A

punch of fear rose through his guts. Ellie. A bolt of love shot his heart. And in a flash, he knew what he had to do.

He had enough to get there but Bob had his money and it didn't look as though he was going to hand it over. Bob marched towards the door with Jules hot on his heels but as they left the bookies Bob broke out in a run and Jules found it hard to keep up. He'd thought Bob was his friend. People said that gamblers were thieves and liars and now he knew it was true.

Just when he was thinking the worst of Bob, he came to a halt outside the flight shop and went in.

'Why did you run off?' He asked, struggling to get his breath back.

'It was the only way to get you in here and stop you losing your winnings. You had that look in your eyes. You were going to carry on playing. Don't deny it.'

AT THE AIRPORT, he remembered the scratch card he'd bought. He was on a roll and it might be another win. He ordered a small whiskey from Wetherspoons. He had a ritual, a sip then a scratch, a sip, a scratch, taking his time. He scratched off two, five-hundred pounds. His heart raced, his palms sweaty he held the two pence coin ready to scratch the last number. He wanted to prolong that moment with one square left to scratch and until it was scratched, he was a winner ...once that coin rubbed his fate away—he might not be. His hand hovered over the card and he realised he hadn't checked the flight board for a while. He dashed to the board. Gates boarding it read. Shit. He dashed back to his table, but the whiskey was gone. The staff had swiped it. He hastily scratched the card and when he saw that it was a third five- hundred he couldn't believe how his luck had turned. First a horse race and now a lottery win. He checked the board. They were boarding. Sweat poured from his brow. He needed the money. He ran over to WHSmith to claim the win, but the queue was snaking around the shop, but despite that, he joined it. They were still waiting at the gate, he'd have time. The plane wasn't leaving for at least another forty minutes. His heart raced as he willed the queue to go down, keeping a close eye on the time. Ten minutes seemed like twenty. There were only five customers in front. And then an announcement came over the loudspeaker. 'Would Mr Jules Newton please go to gate twelve. Your flight is leaving in ten minutes.' His gut was knotted, he needed the loo, but he turned and ran to the gate, pains rattled across his chest because he wasn't used to running.

His scratch card was safely in his wallet. If only he'd been able to cash it. A new thought shimmied into his mind. The trainfare. Shit. He'd almost forgotten that he needed train fare to get to work, If he didn't pay for the fare he'd be out of a job. If he could cash the scratch card and place a bet with some of the money, he could get a train season ticket. That was the answer. Everything came down to win or lose with him. It was a muddle. His head spun with the constant juggling of schemes, how to pay for this, how to pay for that, a never-ending circle of bills and responsibilities. The high of his wins crashed, as they always did when the adrenaline subsided. He wished the plane would crash and put an end to his misery.

CHAPTER 33: PANDORA – 2018

The raw edge of evening closes in as dark clouds form across the sky bringing light rain. It's gone eleven and there's still no word from Ellie. I trawl the streets peering in every restaurant window near to where she'd stormed off. Just catching a glimpse of her would be enough to settle my mind. I'd wait outside the restaurant for her, just to know she's safe. I scan the people and everywhere there are Ellie lookalikes. It's as if there are a hundred mirrors and I'm calculating which is the real Ellie and which are the fake. Sometimes I think I see her running ahead and I crane my neck, but her handbag is black not beige, and her jeans are loose not the tight fit that Ellie prefers. She'll be back my head tells me. My gut says she won't and it churns with worry.

I have walked up and down and in and out of every restaurant and down to Quincy Market to do the same. It's late but the coffee shops and restaurants are still sucking in trade. I convince myself she'll be back at the Airbnb.

Taking the subway, the train halts a hundred yards from the station and a voice announces a short delay. I check my phone while we wait but there's no signal. What if she's trying to reach me? A wave of nausea grips me. Ten minutes pass but it feels longer. People around me are muttering and craning their necks at the window. Closing my eyes, I breathe deeply, distracting myself, flexing my fingers and despising the train company. My nails have made indentations in the palms of my hands.

The train lurches forward, then jolts and another announcement informs us that the train won't be stopping at the next station. There has been an incident and so it will be stopping at the one after. I want to know what kind of incident. What could be more important than Ellie being missing? Panic engulfs me as I watch passengers shift and mumble, tutting in despair. Why has something happened at my stop—is it Ellie?

Disorientated, I head for the steps, confused about how I'm going to get back. The other passengers seem to know where they're heading. They've made plans in their heads and don't need advice to get home.

On the street the sky is leaden. Police sirens pierce the night air and buildings are bathed in blue. Something is going on. I worry about Ellie more with each passing minute. How long has our station been closed and will she have the same problem that I had? Every man on the street is out to get her. I've been focused on one homicidal maniac, but the train situation has opened the way for thousands of them to flood to my head. I focus on hailing a cab and try to dispel images of Ellie as I try to remember the address of the Airbnb, but I've clean forgotten the damned address. I can't focus. My mind is a sandstorm and the information I need swirls incomprehensibly in my addled head.

'I can direct you from the next subway, it's just up the hill from there,' I tell the taxi driver.

'The roads around the subway have been closed off ma'am. There's been an incident.'

'What kind of incident?'

'It's unclear exactly, but an SUV hurtled into a crowd of pedestrians leaving the station.'

'Oh shit, oh my God, my daughter. Do you know if anyone's been killed?'

'Yes, and according to the news, several have been taken to hospital.'

'Please could you turn your radio on, I'm really worried that my niece was involved. She's been out all evening and I've no idea where she is or when she's getting back.' Shit, shit. I shouldn't have left her.

'You can call the Boston police. They'll be able to give you some more information.'

Ribbons of panic coil inside me as I realise the incident might be terrorist related.

As I get out of the taxi, the first thing I notice is that the house is shrouded in darkness. I had hoped beyond hope that Ellie would be back already. Tendrils of fear tighten around my chest when there's no sign of her inside the apartment. I call the police, explaining what's happened. They promise to call back when they've checked the names of the casualties.

As I end the call, Jules phones.

'I'm at the airport.'

'What? You're not serious.'

'I'm at Boston Airport.'

'Oh, for fuck's sake Jules.'

'I need to make it up to her.'

'What the fuck. You can do that anytime. You've had twenty-two years to prove yourself as a father.'

'Don't start, I know I've messed up and I'm proving a point —that most of the time I'm a waste of space but I'm prepared to fly half-way across the world to sort it.'

'I've been trying to call you for the past three days.'

'I've been too focused on getting over here to answer the phone.'

'You wouldn't be coming if you had no money, so how did you get hold of enough to get here?

'I'll explain later. Can you and Ellie pick me up?'

'If you'd bothered to answer my calls you could have spoken to her and persuaded her not to go on a date with a random guy, but now she's not here. She went on a date this evening and she's not back yet and I'm worried sick.'

'Jesus and you didn't stop her?'

'How could I stop her? She's a grown woman.'

'Have you called the police?'

'Of course not. But if she's not back by the morning, which I'm sure she will be, then yes, I will. Although I'm scared witless, technically she is not a missing person yet.'

In my distressed state, I'm pleased to hear his voice and relieved to have somebody here in Boston to take care of me. I haven't felt this way in a long time. Jules has always been the needy one. When I think of Jules, especially after what he did to Mum and Dad, I feel pure anger and resentment. How could I be related to somebody like that? But in my shrivelled state, I don't care how he got the money together to come here, the fact is he's here and I need him.

I swallow, drained from the weight of the fraught evening.

'Wait at the pick-up. I'll be as quick as I can.' I don't tell him about the incident at the subway. He'll freak.

Light drizzle turns to heavy rain as I get in the car. The engine coughs to life and I reverse out of the driveway, almost hitting a passing car because the road is poorly lit and he's driving too fast. The driver waves an abusive gesture and we exchange furious bursts of car horn— but mine are more desperate. There's still activity around the subway. Strobes of blue light remind me of a rave. With the roadworks and construction on top of the calamity at the station, it's hard to work out the road diversions. I navigate around the maze of roadblocks and type in airport into the sat nav while sitting at the traffic lights. My phone is silent on the seat beside me. I thump the steering wheel willing the police to call back.

As I sweep into the pick-up area it takes me precious minutes to spot Jules.

'What's happening,' he asks when we settle into the drive. 'Has she called yet?'

I explain about the incident at the subway and he freaks and starts shouting at me.

'A terrorist incident?'

'We don't know for sure, but it seems to be.'

So much for feeling reassured that he's here. He's adding to my stress and suddenly I wish he was back home.

'Jesus Pandora, you should never have let her go. Christ, she met him online? What were you thinking?'

'Oh, just fucking shut up. Shut up alright.' Unable to contain myself pent up tears spill. 'Pass a tissue.' I point to my handbag. He reaches to the footwell to rummage in my bag. I wince. I'm uncomfortable with him fishing around in my bag. It's terrible to have to be like this with my own flesh and blood. I don't want to be on my guard all the time. I want to be able to trust him.

I can't see ahead through tears and the rain is beating a steady tattoo on the windscreen. I nearly hurtle into the car in front. I swerve recklessly and Jules screams at me to concentrate. I wish he'd show more empathy. For goodness sake, I'd like to see him drive in Boston. He's a bloody backseat driver. He hasn't driven in years and can only afford a bicycle. This is not what I need.

'Why haven't we got the news on?'

'I can't concentrate over the radio.'

'We need to find out what's happening.'

'There appears to be a major police emergency unfolding in Boston tonight. Details are just beginning to come in. We do know that President Trump has been briefed and is in contact with security officials. There are disturbing and chaotic scenes in three locations across Boston. The news is still fresh but if these incidents are connected it looks as if this is terror related. Stay tuned for regular updates as they come in.'

'Shit.'

'Eyewitnesses say that a car ploughed into pedestrians in each of the three locations. Let's go now to eyewitnesses on the scene...'

'I can't bear to listen to anymore, Jules.' I scream and kill the radio.

'Calm down sis, it's going to be all right.'

I cringe. He hasn't called me sis in years, and it doesn't feel right. I can't get cosy with him, the memories of the pain he caused run deep.

'We need to listen.'

He presses the radio, but I push his hand away. I don't want my worst fears to be true.

CHAPTER 34: JULES – 1997

J ules didn't call 999. His world collapsed in a single moment as he stared down at his wife lying in a heap at the bottom of the stairs. A single act was all it took for reality to alter forever. Rooted to the spot, there was a numbing moment of disbelief to anaesthetise his fear and stop him from racing down the stairs to find out if she was still breathing. He looked away focusing for a moment on a patch of damp and bubbled peeling paintwork. Why hadn't he got around to decorating? He never got round to anything. There were always things on the stairs, bits and pieces waiting to go up. He stared at the weapons, a hairbrush, a bottle of shampoo and a few pieces of Lego. Rather than taking things up with him, it was his habit to ignore them as he passed. He swore as he wondered where this lazy habit of leaving stuff on the stairs had come from.

She was slumped on her face, like a crumpled doll. A cold, iron paralysis tightened around him. He was an automaton, powerless to move.

Blood was splattered across the wall like a messy child's

painting. One of her red stilettos had come to rest on the bottom step, intact and unbroken—more resilient than the human skull. The other shoe lay beside her, the five-inch heel pointing to her head, like the barrel of a gun.

The ringing of the doorbell broke the silence of the night, Pandora was here to babysit. Her first words when she saw the carnage jolted him, like a defibrillator.

'Fuck Jules, what have you done?'

'Argument. Tripped. Stilettos.' Tears sprung to his eyes and he buckled, leaning against the wall for support. Words weren't coming out in coherent sentences. The hall was spinning. He collapsed to the floor, pulled his legs up and bent his head between his legs. He couldn't touch her, as if she was made of china, he didn't want to. He wanted to run, to get as far away from the house as possible. He needed to hide. The last half hour was a muddle. He remembered everything coming to a head. He revealed the true extent of his gambling to Vicky. It had escalated again—since the last time he'd revealed the true extent to her. She discovered that he'd gone behind her back, she was screaming about deceit. He'd forged her signature to extend the terms of the mortgage and to take out several bank loans—again. Due to his job, their credit limit seemed endless and the more he wanted the more the banks gave.

They were going to a party. It was going to be fun. They were on the landing, close to the stairs when she started on him. 'Those bloody stilettos,' he'd said, trying to get her off the subject of his gambling before the evening was ruined. She twirled round and shouted at him, with venom in her voice, with a crazed expression on her face. Had she been holding the banister? Did he push her? Maybe he'd done it in the heat of the moment to stop her nagging but he couldn't remember. He couldn't fucking remember. One minute she was at the top of the stairs, the next she was at the bottom.

'Don't you criticise what I wear, you bastard. You've got a fucking cheek. I hate you. I know exactly what you've been up to. Are you in debt again? What have you been spending our money on?'

He told her he'd lost everything they had.

'Have you called for an ambulance?' Pandora asked, breaking his thoughts.

He stared at her blankly.

'I don't know'

Vicky was alive. She was conscious and struggling to breath when the paramedics arrived.

'Female still breathing,' the paramedic said, requesting an ambulance.

The gurney crashed through the doors. She was alive. She had a CT scan which revealed a number of fractured ribs, a fractured shoulder blade, and a punctured lung. Air was escaping into her pleural cavity and a drain was put in place to reduce the pressure. The worst of her injuries—and the one that killed her was a subdural haematoma where her head had impacted with the wall.

The police treated the death as suspicious and arrested Jules. The neighbours had heard shouting and banging of doors and had called the police. The facts were investigated and the coroner concluded that she had suffered a fall causing catastrophic injuries. The level of alcohol in her blood and the stilettos had played a part in her death. There was no sign of a struggle and Jules' account of what happened couldn't be disproved.

Had he pushed her? He couldn't remember. His recall of those minutes had simply vanished, probably due to amnesia. They were at the top of the stairs and the next minute she was in a heap at the bottom, everything else was a blank. Guilt smothered him like a blanket, but it also drove him on—guilt drove him into the security of the bookies where he could park his troubles and escape the horrible reality that he was responsible for his wife's death. It was true that he didn't remember, but deep down he knew.

CHAPTER 35: PANDORA – 1997

I'm at their doorstep, about to knock. I tilt my head to listen and hold my breath. I'm sure I heard banging coming from inside. It was as if a piece of furniture had been hurled down the stairs. But all is now quiet. I knock, rather than ring the bell. They'll have Ellie settled, the last thing I want to do is wake her and have to cope with a fractious child all night. Vicky's days are fraught. Tonight, is a much-needed evening out for both of them. After the day I've had, I'm looking forward to curling up on their velvet settee with a good film. Today is the anniversary of Richard walking out on me. He left me for a younger woman, and I have my own agenda that includes a nip of gin or two. He sacrificed our long-shared history for somebody ten years younger. The sting is as palpable now as it was then. 'But you're pretty and intelligent and you'll find someone to love you.' I heard it repeatedly as word leaked out. It helped a bit, knowing that others saw beauty in me, even if it wasn't enough to keep my husband. After he left my life was so empty and lifeless. We'd focused for so long on having a baby, it had worn us down. I still wallow.

They're taking a long time to answer the door. I peer

through the side window but can't see either of them. I'm looking forward to drowning my sorrows in a mug of hot chocolate before hitting the gin. The old feelings of self-loathing that I thought I'd recovered from have returned with a vengeance. Today I bumped into the wife of a friend of Richard's in the pizza aisle at Iceland. 'Richard's new partner is having a baby, did you know?' She said, all mealy-mouthed and impervious to my feelings. I smiled and pretend the news didn't hurt, but of course it did and she must have known that it would. Was it really necessary for her to tell me Richard's news? What did she think I'd get out of it? I can't be happy for them because that should have been us. I couldn't give him a child, so he moved on. I am the reject. The equipment that didn't work in this throw-away society of ours that no longer makes do and mends.

Jules, white-faced opens a gap and peers through.

'Come on, open up, I'm freezing out here.' Pulling my collar up I make shivering noises but Jules doesn't stand back to allow me to come in.

'I've got the right day haven't I?'

'Yeah, but I've got a bit of a problem.'

Opening the door I then see why. I am so shocked at the sight of Vicky slumped at the bottom of the stairs that I can't speak. Crying or screaming isn't an anatomical possibility either. I stare, stupefied, knowing that the scene before me will stay with me forever. The silence is suddenly broken by my barrage of expletives and questions and my brother's croaky grunts.

It doesn't occur to me to check whether Vicky is breathing until the paramedic on the phone asks me if she is. I kneel beside her and put my face close to hers. Jules is motionless, as if in a trance. Fumbling in my bag for a lipstick mirror I put it close to her lips. She's breathing, thank God. Her eyelids flutter briefly. She's going to be okay. They'll fix her.

'What the hell happened?' I ask Jules. 'Did you push her?'

'I don't know. I honestly don't remember.'

The paramedics are taking her away, the police have arrived. It's chaos. Jules goes with the ambulance while I look after Ellie.

Three days later, Vicky is pronounced dead when the medics switch her life support machine off. The coroner concludes she suffered a fall causing catastrophic injuries. When the facts are investigated, the level of alcohol, the stairs which were steeper than they should have been, and her stilettos all play a part in her death. There is no evidence that she was pushed, or that there was a struggle and Jules' account of what happened stands up. But I don't understand why he can't remember what happened. It's as if he's covering something up. There's a missing piece to the jigsaw of Vicky's death.

When the machine is turned off, he goes to pieces and can't cope. Grief rises from him, like a haze of heat, altering the landscape of his life and pulling him further into the gambling world. It's a warped but predictable reaction and it makes me mad. His gambling led to Vicky's death and now he's driving his daughter away too.

'Please Pandora, look after Ellie. Just for a few days. I don't want her to see me in this state.'

'You're her dad, she needs you. I know it's hard but you've got to get a grip. She's what you need and you're going to get through this. You've got to stop gambling.'

'I can't look after her right now. I just can't. And if I can't they'll put her into care. Please, you need to understand how hard it is for me.'

I wish I could stop him.

Vicky's death changes everything. For me. For Jules. And for Ellie. Bizarrely she is the answer to my prayers. I have a child to love. When we walk around the town people think I am her mother. The weeks race by and each time we visit Jules he begs me. 'I'm not in a good place. Please Pandora. She's better off with you.' Or he claims poverty. 'I can't give her what she needs.'

I don't know how much more I can take. As the weeks turn into months all I can think is that he's a selfish pig and doesn't love his daughter. If he did then he wouldn't want to be apart from her. So, she's better off with me.

'My head's all over the place, now isn't a great time to take her back.'

'If you stopped gambling then maybe you'd have a chance.'

And his usual reply came, 'It's not that easy sis. You don't know what it's like.'

CHAPTER 36: ELLIE – 2018

I'm not creeped out by the fact that I'm dating—or should I say having an affair with—a guy who remembers when a piece of bubblegum was half pence. A big age gap works for aging pop stars and President Trump. Andy's cooler about all sorts of stuff than guys of my own age. It's a terrible cliche to refer to him as my silver fox but he is, and I frequently remind him that he's the spit of George Clooney. He remembers a world before twenty-four hour tv and when shops stayed shut on a Sunday. I think that's rather quaint.

And better still, he's in Boston, on business. I think he deliberately arranged it because I was here. I said something to him along the lines of, 'I'll be with my auntie for a whole week, I may need a break.' He's a smooth operator and waited to surprise me. The evening we arrived in Plymouth he told me he was staying in downtown Boston for a few days.

It was easier to tell Auntie that I was chatting to a guy on Tinder. Everybody's on Tinder, it's the modern form of social media, a bit old hat. She went overboard in her concern for me. I wasn't expecting that. Bless her. She means well. But I don't get why she's so worried. This is America. They speak English and I'm hardly likely to wander off into the unsafe areas of town. Boston is a pretty safe city. If I had told Auntie about Andy she would have freaked and I dread to think what she'd say. He has to remain a secret. I cringe when I imagine having a conversation with her about him. 'Oh by the way Auntie, I'm dating my married boss. He's forty-seven—yes you heard—yes that's only five years and three hundred days younger than dad, I've done the maths. Yes, he's married, I can hold my hands up to that ugly crime.' If I was sitting in front of a therapist, I know just what they'd say. They'd analyse the psychology of why I'm dating an older man and conclude that I'm searching for a father figure because of my shitty childhood. I don't want to have to analyse my reasons, it just happened one day. His wife was away on a course in London and he was at home working in his study. I took him some important correspondence and we got chatting. I don't think he'd even noticed me until that day.

I'm not with him for his money, although it certainly helps. He treats me—a lot. Guys of my age are always skint and they aren't chivalrous. They expect to go halves on everything. Andy's from another age when possibly feminism didn't exist. He knows how to treat a woman properly, opening car doors, walking on the outside along a pavement and bringing flowers to a date—never garage forecourt flowers with an aroma of petrol. I don't know many guys of my age with a car. Their mums pay for driving lessons but because insurance is astronomical, they can't afford to drive. They'd rather stay in playing computer games than go to a nice restaurant. And guys my age orgasm too quickly and it's all over in two minutes. Andy knows how to hold back.

I'm so distraught as I get to the restaurant where Andy and I are meeting that I walk straight past him, through a veil of tears. Stopping at a lamppost I almost retch. I hear my name being called and forget about self-pity puking.

'Hey,' Andy says out of breath, 'you walked straight past

me.' When he realises that I'm upset he wraps his arms around me and I am cocooned in his love.

'What's wrong?'

I sniff and wipe my nose inelegantly with the back of my hand.

'Oh, just about everything.' I start walking because it helps me to compose. 'My dad isn't the man I thought he was.'

'You mean your mum had an affair and your real dad's out there somewhere?'

'No.' I stop abruptly and stare at him, shocked. 'Nothing like that.'

As I explain about the addiction my words float meaninglessly over the pounding of blood in my head. I can't fathom any of it.

'I thought I knew my dad. But it turns out everything's been a lie. I feel cheated. Now I know the real reason why my auntie brought me up. She was trying to protect me from my father. It makes her a liar too. God damn it, I hate them both.'

'Sit down a minute.' He guides me to a bench, and I rest my head on his shoulder.

'He borrowed some money from me the other week. I didn't think much about it, he's my dad, I expected him to pay me back.'

'Don't worry about it. I'll give you the money.'

'You don't get it, do you?' I snap.

'I do. I just don't want you to worry about losing the money. You don't earn much.'

'It's not about the bloody money.' What is it with men? Women look for sympathy and to offload, but men try to find a solution. There is no solution. My dad has screwed my life up —and my mum's life.

Putting his arm around me he says, 'Just like parents have to accept the choices children make, we have to accept the choices they make too. And those choices aren't always good or wise ones.'

His words are a comfort blanket around me. I'm unaware of the world outside our bubble but realise that we are now walking towards the restaurant. 'We expect better from our parents, they aren't expected to fail. I know you're feeling raw right now. I'd be the same. It's a massive shock.'

'I don't want any more to do with him. I feel so let down.'

'That's understandable. I'd feel the same. All sorts of people bring children into the world. You don't need a passport, a qualification, or a training course. A rumble in the sack is all it takes.'

'Now you're getting all philosophical on me.'

I feel better for just having him with me.

We laugh and walk into the restaurant.

It's lovely not to worry about somebody recognising him. We can forget about his wife. He's usually edgy, looking around to see if there's somebody he knows. He normally chooses a table at the back of the restaurant where we won't be spotted. I hate it and want to be shown off. Tonight we sit by the window, like a pair of goldfish, gazing out onto the bright lights and tall buildings of Boston. I have him all to myself.

His hand reaches for mine but staring at my chest he slays the moment by saying, 'Pull your top up love, your cleavage is showing.'

'This is America, not Saudi.'

The waiter arrives and puts a bowl of oysters in ice on the table and we spring apart like two teenagers caught on the front porch.

'Sorry, you look lovely. I'm always on high alert, worried we'll be spotted—it's habit I guess.'

I sigh and help myself to bread automatically, without really wanting it. It shouldn't be like this. I want him to relax and pretend just for one evening that he's not married.

'I haven't told you this before, but I lost my dad many years before he died. He drank himself to death.'

I gasp. 'I'm sorry. I had no idea.'

'All the help we tried to get him failed, from detox programmes to rehab, to psychiatric sessions, they all failed. He chose to drink and it was a choice he made over us. It took me a long time to accept that he had a disease. My anger was over before he died. I took the brunt of it. No one should have to beg their mother to get a divorce, or their father to stop drinking and choose them over alcohol. It's outside of your control.'

'That must have been frightening.'

'I don't know much about gambling, but like alcoholics he'll be secretive about what he gets up to. Now that it's out in the open you all need to come together and talk about it.'

'It just feels as if he's stolen my childhood. Packing me off to my Auntie Pandora was a horrible thing to do and then there's my mother's death. Did she really fall down the stairs? What's to say he didn't push her?'

He squeezes my arm and I feel myself soften and grow warm with his reassurance.

'It happened a long time ago Els. It's best not to rake it up again.'

'But she was my mother. I just want to know the truth.'

'You're reading into what happened. Let the ghosts of the past settle.'

My phone rings again.

'Don't mind me,' he says. 'Answer it.'

'No, I'm not going to.' I swipe to turn it off, not wanting to be disturbed. Why does she keep phoning me? She knows I'm on a date and she's determined to ruin my evening. All I want is a few uninterrupted hours with a wonderful man. Is that too much to ask? Next week we'll be back in the house and I'll be padding about discreetly, never speaking unless spoken to. I'm like a servant in Downton Abbey.

'You're a stubborn girl.'

I cringe. Does he have to call me a girl, emphasising our age difference?

'She just wants to know what time you'll be getting back. That's reasonable enough. You're in a city you don't know.'

'You're mollycoddling me. I've been travelling on my own, I can look after myself.'

'Well, tonight I'm looking after you. You're my responsibility and I'll make sure you get back safely.'

'I'm fine getting the subway on my own. I know what I'm doing.'

'You'll do no such thing. It's not safe for a girl at night.'

'Stop calling me a girl. I'm not fourteen.'

'I'm only looking out for you.'

'You sound like my auntie.'

I'm not sure I want him to leave his wife. There are times when I do, but it's times like this that I realise how much his comments irritate me. He'll never leave his wife, he's got too much to lose. And I can't be bothered with the fallout. What we have is good, for now. Time—as in the number of years he's been on this planet—creates wisdom and experience but it also creates responsibilities and complications. If he announced to his wife that he was leaving her it would be like swinging a double rod pendulum. I can't begin to imagine the chaos it would cause. I'm baggage free, carefree, responsibility-free, wrinkle-free. It's a great place to be. This time next year I'll be training to be a teacher. Who knows who I'll meet. Don't get me wrong. I'm not condoning what I'm doing, I'm not proud that I'm sleeping with a married man, but it's a passing phase in my life. It's an experience and a box ticker on the bucket list in the same way that climbing the Himalayas is. I don't care about his wife—or his kids, why should I?

After eating a very expensive meal—I had his dessert as well as mine, we walk around the harbour area, watching street entertainers. The hours fly by. After a bottle of champagne and several cocktails we head to the subway to say goodbye, but something's kicking off. Sirens grind into the street. Blue lights flash and pop, the street is awash with blue and there are crowds of people all over the place, running around in confusion.

'It looks as if it's closed. We'll get a taxi instead.'

'Two taxis. We're not going in the same direction,' I correct him.

It takes us ages to hail a taxi because they are all full of passengers. There are people milling everywhere, all wanting transport.

'Can't we just walk to the next subway?'

'If we can't get a taxi.'

When it proves too difficult, we leave the crowds and the strobing lights and head for the next subway, but it's closed too.

'What the hell's going on?' I ask as I switch my phone back on, a flood of auntie's missed calls hitting my screen as I check my news app.

Andy hails a taxi and as we drive I read the new flash to him.

'Oh my God. It's an emergency. Shit, I hope it's nothing serious.'

'Don't worry, there's always something kicking off, it's easy to forget we're in a big American city. I'm sure it's nothing serious.'

The taxi driver glances in his mirror, alarm on his face.

'They're saying that it's a terrorist attack and that's why the subway's shut. I'm taking the long way, as a lot of roads are blocked off.'

When I step out of the taxi at the top of the hill where our apartment is the scene below is a hive of activity, it's pandemonium. The area around the subway is full of wailing police cars. Our apartment is shrouded in darkness and it's only now that a cold chill washes over me. *Auntie, where are you?* It's late she should be back. And then I realise she's probably in bed but notice that the car is not on the drive.

Andy picks up on my anxiety. 'I'm going to come up to make sure you're okay.'

'No, you can't. I'll be fine.'

'I insist. Just until you know she's okay.'

I don't have much choice, he's sent the taxi away and he's following me in. If Auntie is here, I'm going to have to think of something—fast—to explain who Andy is.

The apartment is quiet so I turn the lights on and scan each room while Andy hovers on the doorstep.

'I wonder where she's gone. The car's not there. It's very odd.' I check the time and it's gone one.

'I'm staying until I know you're okay.'

'Just for five minutes, I don't want you here when she gets back.'

'You make it sound as if you're ashamed of me.'

I put my arms around his neck and kiss him lightly on the lips. 'You know what I mean.'

He pulls me in for a snog. The taste of his mouth, his scent and the warmth of our embrace sends my senses spiralling. A pulse beats below, as if I have a spare heart tucked in my knickers and I feel his cock twitch against my thigh.

'Let's not get carried away, Auntie could be back at any moment.'

'Yes, getting caught in the act wouldn't be a great idea.'

It's too late. We hear the pounding of feet on the stairs, more than one pair. I hope to God that Auntie hasn't pulled a bloke. That's something I couldn't cope with. Surely, she wouldn't do that? That's not her style. I know my auntie.

My mind races as I try to formulate a suitable scenario for why Andy is standing in our apartment at gone one in the morning, but I can't think of one. I'm hopeless at lying and I have no imagination. The nifty bastard has undone my blouse, I fumble, trying to do up the buttons as the door opens and we are like rabbits caught in the headlights.

'Ellie, oh God I've been so worried.'

Her reaction to seeing me is unexpected and completely overboard. It's embarrassing. I feel about five years old.

'I'm an adult, what's the big deal?'

'Don't you get news flashes on your phone?'

'Sorry, yeah of course. It's terrible. Luckily neither of us was anywhere near it.'

Andy doesn't move and Auntie doesn't seem interested in who he is. It's as if he's invisible. It doesn't occur to her that Andy is my date. He's just three years younger than her, I remind myself, shocked at the thought. They are contemporaries, in the same secondary school cohort. They remember the same kids' tv programmes and chart hits. The mask of age he wears is disguise enough and I know that there won't be a tirade of questions.

'Thankyou...' I say, turning to Andy, but the sentence needs completing. What am I thanking him for?

Andy looks awkward and I wish he would take his cue before I need to add more words.

'Surprise,' Auntie sings, waving her arms and sweeping Dad, with his enormous suitcase through the door.

'Dad.' I'm aware that my voice is flat. 'What the hell are you doing here?'

I hoist a small smile but I'm reeling.

'Charming. Nice way to greet your dad.'

I cringe at his title, dad. It doesn't feel as if he is my dad. Dads don't gamble, they're responsible people.

'But why are you here?'

'Because we need to talk.'

'I'm not sure that we do. You should have waited until we got home. We don't have a room for you.'

'Yes, we do,' Auntie laughs. 'He can take the bed settee. That okay Jules?'

'Fine with me.'

Remembering Andy, hovering next to me, I realise that I need to get rid of him.

'Thank you for the lift...I'd better let you get off.' I reach out to shake his hand, aware of how formal this is but Andy goes along with it, squeezing my hand with his thumb before letting go.

Auntie and Dad focus on Andy.

'This nice man gave me a lift home. I was waiting for a taxi and he stopped for me.'

Auntie and Dad look aghast and I know what they're both thinking. Is she really that dumb, accepting a lift from a stranger, have we taught her nothing about personal safety over the years?

'How kind, thank you,' they say in unison with forced chirpiness.

Blood rushes to Andy's face as he stammers an answer.

'Stay for a coffee,' Auntie offers.

'Auntie it's very late.'

'That's a great idea, I could murder a coffee,' Dad says, his eyes swivelling around as if he's working out which room to park his suitcase in.

When we are settled around the kitchen table, the questions to Andy, come thick and fast. 'You're English, are you on business here?' Auntie asks. 'Where are you staying?' Thankfully he doesn't need to lie but he's nearly caught out when Auntie asks him where in England he lives.

'Ba...' He's about to say Bath, which will give the game away and they'll put two and two together. He realises mid-syllable and changes it to Barcombe. Where the hell is Barcombe? For a name that he's plucked out of thin air, he seems to know a lot about the place, but the problem is Auntie and Dad know it too. Andy is well-travelled and is able to answer all of their questions. I learn that they used to go boating there as kids and that there's a nice pub next to the river.

'So how was your date? Nice chap?' Auntie asks in a forced jolly tone that I see straight through.

'Yes, thanks I had a wonderful evening.' I avoid looking over at Andy but I'm glad of the chance to tell him how lovely the evening was. 'He was a perfect gentleman.'

More questions follow. 'What does he do? Where does he live? What did he tell you about life in Boston?'

I'm forced to fictionalise my answers to keep her sweet, but while I'm speaking I keep thinking what the hell is Dad doing here?

After Andy's left Auntie explodes, red-faced, her finger pointing at me.

'You really don't give a stuff, do you?'

I stomp towards my room. It's late. Why is she picking on me? I'm back and all is well.

'You were ringing long before the incident kicked off,' I mock.

'When you heard what was going on, you should have sent me a text. Anything to stop me worrying. I can't believe how selfish you've been.'

'We've both been worried sick,' Dad said from behind Auntie.

'And to get into a stranger's car Ellie. Why did you do that?'

She's in my face, screeching, Dad is lumpish behind her, clearly floundering and wondering how best to handle me, the inexperienced parent that he is.

'It was fine. I was fine.' I pick up my washbag and head for the bathroom.

'That man could have been anyone. He was anyone. He

could have raped you. Murdered you. You'd be tomorrow's headlines if something happened,' she spits.

'Clearly, I wouldn't be. The terrorist incident will be splashed all over the papers.'

'Don't get all smart and cocky with your auntie, she's got a good point.'

'Well he wasn't just anyone,' I retort.

'What do you mean?'

I don't want to tell them, but I blurt it out to hurt them.

'He was my date. He's old, yes, but don't judge, you've been through enough women since mum. He's my boss. In Bath. Satisfied now? Can I get washed?' I put my bath hat on, smile through gritted teeth, turn and go into the bathroom, slamming the door behind me. I know I'm a complete bitch, I guess they did have every right to be mad with me, but I can't help myself. I want some freedom. I don't want them breathing down my neck. I want trust for the decisions I make.

When I come out, they are sitting as rigid as cardboard cut-outs in the lounge, my news has stunned them into silence. They barely register my presence and it's my turn to be gawky, hovering at the doorway, muttering goodnight.

'We'll talk in the morning,' Auntie says, barely looking at me. Dad stares at the floor as he mutters goodnight. He clearly can't handle my dating somebody his own age.

CHAPTER 37: PANDORA – 2018

The kitchen worktop is a burial ground of dirty plates and cups. I let the tap run until it's warm enough to wash up.

Last night I didn't fully register what Ellie told us because I was lost for words. Ellie is a sensible girl and it isn't like her to date an older man. A trickle of sadness and disappointment works its way through my stomach. I want to shake her and ask her why she's being so stupid. She's a bright, beautiful girl and could have any guy if she wanted but she chooses a man who's unobtainable. Is her self-esteem that low? I don't know what to say to her to make her see sense without driving her away and making her more keen on him.

I try not to think about Ellie and an older man because it will only wind me up and fill my head with disgusting thoughts about them in bed together. I try hard to focus instead on the day ahead. We're leaving Boston today and heading the short distance north to Salem. Salem is famous for its 1692 witch trials, during which two hundred local people were accused and several were executed for practising witchcraft. The episode is one of Colonial America's most notorious cases of mass hysteria, and I guess serves as a cautionary tale about the dangers of religious extremism.

The Salem trials were not unique but one example of a phenomenon of witch trials happening across America and Europe. In the days before the rise of science and in the absence of knowledge, it must have been easy to falsely accuse somebody of being a witch when you didn't have a plausible explanation for things that happened.

My thoughts are broken when Jules, with his hair dishevelled and wearing baggy boxers, comes into the kitchen. He slumps onto a chair with a grunt and a yawn. I flick the kettle on and open cupboards for cups.

'Where are we going today then?' He asks.

'We're off to the next bed and breakfast today and then we're going home tomorrow. You do what you like.' His assumption makes me bristle and I know that my tone is cold and unfriendly, but I can't help myself. Last night we were focused on Ellie but now that she is safe— being with him again, after six years is hard. Time doesn't always heal when the wounds run deep and surgery won't fix the hurt he caused me.

'Don't be like that sis.'

I grit my teeth. I swear that I will lash out if he calls me sis once more.

'You haven't said how you got here. Who gave you the money for the flight?'

He looks affronted. 'I did.'

'Really?'

'Yes.' He doesn't elaborate.

'But there's just one problem...'

'The answer is no Jules...' It's bound to involve money, always does.

'You don't know what I'm going to say.'

I feel the cracks between us widen as I stiffen, remembering how he worked his way through his share of our parents' inheritance. Two hundred thousand pounds went down the drain in a matter of months on those evil fixed odds betting machines. My blood boils when I think of Ellie's university fees— fees I paid. The money could have bought her a small flat and he doesn't seem to care. He squandered the lot. I don't get a sense of remorse and it hurts. He paints himself as the victim of the gambling industry. How convenient of him. 'I'm an idiot,' he'd say. 'I need to stop.' He's pathetic. He knows the wretched machines swallow money but he carries on. I don't understand why he doesn't just stop, especially after burning his way through thousands. What's he hoping to achieve? He had a house, once upon a time, with Vicky but lost it after she died. He's an idiot, he couldn't keep up with the mortgage payments. I can't understand what goes through his head. He earns good money and doesn't need to gamble.

I make coffee and hand him a cup, pained bewilderment replacing the anger I felt when I found out what he'd done.

'Go on...'

'If you want me to find accommodation for tonight and a taxi back to the airport for tomorrow, plus food and sightseeing I need to borrow some money. I'm skint.'

'What a surprise. For God's sake Jules. It's like dealing with a child. When are you going to pull yourself together? You've got another child on the way for pity's sake. Do you really want to make the same mistakes all over again?'

Ellie is straightening her hair and applying make-up when I take tea into her room.

'That's swimming in caffeine,' she says taking the cup. 'Are we out of green tea?'

'No, but I thought I'd give you a break from that gnat's piss. Did you know that someone died from drinking too much of it?'

'That's rubbish,' she laughs. 'But someone did die of acute

liver damage from too many green tea supplements. I don't take the supplements.'

She gets up and shuts the door so that we can't be overheard.

'Why is he here? He didn't answer when I asked,' she whispers.

'He wants to talk to you about things. And he was worried about you looking at men on Tinder.'

'He's never worried about me.'

'You worried us both.'

'It's a bit drastic though to come all the way over here, for how long? We're going home tomorrow.'

She pulls a face pretending to be a moron and sticks a finger to her temple.

'I think he realises he needs to change. This baby could be the incentive to quit gambling.'

'I'm not interested in the stupid baby. But jeez, what sort of idiot would gamble? How much are we talking about and over how long?'

I sigh. 'A lot of money.'

'Is that why he never invites me round? He's ashamed of where he lives? He doesn't own a house does he?' She flings a pillow on the floor. 'Stop covering up for him. Just tell me the truth. I want to know everything.'

There's a knock at the door.

Ellie folds her arms and stares out of the window, an irritated expression on her face when he calls out, 'Can I come in?'

'Yeah,' I reply.

He's washed and dressed and there's a powerful whiff of Lynx that makes me gag.

'I'm sorry. I know I've fucked up.'

I pick at a loose thread on the duvet, wishing he hadn't come because nothing will change, and the damage has been done.

'Save it for later, till we're on our own. It's not fair on Ellie.'

'I'm not a baby. I'm sick of being pushed aside as if I don't matter. I want to know everything. How the hell did you get into such a mess Dad? Why aren't you getting help?'

'It's not that simple. I did go on a GamCare course. It was interesting but there isn't one local to me anymore. They've cut back services and I can't get there.'

'You've got a car.'

'No, I haven't.'

'So that's another lie.'

'I had to sell it.'

'But you had Granny and Gramp's money when they died. What happened to that?'

'Jules,' I say in barely a whisper, nudging him to spill the truth as if it's a dare.

A sense of awkwardness settles over him and he walks over to the window as if interested in the view over Boston, his back to us and he doesn't speak. A million questions hang in the air like a length of rope.

'It's all gone, the lot.'

'Why?' Ellie screams, jumping from the bed, in a manic fashion, her face is contorted, eyes flashing fear as she punches out a string of expletives. Her reaction brings it all back to me as if a healed wound has been reopened.

'I'm an idiot,' he shrugs.

'That money could have paid for university and now I'm thousands in debt. Why do I have a wanker for a dad.'

'Ellie, stop it.'

I flinch because she's right, but I hate the way she speaks to him.

CHAPTER 38: PANDORA – 2018

'Before you judge me Ellie, there are all sorts of people who get into gambling for all kinds of reasons.'

'You're just looking to blame someone else,' she shoots. 'You're a grown man. You know exactly what you're doing.'

He tells us everything, standing at the window, with his back to us, as if in court not wanting to face judge and jury. His words tumble, like knotweed, a story that goes back decades to when he was young. I hold Ellie tight as we huddle on the bed as if he's an intruder holding us hostage––but in our case we're huddling from the impact of his words. A bomb of emotion hits my gut as shock, fear, disbelief and guilt flood through me. My brother has spent a lifetime trying to forget the events of his childhood, one so different to mine, though we shared the same house. I knew nothing about it even though I was there under the same roof—in the next bedroom. He's spent a lifetime dealing with it, mostly on his own. A rush of love fills me. Why didn't I know what was going on? I scan my brain for memories but there no bad ones. Dad was away working, and I was studying for exams.

Tears build behind my eyes. I feel like throwing up. Taking the cold tea from Ellie's hand I sip it, feeling my stomach settle.

Silence unfolds between the three of us as he finishes his story, symbolising the feeling of loneliness he must have felt being a member of our family.

'Remember the time he got us to pose in the woods with our bare bottoms to the camera?' Jules turns for the first time as if gaining in confidence as his story unfolds.

'What the heck?' Ellie says.

'That was just a laugh Jules. I didn't take it seriously. He was always after a good photo.'

'Maybe it was a laugh, for you. Not for me.'

'What happened?'

'I don't want to know,' Ellie screeches. 'Stop.' She covers her ears with her hands.

'Neither of you need to know the horrible details. It doesn't matter anymore. It's all in the past.'

'But it does matter,' I assert. 'Because it's affected you, it's destroyed you and it's cast a long shadow over our family.'

'Can we go out now,' Ellie asks as if she's just sat through a bad play, slipping sandals on and yawning as she gets up.

I'm too stunned to process what he's saying.

'Let's talk about it later, Jules.'

'Yes, I've got a headache now, I need some air,' Jules says. 'Salem with two witches.'

His attempt to lighten things falls on deaf ears as Ellie leaves the room.

'Is it okay if I go for a walk, just for ten minutes to clear my head, then we can head off?'

'Yeah, fine.'

I follow Ellie into the kitchen, scoop her into my arms as she crumples against me, her face wet as pent up emotion spills. I have to tread carefully regarding her middle-aged boyfriend. She has a lot on her plate without confrontation about him.

'It's such a shock. It's as if I'm seeing him for the first time. I know it sounds stupid, but dads are supposed to be a source of strength, he's the person you look up to and respect, but all I can see is a vulnerable and weak man. And Gramps, I can't get my head around it. Is Dad telling the truth? What if he's lying to justify his gambling? How would we know?'

'I believe him.'

'What makes you so certain?'

'Some odd things I read in Gramp's diary. Now it makes sense.'

'I kind of need my Dad to be the standard against which I can judge other men if that makes sense.'

'Is that why you're dating an older guy?'

'I didn't intend for it to happen, it just did.'

'Contrary to what you think, I'm not judging you. I'm surprised yes, but the last thing I want to do is to judge.'

'I know what you're thinking. That Andy is a replacement father.'

'Sort of.'

'Maybe, I don't know. I feel safe with him. He believes in me.'

'If he makes you happy. But just think about the future. In twenty years' time you could be nursing a sick man. And think about whether you want kids. He may not want any more.'

'Auntie. I won't be with him that long.'

'That's what you say. But it's hard once you get attached to someone.'

'I don't think there is a Mr Right. There's only Mr Right now.'

'Good cliche but true.'

She nuzzles into me and rubs my back. It's soothing to be in her arms after the shock of Jules' story.

'I'd like to see you find someone nice Auntie, to look after you.'

'Would I be comfortable with never finding someone? I don't know. In a sense, I've got used to being on my own. Breaking up with Richard was painful. I feel comfortable with myself and I think that's the most important thing. It makes life simpler. There you are, that's my tip for you.'

Pulling away Ellie beams at me, my words resonating with her.

'There's no pattern to what life should look like. It's a blank canvas to paint what we like. That's how I feel about my life. I'm painting and I'm choosing bright, bold colours—but one day I might choose pastels.'

'That's very philosophical.'

'I feel really sad about Dad's life. I wish he could forget the past and let go.

WE ARRIVE in Salem and circuit the town for a parking space. I nudge the car into a tight space but the bonnet overhangs by several inches.

'It's fine Auntie, what's your problem?' Ellie says, stropping off up the road.

'Come back,' I call, 'we might get fined if we stay here.'

With hands on hips, she rolls her eyes.

Please don't do that, it's disrespectful. I don't want to get fined alright? It's not you that'll be paying the bill.'

While Jules gets out and checks the kerb, Ellie walks off to look in a shop window.

'You've had it hard sis, I can see that.'

I grit my teeth. He has no idea about being a real parent. If I tell him I'll lose my rag and we'll brawl on the street with poor

Ellie witnessing the spectacle. Spotting another space further along I move the car.

The centre of Salem is a theme town, a string of gift shops reminding me of Diagon Alley in Harry Potter. Window displays are adorned with spell books, scented candles, crystals, charms, potions and cauldrons, and there's even a black cat curled up in a window. Women in witches outfits with mauve hair and oppressive make-up lurk behind counters. Shop assistants wearing black lipstick and wearing Wicca t-shirts is so typical of America – where everything has to be transformed into a Disney experience or in the case of Salem a brash, tacky experience. I prefer the natural look— The Witch House is far creepier and the only building still standing in Salem with direct ties to the witch trials. Judge Corwin lived there and was called upon to investigate when a surge of witch accusations arose in town.

There are clairvoyants, mystics and fortune tellers huddled behind makeshift curtains in the shops. Floral notes of violet and jasmine tickle my nostrils one minute, to be replaced by cedarwood and patchouli the next. The array of smells pulls us along the road. The cultural identity of the town is firmly planted in the witch trials. I notice police cars with witch logos, a school is called Witchcraft Heights and the athletic team is named The Witches. A trolley bell rings as an old-fashioned bus rolls over the cobblestones on Essex Street.

We get to the Salem Witch Museum and join the queue.

'Do you remember doing Arthur Miller's Crucible for O Level?' Jules asks me.

'We did Macbeth, also about witches,' I reply.

'I don't remember much about The Crucible only that the Salem Trials featured in it.'

'Were you lazy at school?' Ellie asks Jules.

'Cheeky mare. I wasn't as clever as you.'

'You did alright for yourself though. Kind of.'

'What's that supposed to mean?'

'Let's face it Dad... are you going to spend the rest of your life gambling away your wages? Why don't you get help?'

'I will. It's not easy to just give up.'

Jules rubs his forehead, it's clear Ellie's questions are stressing him.

'Tell me about *The Crucible*,' I ask, to distract the conversation.

'It's about mass hysteria and how Salem was stirred into madness by superstition, paranoia and mindless persecution,' he replies.

'Like McCarthyism in the nineteen fifties,' I add, turning to Ellie. 'In the fifties there was a fear of Communism and it led to a national witch hunt for suspected communist sympathisers and supporters. People were accused and McCarthy was the politician who whipped up the idea that Communists had infiltrated all areas of life and had to be weeded out. It was a difficult time, we were in the middle of the Cold War, tensions were high between East and West and our greatest fear was another war. The term McCarthyism has come to mean people being wrongly accused.'

'So if there was a modern-day McCarthy, you'd be accused of being a racist, Auntie.'

'Hey stop that.'

'Well, you would.'

'Racism is a strong word, but you snowflakers band it about all the time like confetti. We can't give any opinions these days. It's as if I'm being gagged by your generation.'

With a smile, she nudges me playfully.

'Hey, don't start another argument please, young lady.' I laugh.

Salem Witch Museum is not really a museum, it's more a show with clever visuals narrated as a re-enactment.

When we pay for tickets, Jules hovers to the side. I'm not

sure if he's changed his mind about going in or is waiting for us
to pay.

'You two go in, I don't think this is my kind of thing, I'll wait
outside.'

'You're coming,' I insist, knowing the real reason he won't
come in. 'You haven't had a day out with your daughter in God
knows how long.'

'Come on Dad, you've flown all this way, you've got to
come in.'

'It's okay, I've got a headache, I'd prefer a walk.'

I know he's skint and irritation springs to my gut when I
consider this is only our first port of call. Will he have money
for lunch and dinner I wonder? With a sinking feeling, I don't
persist. I'm not bothered whether he comes into the museum or
not. Like all of the other times that he could have stepped up to
the plate and been the father he should have been, but it's his
loss. He has to take responsibility because I can't bail him out
anymore, I refuse to. There have been too many occasions, like
all the birthdays and Christmases when I bought two presents
for Ellie - one from me, one from him. It's his burden to carry.

'I enjoyed that, but there are aspects they didn't discuss.'

After the darkness of the museum, our eyes start to adjust
to the sunshine

'You're the expert on American history Auntie.'

'They didn't mention the theory that the town's rye crop was
to blame.'

'They can't cover everything.'

'Ryegrass was susceptible to a fungus. There's something
called Ergot poisoning which causes lots of symptoms from
psychosis and hallucinations to vomiting. Ergot poisoning was
a problem throughout history but it's possible that it fuelled the
witch trials.'

'That's interesting.'

'Anyway, enough of witches let's find dad and get something to eat.'

'I'LL JUST GET A SANDWICH, you two can eat in the cafe.'

'Dad don't be pathetic, you're coming in.'

'Really, I'm fine. I've imposed on your holiday. It's not fair.'

'Cut the bullshit, just admit you're skint.'

'Yeah, that's the sum of it.'

'I'll pay for you Dad, but you've got to get treatment when you get back. Promise me.'

'I can't promise.'

'No lunch then.'

'Hey, don't be cruel,' I say. 'I'll pay.'

As we take our seats in a cafe, I realise that this is the first time in many years that we've eaten together. I haven't forgiven him, I'm tolerating him, for Ellie's sake but I realise that a lot has changed since this morning and I'm still reeling in the shock of his revelation.

He raises his cup to ours, but the cups are plastic, like us, fake. We can't chink and somehow this symbolises the nub of the problems. We have to reconnect and be the family we should be. Plastic bends and like us, we have to bend and reshape. The addiction he has is so powerful it has robbed him of the power to decide for himself.

Jules chooses the cheapest thing on the menu.

The food arrives and nobody speaks for a long time until Ellie pushes her plate aside, her voice low but passionate, 'What happened Dad?' Please tell me what happened. Please just talk about mum's death, will you? I know it must be the hardest thing for you both. But it's so long ago now.'

CHAPTER 39: JULES – 2018

I s it? Jules asked himself. In actual years maybe it was a long time ago, but it's only a second away in his thoughts.

Jules waited for Pandora to speak but Ellie turned to him and said, 'Dad. Say something. Please. Someone. Stop blocking it out as if it never happened. You knew her, I didn't. How do you think that is for me? She's the mother I never knew.'

'You know what happened,' Jules said quietly, the words were forced from unwilling lips. 'I told you.'

'You were so little,' Pandora said, 'I didn't quite know what to say to you.'

Ellie's face was tense with trepidation. She looked as if she was bracing herself, compelled to ask the questions she knew neither of them wanted to answer.

Jules said nothing, his head bowed and Pandora felt obliged to respond. 'What more do you want to know? It was a terrible accident. She fell down the stairs. Why do you need the details?'

'Because neither of you have ever properly spoken about it. Not for my entire life. And it's the first time I've got you both alone together. I've always avoided asking, because I know how upsetting it is. But not talking about it, not talking about Mum is kind of weird don't you think? We ought to be able to talk about her as a family and now is a good opportunity.'

Jules looked at Pandora. For a split second, he met her eye.

'I know you lost the person you loved Dad,' she continued. 'But I lost her too. And lately...memories, I think they are memories, I don't know what they are but lately, something triggers a thought. A song, a picture, a glimmer of a something that stops me in my tracks and leaves me breathless. I close my eyes, take a deep breath. I can't separate the real from the imagined.'

'Ok,' Pandora said folding her fingers, 'Ok sweetheart, I'm sure you're right. Sometimes it's easier to stay quiet, it wasn't deliberate.'

'Did she used to sing Connie Francis songs to me? I heard a song in a bar a few months ago and it gave me a really weird feeling and then I had a dream and she was singing *Lipstick On My Collar* to me as she looked out of the window. And did she bath me in the sink? It's like a jigsaw puzzle. I just want the pieces to fit.'

'I've had nightmares since it happened,' Jules whispered.

'Really?' Pandora said. 'You never said.'

'It's always the same. I wake up in a cold sweat.'

'What happens in the nightmares, Dad?'

Jules took a deep breath and fiddled with his napkin. 'I pushed her.'

Ellie frowned, a puzzled expression on her face. 'But you didn't really push her. You feel responsible that's all. It's natural.'

For many years Jules never knew, looking back and wondering how it happened. They were arguing and she lost her balance, but there was a gap in his memory. The nightmares triggered a memory, the missing link to what happened that evening. In his stressed state, it was too horrible to remember. It was as if his brain had flooded with chemicals, blocking out the details. He'd tried so hard to piece it together. And now it was as clear as rain. He remembered the guilt he'd felt when Vicky had discovered the falsified agreement to extend their mortgage and taken out a loan to cover debts. The guilt bubbled that day and had tracked him for years, it was an ugly shadow that walked beside him. Guilt was like a light on the dashboard of his brain, filling him with self-loathing and he'd lashed out. He hadn't hit her, he hadn't tripped her, he'd shouted in her face. But that was all it had taken. He wanted to stop the wrath of guilt burning inside. When the nightmares came, her face was welded to his mind, the horror, the shock when he shouted in her face. He never normally shouted as it wasn't in his nature, but she'd driven him to a point he couldn't return from, his anger all-encompassing. If only he'd taken a breather, gone to the bathroom, out of the back door, anything to calm down, it wouldn't have happened. It was the heat of the moment and he knew with that he was to blame. Ellie deserved to know the truth, but this would be one step too far. Pandora was still struggling with what had happened when their mum died and this would push her over the edge, she'd never speak to him again and a wedge would be driven between them. He couldn't do it, he had to bottle it and erase it from his mind.

Eventually Pandora and Jules stopped talking, Jules having done most of the talking, Pandora picking up the story at the point she had knocked on the door. Their faces were stony as both spoke hesitantly, almost detached as they told their tale, but as the words gathered momentum, they were unstoppable. Ellie thought there were too many weird details. They talked about the paint mark on the carpet, the canary yellow colour of her mum's knickers and how they didn't match her letterbox red dress and shoes. It only took minutes to recount the details of that terrible evening, a story Ellie had wanted to hear, and not wanted to hear, her whole life.

'If it wasn't for your gambling, Mum would still be alive,' Ellie cut in. It's a matter of fact dramatic statement, and she's not looking at either of them, her eyes never moving from a fixed point on the other side of the cafe.

'We shouldn't have argued at the top of the stairs. It's not a good place when emotions are running high.'

As if blocking his voice from her trail of thought she continued. 'And Mum's death had no effect on your addiction. You carried on wasting money, despite having a child to bring up. What's it going to take for you to quit Dad? Fucking hell, wake up will you.' Her eyes shone with accusation.

Unnerved by the hurt lacing through her words he tried to reassure her, reaching across the table for her hand, but she pulled it away and folded her arms defiantly. They sat in awkward silence.

Slamming her hands on the table the plates juddered.

'And I want to know why you two don't speak to each other.'

'We do. I'm here now, aren't I?' Jules said.

'Don't treat me like a kid. Something happened. It started at Granny's funeral when you were arguing at the wake.'

'No, we weren't.'

'Dad don't deny it. You were yelling your head off at Auntie in the carpark.'

Pandora stared into the dregs of her tea, holding herself together.

Faltering, Jules was unsure how to begin without accusing Pandora of not helping when their mum was ill. It was best not to re-open old wounds but there was no escaping it. Ellie wanted to know what had caused the rift between them. He felt sick to the bone when he thought about what he'd done and wished that the floor would open and swallow him.

'You tell her Pandora,' he said and then turned to Ellie. 'I'm not proud of what I did. I want you to believe that. And if you hate me after hearing what happened I'll understand.' He faltered. 'I don't expect your sympathy and yes I'm a shitty person. If I could change that one thing about myself, you'd see that I'm not really bad.' Tears were gathering in the corner of his eyes and he sniffed them back.

'As you know Gramps died years before. And I can't say that I was sad. Just numb. I was glad that I could put it all behind me. He cast a long shadow over my life. I loved him but I didn't like him if that makes sense. And then there was Mum—your granny—she got ill and needed one of us to check on her twice a day. Your Auntie was busy with you and working.'

'Don't give her the edited version. The truth will come out,' Pandora hurled.

Ellie shuddered.

'Okay, I will but it's not pleasant Els. Whatever your reaction remember that I'll always love you.'

'Just get on with it,' Ellie said sharply.

'I went to look after Granny and ended up staying for months.'

Pandora sniffed primly and raised an eyebrow.

'Auntie...?'

'I don't think your auntie liked me living there, but I had nowhere else to go and yes I probably used the place for my advantage.'

Pandora crushed her cup in her hand, a daggered look in her eyes.

'She wants to know the truth Jules,' Pandora snapped. 'I'm sick of covering up for you. Your reckless gambling has ruined this family. That is the simple truth Ellie. Sorry Jules but you're a loser, a waster. I can't see you changing.'

Ellie shook her head. 'Jesus. I wish I had a normal family.'

Pandora held her nerve and resumed the story. 'He gambled

Granny's engagement ring, having stolen it from her jewellery box.'

As soon as the ugly secret was out, Pandora felt dreadful. Ellie didn't need to know this detail, but she felt under pressure to tell.

Ellie's mouth fell open in horror. 'That's mean Dad. How could you?'

'The worst of it is he emptied her bank account the day she died. He frittered the money away—and that's not even the worst thing— he delayed calling an ambulance.'

Pandora clicked her fingers to demonstrate the ease with which Jules had lost the money.

'Thanks sis.' Jules hung his head and rubbed his forehead. 'So there we are.'

'And let's not forget how you gambled her pension. Your Dad gambled his own mother's pension. That's how low he stooped.'

'That's not strictly true.'

'Yes it bloody is.'

Heads turned to stare.

'Oh my God,' Ellie gasped, her face pinking in shock.

'I always made sure she had enough food and everything she needed.'

'That's not the point. It was her pension. And you took it.'

CHAPTER 40: PANDORA – 2018

I feel the weight of the secret lift from my shoulders, to be replaced by a new worry. Ellie's relationship with her dad was in shreds. I didn't want it to be damaged by this but it was inevitable. Was it really necessary for her to know all of the details? I feel dreadful for attacking her father, but a fear snags in my head. This needs to be out in the open. Jules' actions have to have transparency, for Ellie's own financial security. I chastise myself for thinking this and being so untrusting of my own flesh and blood. I don't trust my brother, not after fleecing his own mother. It is still shocking when I relive those events in my mind. It's the simple things. If he stole from his daughter next, she'd feel responsible. If he found out her pin number she could lose everything. I love him but he is suffering from a leeching illness, it's an addiction and there's no telling what he's capable of. That's the sad truth. Gambling is in his blood and it will take so much for him to stop. It has gone on too long. I don't think he can change. And those machines he plays are the work of the devil. Measures are needed to protect vulnerable people like Jules. Is he vulnerable? I've never thought about him in that way, but yes, he is and everybody close to him is vulnerable too. The stakes on these machines need to be reduced. They are too high.

I wish the government would do something because that way it will be taken out of my hands. But that won't be the end of it. Gambling is insidious and has crept into every corner of our lives without us barely noticing. They estimate that there are four hundred thousand compulsive gamblers in the UK and a further two million at risk—and this is probably a gross underestimation. Betting shops used to be filled with old men, who enjoyed watching a horse race but now all sorts of people go in betting shops—students with time to kill between lectures, businessmen and women seeking a bit of fun between school runs.

There should be a *whistle to whistle* ban on gambling advertising during live sport, there should be a special tax on gambling companies to finance therapy for problem gambling, and a ban on betting with credit cards— it's often money people don't have. And most of all I'd like to see fewer betting shops on the high street. They are on every shopping parade, a blight on our landscape and they are always dotted around poorer areas.

The Labour party got it wrong when they liberalised gambling laws a decade ago, because they failed to predict the impact of technology. Under Tony Blair's leadership restrictions on advertising for gambling were lifted. The money spent on advertising gambling is going up year by year. This needs to stop if lives are to be saved. I've always paid attention to any news to do with gambling laws and trends because of my brother.

Part of the problem is the National Lottery which normalised gambling in Britain and has changed our perception of the dangers involved.

I'm partial to a scratch card because they sit on the counter when I pay for petrol and I don't notice the pound I'm adding to my fuel bill, looking forward to sitting down with a cup of tea and a scratch card. I'm on my own now that Ellie has left and apart from watching Eastenders there are few pleasures in my life. It's about the small pleasures they say, and it is going to charity after all, so that makes it okay. It's not really gambling as such. But I blush when I think about the money I spend on scratch cards. It began as a flutter, a pound a week if that. I don't want to admit it to myself but it has escalated to thirty pounds a week on scratch cards. What began as an add on to my petrol bill has soared. Thirty pounds is a lot, but it is for charity. I don't go in charity shops and I don't put coins in charity boxes so this is a replacement—I'm doing my bit. I don't notice thirty pounds leaving my bank account. It's not a big haemorrhage, it's pound coins here and there, money I don't notice. Am I addicted too?

CHAPTER 41: ELLIE – 2018

There's a shift inside me. I don't know where it comes from but it's as if a tiny bud is pushing through snow to grow. The shift is painful because my head screams for me to hate Dad for everything he's done to destroy my life and I don't want to forgive him, I can get on with my life alone. It's always been just Auntie and me. A voice inside stirs and tells me that I can't change him or the direction of his sails, but I can change my reaction to what he's doing. There's no point in fighting what's happened. The money isn't going to miraculously come back. It's gone and actually even though money's important and I'd like to be earning lots of it, it isn't the be all and end all. As we sit around the table in the café it's family that matters. It feels good that we are all here, together in Boston. It's taken my foolishness to drag him here. Dad's fucked up but I can harbour a grudge for the rest of my life—or I can let go. It feels as easy as blowing a feather from my fingers. I'm not a kid. I'm not going to make my dad's mistakes. I'm a different person. I'll find my own mistakes. He's responsible for the failures he owns and there's nothing I can do.

'Dad, I've got an idea. You can take it or leave it.'

'Oh yeah?'

'I want to come with you to a support group and help you through this. You can do it. Maybe you can set up a blog to publicise gambling as a problem which would help others.

It's nice of you Els. But you're in Bath. How would that work?'

In my enthusiasm I hadn't thought about that. My heart sinks. He needs me and I can't be there.

'Well, I'm going to research gambling recovery and help you get over this. Already I've done some research. There's a drug you can get from the doctor to stop cravings and I've been reading about the Twelve-Step Programme. There are religious elements to some of it though which is weird.'

'I don't want to take any drugs. I am cutting down on how much I gamble. It's been hard but I finally feel as if I'm getting a grip on things.'

'Really?' Auntie gives a sceptical look. I don't think she believes him. She's heard his talk too many times. My heart sinks again feeling helpless. His words are just gambler talk to shut people up.

CHAPTER 42: PANDORA – 2018

Our final bed and breakfast is on the outskirts of Salem, a white weather-boarded house with a pink door and pot plants along the ledge. Our host pings a message inviting us to 'just go in and your rooms are up the stairs marked the Mary Walcott suite and the Giles Corey suite.'

'Three guesses ... named after people accused of witchcraft,' Jules says.

We park on a sand driveway and out of habit and politeness knock on the front door and then go around to the back door.

'She said to go in,' Ellie says.

'I don't like to. Feels weird.'

The door is on the latch and we trundle up the stairs to dump our bags in the rooms. Luckily one of them has twin beds. Ellie and I will sleep in that room. We have the house to ourselves, for a while and it's tempting to have a nose around. The lounge is littered with ornaments. A row of hats covers one wall and there are candles in teacups. Everything is available to buy and has a price tag. There are scones on the table with condiments, an antique Chinese cabinet, an old gramophone and, a Victorian birdcage. A tatty curtain hangs across the door frame to the kitchen. We push it aside and gasp. This is without a doubt the filthiest kitchen I have ever seen. The stove is caked with grease and grime from years of build-up. The walls are filthy and the floors pitted. Piles of dirty plates with congealed food sit on every worktop. Dirty saucepans and frying pans are soaking in soapy water on the floor and there are broken mugs on the floor. My mind boggles. This is worse than a grotty hotel in Blackpool.

'Jeez. What the heck,' Ellie says, hand on mouth.

'Oh my God, when she asks what we want for breakfast tell her we're leaving early for the airport.'

'We're lucky it's only for one night,' Jules says.

'Can't we leave and find somewhere else? There are probably cockroaches and bed bugs.'

'No, we've paid now,' I say, but the thought of bed bugs is making me itch.

'We should put a bad review up.'

'I'm surprised there aren't any. I checked them before booking.'

'I'll just nip to the loo then we should go out for something to eat. While we've still got an appetite.'

'I don't mind staying here, I'll find something to eat in the kitchen, you go out and enjoy yourselves,' Jules says.

'You're having a laugh? Find something in that shit hole?'

'For God sake Jules, we know you're skint, I'm paying, but when we get home don't expect any bail-outs. You need to sort yourself out.'

The bathroom walls are covered in Dutch Delft tiles depicting rural scenes, and as I approach the toilet, labelled Ministry of Magic, it burbs and splutters and the lid rises. Somebody has forgotten to flush it and there's a huge turd lurking at the bottom, the water's a murky brown. Still gurgling as I tinkle, I hurry to get up and wash my hands and gag for the second time - there's a bowl of old scuddy soap pieces swimming in mucky water by the sink. Talk about penny-pinching, this is beyond a joke.

We rock up at a harbourside seafood shack in Salem. It's ramshackle but it's busy which confirms it's a good choice. I order cocktails for me and Ellie, but Jules insists on coke for him. He knows I'm paying and doesn't take the piss.

'Do you have ID?' the waitress asks Ellie. She pulls out her driving licence.

'We need a passport.'

'I'm twenty-two. And I don't carry a passport around.'

'We have no means of checking your driver's licence.'

'What the hell.' She rolls her eyes.

'Be grateful they're asking. I'd love to be mistaken for being younger.'

'That's not very helpful Dad. I was looking forward to a cocktail as it's our last night.'

When my cocktail arrives I fish out the ice. 'For God's sake. Why do Americans love ice so much? I feel cheated. There's hardly any drink, the ice takes up all of the room. It's like clutter in a house. Who needs it?'

'Stop complaining Auntie, at least you've got a cocktail.'

'You drink it, I'll order another. Mind they don't see.'

I consider ordering a whole lobster but at thirty-eight dollars I can't justify it. New England is famous for seafood and eating it is a must. There are odes to its lobster rolls across the walls alluding to their size, beauty, and succulent taste. It's death by lobster. Lobster rolls are legendary across Massachusetts but more so in Maine— they are served in mayo-laced brioche, so that's what I choose. Any longer here and I think my immune system would reject the mere idea of seafood but on our last night, my taste buds are still functioning with an insatiable desire for lobster.

Jules chooses the cheapest item on the menu, burger and chips, it's his usual fare and we settle into conversation.

Ellie's phone rings.

'Sorry Auntie, got to answer it,' and she slinks off towards the toilets.

A palpable sense of excitement follows Ellie as she breezes back to the table in a fluster and Jules and I wait for her to spill the beans.

'You're both going to love this,' she swoons.

'What is it?'

'Andy's got Dad a place at The Priory. It's a residential rehabilitation course. These places are gold dust and are so expensive.'

Jules looks guarded and it's hard to tell what he's thinking. This is just what he needs and how wonderful that Andy is prepared to pay for it. But like leading a horse to the water Jules cannot be made to drink the therapy. He's got to want to go. Want to change. Want a new start. I don't see it happening, he hasn't got the backbone, he's consumed by the addiction.

'What do you say Dad? Worth a try? You don't have to pay a penny.'

'What's the catch?'

'Don't be cynical. It's a kind-hearted gesture from my boyfriend to you.'

'Why would your boss want to help me?'

'Because he loves me.' Ellie's face is crimson as she lays bare his feelings for her.

Jules rubs his empty glass as if he's calling upon the assistance of a genie–– but says nothing. His expression is blank and I can't tell if he's considering the offer, or hoping that it will go away. He could be thinking about his daughter being bought and objectified by a middle-aged man.

'Tell him thanks... I'll see.'

'What do you mean, you'll see?'

He shrugs. 'I'll think about it.'

'You're looking a gift horse in the mouth.'

'I'll let you know what I decide.'

'Dad this is crazy. This is the best offer of help you've ever had and you're telling me you need time to think?'

'Mandy took me to Gamblers' Anonymous. They have the twelve-step programme. I don't like some of the steps. There are creepy statements. You have to submit to a higher power, in other words to God. I don't believe in God. It's not a programme that reflects how I feel. To be honest, I didn't find it much help. I am getting better though. I'm gambling smaller amounts. If I can keep it that way, it's a good start.'

'Really?' She asks her eyes bulging like fish in a tank. 'I don't believe you.'

'Quitting isn't simple. That's what you have to understand.'

'Help me understand then,' she demands, adopting a listening posture. I'm curious to hear what he has to say. I'll lose my rag though if he gives her any bullshit.

'I get a constant stream of emails, adverts on Facebook and banners popping up on my computer. They offer deals, free bets and discounts to encourage me to gamble. My phone company sends me texts about games. They have a way of hooking you in.'

'Just ignore them.'

'It's not that simple.'

Ellie sighs. 'This is annoying me. You're putting up every roadblock you can think of.'

Ignoring her he continues. 'They offer you days out to racing events, hospitality boxes at football matches, free tickets to The Grand National and so it goes on.'

'Why can't you just ignore the emails and the offers? Put it all behind you. You'll end up homeless at this rate. My dad on the street.' Her eyes fill with tears.

'If I ignore them they might close my accounts and then I'll never be able to get my money back.'

'I don't understand,' she says.

'I need to get back what I've lost.'

It's my turn to be irritated. 'You're never going to Jules. We've been through this so many times. All that money of Mum and Dads you blew... it's gone. Accept it. I've had to and believe me I've faced a lot of anger.'

'These betting companies are cunning. With the online accounts, it takes twenty-four hours to actually receive the money, and in the meantime, it's so hard not to cancel the transfer to your bank account and to let it sit in your betting account. That's one of the hardest things–– the long wait.'

'Don't you even want to hear what the course will entail?' Ellies asks, pulling out a bar slip she's scribbled on.

Jules raises his eyebrows with feigned interest and Ellie doesn't wait for an answer.

'It relies on Cognitive Behaviour Therapy.'

'Do you know what that it?' I ask.

'Yeah of course.'

I'm not sure he does, but if he's been for some therapy and counselling in the past he may have come across it.

'They ferret out the underlying reasons and what led you to gamble in the first place. It means going back to your child-hood. Would you be comfortable with that?'

My goodness, I think to myself. I can't believe how calm and adult-like Ellie is being and how well she's coping with the news about her Dad and trying to help him. She doesn't realise though how tough going that's going to be. He's ignored me and my efforts for years. When we get back home, I'll have a chance to talk to her. She's been hit by so many surprises, she'll be the one needing the counselling and support at this rate.

'Erm, I'll think about it. Leave it for now. Let's enjoy our last few hours.'

Leave it for now means no. I'll think about it means no. I just want to pull my brother out of his chair by the scruff of his neck and shake him. Does he care so little about his daughter that he won't accept help? My heart melts. Poor Ellie. I hate to say it, or even think it but she deserves a much better father. His devotion to gambling is stronger than his devotion to her. I don't understand the power of addiction. A real dad would fear the loss of her love more than the uphill battle of fighting it.

'So Els, what about your life. This Andy guy, what's going on?'

'I wondered when that was coming. Auntie's already given me a pep talk.'

'You're young and it's hard to see yourself in the future. It might not seem as if it's a big gap now, but in a few years it will be. And what about his wife? Don't you feel guilty for her?'

'I didn't set out for it to happen.'

'You don't want to waste the best years of your life and regret it.'

'That's rich coming from you Dad.'

CHAPTER 43: PANDORA – 2018

L eaving the Bed and Breakfast early before our host lures us in for breakfast means we have hours to kill before the flight. The small town of Marblehead has been recommended to us as a rare gem. It is one of the oldest towns in America, settled just nine years after the Pilgrims landed and flourished as a fishing port.

As we approach the town at seven-thirty the locals are tending to flowers on a roundabout. The houses are pastel coloured and weather-boarded. On the main street there are white plaques highlighting notable people who had lived in the house— there are various shipwrights, shoe manufacturers and so on. An occasional jogger or cyclist passes us. It feels like being in a bubble of charm and delight. It has a time capsule aura. The centre is lined with quaint streets and beautiful old weather-boarded buildings in bright colours, that were the pride of its first colonists in 1629. There are floral displays in boxes, vibrant pink and blue hydrangeas in neatly tended gardens. There's a nautical clothing shop, an art class in a gallery and a knitting class in a craft shop. This place looks crime free, a backwater and a place that time forgot. I think if I moved here I'd never want to leave, not even to visit the city. It's almost so perfect that I want to peer inside the house windows to check this isn't a film set. I'd expect to find ladders and props or I might find freshly hoovered carpets and plumped up cushions. Nothing about this town is out of place, from the blades of grass along the verges to the paint on the doors.

To our left is the coastline and we can make out Boston in the distance. It's magnificent, craggy rocks and slivers of seaweed adorn the beach and remind me of Cornish coves and pirates. I sense the history of the place. We stop to take photos in a glorious cove. A smattering of large houses keep watch over the still sea and flags flutter as if they are customs houses awaiting the docking of a ship. Seaspray and patriotism fill the air and I sense the history of the place.

We gaze out to sea from the rocks we've clambered on.

'Dad, a question for you. If these pebbles each represented a pound how many would I have to count to reach the amount you've gambled over the years?'

Jules looks around him.

'God knows. Too many.'

'Come on, let's grab some breakfast,' I say to ease the tension—not today, not here surrounded by beauty. It seems wrong to taint the coastline with our dirt. I don't want to stain it.

As we eat, I see a notice on the wall, cash only. This is America. I expect to pay by card everywhere, but it's easy to forget that many towns are behind the times and are cut off from larger communities.

We take our purses out to see what change we have, and Jules gets his wallet out, though I have no idea why. I ponder what it's like dating a gambler. It would be like caring for a dependant. But this is different. We are talking about a grown man, and men of Jules' generation are supposed to take the lead and pay for the lady. Jules lives off people like a parasite. I

think of a tapeworm living inside a host in a very unequal relationship and shudder. The parasite takes all the food from its
host and gives nothing back and so often the host becomes ill
or it causes discomfort. That's what it would be like to date a
compulsive gambler. I'd rather be on my own, than become
entangled in problems of such complexity. I don't blame
Mandy for pulling away, despite having a kid with him. Whatever possessed her to get pregnant, it must have been a
mistake.

My eyes hook on Jules' wallet.

'Is that a scratch card?' Before he can pull the wallet away
I've slipped it out to reveal a five-hundred pound win.

'Sleazy bastard. Why didn't you say you had some money?
You've sat on this for two days and let me pay for everything.
Free-riding Jules as usual, your sense of entitlement is astound-
ing. Well not this time mate, I'm taking it. I'll cash it in when we
get home and deduct what you owe me for meals. You can have
the rest back. I'll tell you what, I'll just leave it at the fucking
bookies for you shall I, save you having to walk to my house.
We wouldn't want to keep you from your precious machines
any longer than necessary. It shames me to say this Jules, but
you are a waste of a human being and I'm ashamed to call
myself your sister.'

'Dad you owe me two hundred. That can come out of it.'

'Come on sis, give it back.' Jules rubs his forehead. Having
us clamour for money will only drive him back to the betting
shop.

'No, I won't. Like Ellie says some of it's hers.'

'You can cash it here and give me the money in dollars. I
don't want to go back today. I've decided to change my flight
and go to Vegas for a couple of days.

I feel something fizz in my brain like a chemical reaction, a
wall of tolerance finally breached. I explode.

'Jules wake up. You've got a serious addiction. You need to

get it sorted. Las Vegas is the last place on earth you should be going. The only fare I'll give you is the train fare to The Priory.'

'Talking of train fares, that's exactly what I need.'

'Good that's settled.'

'Dad? What do you mean?'

'The company are no longer paying our train fares into London. I've had the past couple of weeks off. And I don't have any money to get to work on Monday.'

'Just how did I come to have such a useless dad? I know that sounds disrespectful but it's true.' Ellie's face is red with embarrassment.

I raise my eyebrows to Jules, waiting for an emotional reaction to his daughter's words, but there is none. He still doesn't get, I doubt he ever will.

'Right well in that case I'm taking the money you owe Ellie, it's not right that you've borrowed from your daughter. Don't ever, ever ask her for money again, do you understand? I'll buy you a train ticket with the remainder. I can't keep doing this. You're a shit.'

'Listen, all I'm asking for is a bit of trust. I know what I'm doing. Give me the money back and let me go to Vegas, and I promise I'll bring back more money than you know what to do with. I promise. I'll prove to you that I'm not a waster.'

Ellie is in tears, but he doesn't notice.

I'm done, my voice is heavy with regret. 'You'll get what's left when we get home. We're done, Jules.'

'I know I've been an idiot but I'm trying to change.'

'You keep saying you're an idiot. It sounds wooden. Don't keep repeating the same thing. Do something about it.'

'On top of everything you're prepared to jeopardise your job. You'll be out on the street if you're not careful.'

'The landlord's given me a month's notice.'

'Oh great, so you're not paying your rent either.'

'Look please just get me a ticket to Vegas, I'll find my own way back. This is my last hope. People go there to win their fortunes.'

'And lose their fortunes. Are you that dense Dad?' Ellie doesn't seem to care anymore about how she talks to her dad. I don't blame her. Maybe she can knock some sense into him but I'm done. I have no energy left.

WE DROP into a massive Whole Foods supermarket which leaves me in awe. There are rows of healthy food and alternative foods for people with allergies. The fruit and vegetables are vibrant and tantalising, so much so that you want to eat a carrot or a lettuce leaf. I feel healthier just for sauntering up and down the aisles. We buy smoothies in the small cafe area.

'Oh God I don't believe it.'

I'm in full Victor Meldrew rant mode.

'She's off again,' Ellie says to Jules. 'What's got your back up now?'

'Moan is her default setting.'

'David Attenborough has made us aware of how we are damaging the environment, but we ignore his warnings.'

Heads are turning and scowling but I don't care, I'm off on one and can't be tamed.

'Plastic cups, plastic cutlery, plastic plates. There's no end to it. I'm sick of being served drinks in throwaway cups. We need to wake up and realise the damage we're causing to the oceans.'

'I saw a programme last week with a straw stuck up a turtle's nostril.'

'Next time you use a straw,' and my voice is louder now, 'think of all those turtles with straws stuffed up their nostrils. It's a bloody disgrace.'

'You should have been a politician sis.'

'Maybe I should have been. Don't you care about the planet? Have you heard about the Great Pacific Garbage Patch?

It's a giant island floating in the ocean, an area of about six hundred thousand square miles made up of discarded plastic. It boils my piss. Are we too lazy to wash crockery and plates?'

And with that I pull a plastic fork from its wrapper and scratch my back. When I get worked up my back gets all itchy. A woman passes me, a shocked expression across her face as she glances at me and returning to her table leans in to her friend and says, 'You'll never guess what that woman over there did. She used a fork to scratch her back.'

They glare at me with disgust.

'Come on time to move.'

As we pass their table I say, 'Madam, the fork was disposable. Like everything in this world.'

I am still moaning when we get back to the car. I haul our purchases into the boot while Jules, stands with his head in the clouds, day-dreaming. We have a long flight ahead of us and as usual he is useless.

CHAPTER 44: JULES – PRESENT

After Pandora took her cut the scratch card money was all he had. It was enough for a train ticket. With flushed face and palms burning, he knew he had no option but to gamble it. His head groaned in confusion. It was impossible for him to see that he was earning good money. He didn't need to risk the train fare to gamble, but the creditors were circling like sharks in a pool. When their letters arrived, there was always more interest piled onto his debts. He had to find a way to stave them off. A big win was all he needed—just the one and he'd stop forever.

With these thoughts burning into his skull, his surroundings faded into a dark shadow. From somewhere close by, he heard a piercing scream. 'My baby, my baby, get my baby back.' Like a light bulb turning on, his brain switched back to the present. Pandora and Ellie stopped packing the car to watch the scene unfold. A man was running with a baby. The pram was empty. The woman was distraught. A thousand questions hit his brain. What is going on? Is he the baby's father? Is he an abductor? Sweeping the questions aside he knew he had to act, without delay. He sprinted as fast as he could having been good at sport at school and won a couple of marathons. The car park wasn't very full and there was nobody around to help. He was this woman's only chance and had to get her baby back. Her baby's life was in danger. His trainers smacked the sticky tarmac as he took long strides, gaining ground, desperate to catch him. Maybe a car was waiting. What if he threw the baby in a car and got away? He'd take the registration number. His heart raced, searing pains shot across his chest and radiated down his arms. He was out of breath, puffing, panting, he had to get there. And then the man slowed, he wasn't sure why, maybe he'd reached the car. He was worried a car would pull out of a bay and hit him. That sort of thing happened all the time in the U.S. What if there was a gun? Shit. It was easy to forget their gun laws.

Jules gained enough ground to grab the man's shoulder and pull his arm back without the baby falling. Luckily the man kept the baby close to him while Jules wrestled him to the ground. As he put his foot on top of the man, from behind them came shouting. A security man was running towards them and he heard the screech of a police car as it came to a halt in front on them. He'd done it, he'd saved the baby. Screaming, the mother ran towards them, in floods of tears. Jules pulled away as two police officers handcuffed the abductor and returned to their car. Jules the gambler—was the hero. It felt good.

CHAPTER 45: PANDORA – PRESENT

At the airport the toilet is permanently on flush mode, like an elaborate National Trust water feature and there are no hand dryers, just hand towels, which means more waste. I groan. I must pull myself out of this Victor Meldrew malaise. I read in The Guardian that paper towels generate seventy percent more carbon emissions than air blade dryers. this research comes from a study by the Massachusetts Institute of Technology into the greenest way of drying your hands—you'd think they'd put things right at the airport.

As we head down the moving belt at the airport Ellie laughs. 'You're always saying how much you'd love to move to America. I can't see it. You've complained about everything.'

'That's a tourist's job. To complain. If you find lots to complain about you know you've had a good holiday. If I moved here and that's highly unlikely—unless I can find an American who'll marry me—I'd open a quaint English tea room. I'd serve cucumber sandwiches and scones and jam on fine bone china, and there'd be proper cutlery.'

'That's unlikely to happen Auntie.'

'Well yes but I think I could make a killing. These Yanks must be sick of Dunkin Donuts and Starbucks.'

'Do they look sick of them? Those places are all over the country and that would indicate that they're very popular.'

'Yeah, but Americans love English things. I'd have lacy tablecloths and Royal memorabilia on the walls. Di and Charles teapots, how about that?'

The walk to the boarding gate is lined with lobsters, though not literally. Posters advertise, 'Live lobsters, boxed and ready to go.' There are fluffy lobsters smiling cheekily from gift shops, lobster keyrings, lobster fridge magnets. At least I didn't get food poisoning from eating one.

Our bags and belongings go onto trays and the security officer tells us to take our shoes and belts off.

'He'd be no good on a market stall. He'd never sell a single potato. He needs to shout,' Jules says.

My bag is sent through again. Is it all the Dunkin Donut sugar bags in the side pocket, I wonder? They must look like sachets of cocaine.

'Well Jules, you were the hero of the trip.'

'That poor mother.' He was playing at being humble.

We board our flight to the slam of overhead lockers and a whiff of urine as we pass the toilets with Ellie screeching about Andy's 'bitch of a wife.' 'She's such a bloody control freak, checking up on what he's doing. You'll never guess, she's stopping him from going out on Saturday evening. That's my only night off. It's his chance to escape and leave her to her screaming brats.'

'I thought you said her kids were very nice?' Pandora asked.

'Well they are, but she doesn't deserve to have kids. She doesn't appreciate them and never wants to spend time with them. She's always moaning at them and hardly sees them much anyway. She has no idea what it's like to raise children because she's always had a full-time nanny to bring them up.'

CHAPTER 46: JULES – 2018

His head was a tangled mess. It had only been two days since he'd had a bet. The stress was back, his head was filling with anxiety, needing the machines to relieve the stress. As far as he was concerned Ellie and Pandora didn't understand what it was like for him. He'd be relieved to hit British soil. He knew his daughter meant well, but he didn't know what the people at The Priory would say that he hadn't heard before. There was only so much you could say to somebody like Jules because he didn't feel ready to change. He rebelled when people tried to change him. Everybody had their vices. Some of his co-workers drank too much. One had lost his job because of drink. He had a friend who'd smoked himself to death. You can't die of gambling, Jules reassured himself and it didn't carry a government health warning. Cigarette ads were banned, but advertising for gambling had mushroomed in recent years. The trouble was he was getting further and further away from where he wanted to be. The markers A and B are wider apart and the wider they got the more he looked to gambling as a solution to solve his money problems. When he was in a betting shop or casino, money had no meaning. It was Monopoly money, it wasn't real. Only after he had left the bookies did the extent of his losses kick in.

During the flight home, Jules watched Pandora like a hawk. He was looking for an opportunity to get in her bag and steal back his scratch card. She was wise to him, and didn't close her eyes once, nor did she loosen her grip on her handbag. With every second, the confines of the plane made his stress levels rise. He was sweating and hyperventilating. He was in the middle seat—trapped—the walls were closing in and he sat for hours unable to move—craving the flashing lights and security of the bookies.

The journey gave him time to think. If it hadn't fully dawned on him before it wasn't okay to pass your child to somebody else to bring up—nanny, auntie, stepfather, whoever. He should have manned up and got on with things when Vicky died rather than turning to the betting shop for solace. What good had it done him apart from dragging him down into a soup of pity and despair? Had he ever acted as a father, he asked himself. Had he told Ellie he loved her? His face burned with the realisation that he hadn't. If he had no relationship with this next baby he'd never get the chance to tell his second child either. The thought of that seared through him like a steak knife.

The hostess handed him a menu. He wasn't in the mood for eating. The thought chilled him to the bone that a baby had nearly lost its mother today. Time and chance, that's all it had taken, being in the right place at the right time and with a good pair of legs to run. Because of him, two people were reunited and their bond restored forever. He was prepared to lose this next child for what? To throw hundreds into a machine that lined the pockets of the betting companies. He'd seen recent headlines of the UK's best-paid boss, it was the co-founder of an online gambling firm. Her pay was a staggering two hundred and sixty-five million. What the fuck was he doing getting poorer by the day and was about to be made homeless, to line the pockets of these rich bastards who had no regard for the vulnerable people they were fleecing? He tore open the lid of his orange juice, splattering drops on his leg. It was an outrage. These firms were criminals, sitting on their luxury yachts while their customers queued at the food bank. They were companies that profited from peoples' addiction. Betting firms should supply food banks. There's an idea, Jules thought. A Labour leader had recently declared gambling to be a 'public health emergency.' Betting companies weren't a force for good in the community any more than they were they were a force for good in his life. It had taken twenty-four hours in Boston to make him see differently. Despite his musings over the state of the gambling industry and the pain he'd caused his daughter, he watched Pandora for an opportunity to steal his scratch card until sleep got the better of him and he couldn't keep his eyes open.

Jules wished he was dead. He could have died the day before Vicky had and it would have been for the best. They'd been arguing for days and at two in the morning, he dressed and went for a drive to relieve his stress. Heading out of town into the countryside, down windy dark roads, he turned up the music, stepped on the accelerator and was past caring. He couldn't see a future, wanting to end the spiral of decline. On the brow of a hill, he realised he'd lost control of the car and knew he was about to have an accident. He didn't remember the minutes that followed until he banged his head against the door and found himself upside down and the windscreen shattered. Vicky didn't know he'd gone out until the police called her to say that Jules had been taken into hospital. He wasn't hurt but was suffering from shock.

Stirring from an unsettled sleep Jules peered up the aisle. He'd woken to an epiphany—he was going to change—and for the first time in his life, he meant it. Meaning it and doing it were different things. He didn't know if he was anywhere near strong enough to go cold turkey—but he was going to try. And that was a genuine start, not just empty words this time. Light streamed through the windows. He had no idea how these air hostesses, who all seemed to be in their fifties coped in stilettos on such a long flight. It was mad. But that was women for you. They were copers and got on with things. So many deserved medals just for being unsung heroes and his sister was one of them. He owed her so much, in love and gratitude for being there for him when he needed support. He had to make an effort and couldn't carry on like this forever. It would destroy him and destroy his family.

'The weather in London is a cool twenty-two. It's been a pleasure having you on board and we would like to wish you a good onward journey.'

CHAPTER 47: ELLIE – 2018

Because of what happened to Dad when he was young I can almost, although it's hard, forgive him for the dismissive way he's treated me over the years. But the thing I'm finding hard to come to terms with is how Grandad treated Dad. The Grandad I knew and loved was the best man ever. He was adorable. I spent a lot of time with Granny and Grandad when I was little, especially in the school holidays when Pandora and Dad had to work. He'd take me for days out, we always went on the train to either the coast or London. He was fond of the Imperial War Museum and would show me the planes and tanks and pretend that they were going to take off at any moment. On the train he'd played a game, making out that the seat buttons were really the train's controls and the view from the window was a moving picture with somebody at the end of it winding the picture along. Grandad was kind, he was generous and would do anything for me. He always had a packet of Trebor Extra Strong Mints and chocolate chewing nuts rattling round in his cardigan pocket.

It's been a great holiday, but I know I've been a cow. Sometimes I don't know where my moods come from but when it's the time of the month, I can't control my feelings and I know I'm going to lash out. Auntie was on the receiving end and I feel awful about the way I've treated her on occasions. I've decided that when I've qualified as a teacher and I've been promoted to head of department— in a few years' time— it will be my turn to take her away. It might be difficult though because I will be paying back a hefty student loan and taking on a mortgage, so it won't be anywhere as grand as America. Auntie will have to accept a weekend away somewhere, maybe we'll go to Bucharest or Budapest. It's the least I can do for her. I don't always tell her how special she is, I take her for granted if I'm honest but I'm sure she knows deep down that I appreciate her. I'm twenty-two. I'm not supposed to be all gushing and gooey with endless thanks for everything she does. It's unwritten between us.

CHAPTER 48: JULES - PRESENT

As they waited at the carousel for their bags Jules' phone buzzed in his pocket. It was Mandy.

'Jules, I'm in labour. I'm at the hospital. Mum's ill. She can't be with me. I don't have anyone else I can ask to be with me. Can you get here?'

'I'm on my way. The plane has just landed. I'll get there as quick as I can.'

He slipped the phone into his pocket and with floods of tears streaming down his face he grabbed Pandora and Ellie, hugging them tightly.

'I'm sorry, I'm sorry.'

He pulled away.

'I love you both. I hope you know that. I know it's never felt like I have, but I do.'

And before he had a chance to change his mind he said, 'Book me onto that course Ellie and thank Andy. And I'm going to come down to Bath to see you as soon as I can. I've got a baby on the way. I can't mess up a second child's life. Can I borrow the taxi fare Pandora to get to the hospital? And this time I absolutely promise I will pay it back.'

THE END

Thank you for purchasing *A Time To Reflect* which I hope you enjoyed. Please would you kindly post a short review on Amazon. Reviews are the lifeblood of authors and always appreciated. My Book

You can also visit my website at https://joannawarringtonauthor-allthingsd.co.uk/books/ where you can find details of my other books and my blog which contains among other subjects posts about gambling addiction.

You might also enjoy 'Holiday' which is a similar book.

My Book

Lyn wakes on her 50th birthday with no man and middle age staring her in the face.

"For readers who enjoy British humour." Readers Favorite.

Determined to change her sad trajectory Lyn books a surprise road trip for herself and her three children through the American Southwest and Yellowstone. Before they even get on the plane, the trip hits a major snag. An uninvited guest joins them at the airport turning their dream trip into a nightmare.

Amid the mountain vistas, secrets will be revealed and a hurtful betrayal confronted.

This book is more than an amusing family saga. It will also appeal to those interested in American scenery, history and culture.

EVERY MOTHER'S FEAR & EVERY FATHER'S FEAR

My Book

The greatest fear in pregnancy is that something will go wrong.

We put our faith in the professionals, but they are not beyond making tragic and major errors of judgement.

Based on real events, this is the dramatic story of two lives intertwined by an unbelievable error.

A night in a Brighton hotel leads to grave and far-reaching consequences for Sandy and Jasper.

And Rona finds an unexpected partner in crime when she pushes the boundaries of professionalism to satisfy her intense desire for a child.

FOR FANS OF CALL THE MIDWIFE, Cathy Glass, Nadine Dorries & Rosie Goodwin

EVERY FAMILY HAS ONE

My Book

   Imagine the trauma of being raped at 14 by the trusted parish priest in a strong 1970s Catholic community.

Then imagine the shame when you can't even tell the truth to those you love and they banish you to Ireland to have your baby in secret.

How will poor Kathleen ever recover from her ordeal?

This is a dramatic and heartbreaking story about the joys and tests of motherhood and the power of love, friendship and family ties spanning several decades.

THE CATHOLIC WOMAN'S DYING WISH

My Book

A dying wish, a shocking secret and a destructive relationship.

Forget hearts & flowers and happy ever afters in this quirky unconventional love story!

Readers say: "A little bit Ben Elton" "a monstrous car crash of a saga."

Middle aged Darius can't seem to hold onto the good relationships in his life; now, he discovers a devastating truth about his family that blows away his future and forces him to revisit his painful past. Distracting himself from family problems he goes online and meets Faye, a single mum. Faye and her children are about to find out the horrors and demons lurking behind the man Faye thinks she loves. *For fans of Nick Hornby, David Nicholls & Nick Spalding.*

Printed in Great Britain
by Amazon